THE DARK PLACE

Gideon spun violently just as Julie screamed.

The shining, naked figure crouching atop the rock swelled and reared up over him, gray and luminous in the murky light, the terrible stone ax raised to the zenith of its arc and already sweeping down.

Without thinking, Gideon leaped forward to meet it. . . .

*   *   *

"Glistens with the same Sherlockian deductive feats, the powerful sense of atmosphere and character, and the understated wit that brought critical acclaim to his first book . . . builds to a violent, eerie climax. A stunning shocker starring a fascinating, cerebral detective."

—*Booklist*

"Imaginative, spooky, poignant, and downright terrifying."

—*Ocala Star-Banner*

"A solid blend of deduction, adventure, romance."

—*Kirkus Reviews*

Also by Aaron J. Elkins
Fellowship of Fear
A Deceptive Clarity
Murder in the Queen's Armes
Old Bones
Curses!

Published by
POPULAR LIBRARY

THE DARK PLACE

AARON J. ELKINS

POPULAR LIBRARY

An Imprint of Warner Books, Inc.

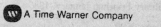

A Time Warner Company

POPULAR LIBRARY EDITION

This Popular Library Edition is published by arrangement with Walker and Company, 720 Fifth Avenue, New York, N.Y. 10019

Popular Library® is a registered trademark of Warner Books, Inc.

Cover illustration by David McKelvey

Popular Library books are published by

Warner Books, Inc.
1271 Avenue of the Americas
New York, N.Y. 10020

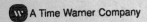 A Time Warner Company

Printed in the United States of America

First Popular Library Printing: January, 1986

Reissued: February, 1990

10 9 8 7 6

Prologue

WITH A CURSE that echoed weirdly in the dripping forest, Eckert sat heavily down on a spongy, moss-covered log. Then he stood up again and shrugged out of the backpack he wore under his poncho, heedlessly letting it slip to the sodden ground. He rubbed his shoulders and stood staring at his moisture-blackened boots, listening to the never-ending soft rain that rustled in the tall trees and pattered on the plastic hood of his poncho like a thousand spidery, scrabbling insects.

He was tired: tired in the base of his spine, and the muscles of his thighs, and the ligaments of his knees. And he was tired of being wet, unutterably sick of the dark, glistening forest with its green, under-the-sea light, ghostly and dim. For two days and nights the rain had floated down in a mist, never slackening, never increasing; just enough to keep him continuously wet, cold, and miserable.

The trail he had been on since eight was too new to show on the map, but the Park Service sign had said, "North Shore, ten miles." That saved five miles and would put him under a hot shower and into dry clothes two hours sooner than the old trail. But now he wasn't sure of exactly where he was, and that made him uncomfortable. Still, it couldn't be more than two or three miles more; it just couldn't be.

He continued to stare at his boots. The thought of taking the right one off to get at the pebble that seemed to be lodged beneath his little toe was almost more than he could bear: untying the tight knot with his chilled fingers, undoing all that wet lacing, taking the boot off, then the outer sock, then the inner sock, putting them on, tying the boot up again—and all in that drenching, bone-chilling fog.

He looked up suddenly at the sound on his left. Twenty feet away, veiled in the mist, a figure had stepped out of the brush,

1

its right hand raised above its head. In the hand was a strange object, hard to make out in the lowering fog. A long, jointed stick? A whip?

"Wait," Eckert said.

The figure's arm plunged down. There was a clacking noise and a whir. Eckert's heart seemed to explode, and the green world turned red and then went black.

On the gravel bar at the bend in the river, Hartman hunched over in the misty rain, trying to focus on the hook and line. He blinked twice and protruded the tip of his tongue in a bleary effort to concentrate. If he didn't watch out, he'd cut his thumb open. Too much brandy. He'd finished most of the pint—his total three-day supply—in the past hour. But it was getting wet and cold, and if he was going to have to spend the night there, he might as well be as comfortable as he could.

He must have taken the wrong turn at the junction where the signpost had been torn out. He'd meant to continue on the Tletshy trail over the divide and out of the rain forest without stopping, but this must be the new Matheny trail, which meant that it was Big Creek he was fishing in, or trying to fish in. He'd have to return to the junction in the morning. It was only a walk of a few hours, but he didn't want to do it in the dark.

He took another swig from the bottle and looked glumly around him. Actually, he didn't dislike the rain forest, but it wasn't anyplace he wanted to spend the night. Still, with the brandy, and maybe with a trout cooked over the propane stove, it wouldn't be so bad.

The hell it wouldn't, he thought; it'd be miserable. The rain forest was getting creepier as it got darker, and he'd be clammy and uncomfortable all night, and wake up in the morning soaked and aching. He hadn't thought to bring a rain fly for the tent, damn it. And of course it would still be raining. Goddamn it, it should have been the Tletshy that branched to the right.

It was growing dark quickly. Hartman wiped the moisture from his eyebrows, shifted his haunches on the sharp pebbles, and frowned again at the hook in his hand.

2

He was startled by a sudden splash at his side. A limb must have fallen from a tree. He looked up. There were no trees overhead; the gravel bar extended far into the bend of the creek, thirty feet away from the forested bank. Frightened, he looked again at the object in the shallow water. It was too straight to be a tree limb, and it had stuck into the stream bed like a javelin. The angle told him someone had thrown it at him from behind.

He jumped and spun around. He could see only a few feet into the dull green mist of the forest. Nothing moved. The only sounds were the gurgle of the creek over the stones and the steady, light patter of the rain. With his heart pounding, Hartman ran for the tent, where his knife lay next to the stove.

He didn't get there. Just as he scrambled from the slippery stones of the bar to the earthen bank, something reared up horrifyingly out of the brush directly in front of him. Hartman stared unbelievingly into a pair of fierce, mad eyes. He tried to stop and turn, but he skidded on the wet stones and fell on his side at the figure's feet. He looked up to see a black silhouette edged with awful clarity against the sky's dying light, its right hand raised high, holding what could only be, incredibly, a heavy, rough stone hammer, a caveman's stone club. Hartman flung his left arm across his face as the hammer came crashing down.

Excerpt from the *Port Angeles Daily News*, April 2, 1976:

SEARCH FOR HIKERS ENDS

QUINAULT, WA—Olympic National Park authorities today announced abandonment of the search for two hikers believed lost last month in the park's Quinault area. Clyde Hartman, thirty-eight, of Portland, Oregon, and Norris Eckert, twenty-nine, of Seattle, disappeared within a few days of each other in early March, apparently in the dense rain forest northwest of Lake Quinault. Senior investigator Claude Gerson said that the search had been "the most exhaustive one ever made" in the Olympic National Park, and there was "simply no trace of them."

One investigator told reporters: "There's just no way. That's jungle in there. You'd need a machete to get through. They could have been six feet off the trail, and we'd never have found them."

Excerpt from the *Seattle Post-Intelligencer*, October 1, 1982:

HIKER LOST IN OLYMPIC NATIONAL PARK
GIRL MISSING IN "DISAPPEARANCE VALLEY"

National Park investigators are combing the Quinault Valley for eighteen-year-old Claire Hornick of Tacoma, who was reported missing late Tuesday when she failed to rejoin fellow campers at the Graves Creek campground near Lake Quinault after taking a solitary hike. According to companion Gary Beller, twenty-two, also of Tacoma, Miss Hornick had gone into the rain forest "to be alone for an hour or two," along the Quinault River Trail.

The Quinault Valley received nationwide notoriety as "Disappearance Valley" six years ago, after a month-long search failed to find any sign of two hikers separately reported missing there. The two have never been found.

1

DR. FENSTER PRESSED his lips into a tight little bud. He wasn't a bone man, had never liked bones. Too much guesswork, especially after they'd been in the ground a while. They shrank, they warped, they were inconclusive cause-of-death indicators, they gave unreliable tissue types. Give him some blood, on the other hand, or semen, or saliva, or best of all a major organ, and you really had something. A pathologist could get his teeth into something like that, so to speak.

He sighed noisily and rearranged the bones on the oak table again, this time in a neat row, but Lau could see he wasn't getting anywhere. After waiting politely for the older man to speak, Lau said, "What do you think, Dr. Fenster? Is it one of them?"

The pathologist shook his head irascibly and pushed his round, wire-rimmed glasses up on his nose. They were the kind of glasses a five-year-old might draw on a cartoon face, Lau thought. All in all, Dr. Arthur Fenster looked a lot like a child's drawing: a rabbit wearing little round glasses. An irritated rabbit.

"How can you tell anything from this junk?" Fenster said. "A few vertebrae, a scapula . . ." He flicked the pieces disgustedly with the backs of his fingers. "It could be Eckert, could be the Hartman one. It's been buried for five years at least. Looks like a male, maybe in his twenties, maybe older. But I'm not even sure it all belongs to one person." He folded his arms and leaned stiffly back in his chair. "This garbage is next to worthless. A waste of my time." He looked at the FBI agent with a mixture of annoyance and disapproval.

John Lau's big, flat, oriental face remained impassive. "Well, it's all we have, sir," he said. "Isn't there anything else you can tell us?"

Fenster picked up one of the vertebrae and thrust it toward Lau. "See that growth on the ventral surface?"

Lau nodded. He didn't know the ventral surface from whatever the others were, but he could see that the ugly, rough excrescence wasn't a normal part of the bone.

"I'm not sure exactly what it is," Fenster said. "Some kind of oddball exostosis—a tumor, or a weird variation of osteomyelitis. Maybe even bone syphilis, although that usually doesn't show up in vertebrae. Anyway, it's a lead. Have a look at Eckert's and Hartman's medical records. If one of them had a bone disease in a highly advanced state, then there's a good chance this is him."

"Okay, that's helpful," Lau said, trying to look grateful. "You don't suppose a physical anthropologist would be able to tell us anything more? I heard Gideon Oliver was working on a dig up near Dungeness. That's only a few hours from Quinault."

Lau had thought it might be a mistake to mention Gideon Oliver, and it was. Fenster snorted, bringing his glasses down over his nose again. He pushed them back up. "Oh, God, spare me, will you? I know you think his reports on the Schuster case and that kidnapping in New Mexico were God's gift to the world, but I'm a pathologist and I *know*. They were fantasy, garbage, crap. He was lucky. Maybe he knows his anthropometric theory—*maybe*, I say—but his conclusions are . . . speculative." He rolled his mobile lips around the word as if it might befoul them.

"Still," Lau said, knowing it was pointless, "he might—"

"Good Lord, the man's an *academic!*" Clearly, that closed the case. Lau nodded resignedly. It would have been nice to have the pathologist recommend asking Oliver's help, but it wasn't required.

The telephone on the untidy desk against the wall buzzed, and Lau turned in his swivel chair to reach it, glad for the diversion.

"Lau," he said; then almost immediately, "Where?" He sat up straight and rummaged through the desk with both hands, twisting his neck to hold the telephone between ear and shoulder. "How many?" he said, writing on a yellow notepad. For a while he listened erectly and wrote, then fell suddenly against the back of the chair. "Oh, God," he said, "that's all we need."

He hung up and turned toward Fenster, slapping the pad on the worktable in front of him. "Five more bodies found."

"Bodies or skeletons?"

"Skeletons. Mostly just a few bone fragments, not in good shape. Some are just four or five fragments in a basket."

"Come again?"

"Some of them were buried in baskets."

Fenster pursed his tiny red mouth like a child holding his breath and burst out suddenly: "This is ridiculous! I'm not going to spend any more time poking around a bunch of bones in baskets. They're probably just old Indian burials anyway."

6

"Probably, but you know, there are unverified reports of people disappearing around here for fifty years."

"Yeah, sure, also unverified reports of the Abominable Snowman clumping around stealing sheep and scaring little kiddies."

His eyes on the pad, Lau smiled slightly. With slow, heavy strokes, he circled the last word he'd written. "Bigfoot," he said aloud. "You hit the nail on the head, sir. They've found some eighteen-inch, humanlike footprints nearby. They look like Bigfoot tracks, the locals say."

Fenster took off his glasses, finically disengaging the wire loops from one ear at a time. Silently he inserted the glasses into a case and snapped it shut with a sharp, terminal click. Then he rose. "I'm not going to be involved in this, Mr. Lau. I deal in real things, not fairy tales. I'll look at your five baskets of bones this afternoon, and then I have a case waiting for me at headquarters. A *hallux major*." He paused, looking at Lau as if he expected a challenge. "A woman," he said precisely, "has bitten the big toe off a would-be attacker. The toe has been recovered, and I mean to identify him from it. Now, *that* is the real world."

Lau barely repressed his grimace. Fenster took his jacket from the back of a chair and shrugged into it. "If you need more help than my poor abilities can provide, you have my sincere encouragement to bring in Gideon Oliver from Fantasyland University."

2

JOHN KNEW THAT Julie Tendler usually showed exactly what she felt, and now her black eyes sparkled with surprise as she put her ham and cheese sandwich back down on its waxed-paper wrapping. "You mean you know Gideon Oliver? *Personally?*"

"The doc? Sure, why not?" He was having a cup of coffee at her desk to keep her company. As chief park ranger, she had been out with the crew that had been digging up the new burials, and she'd missed lunch. "He's an old pal."

"I thought you just knew him because he'd consulted on some cases with the FBI."

"No, I knew him way before that. Met him when I worked for NATO in Europe, and we kicked around together for a while. We still get together fairly often. Why so amazed?"

"I'm not amazed," she said, picking up the sandwich again and nibbling at it, "I'm impressed. When I was finishing up my anthropology minor a couple of years ago, we spent a whole quarter just discussing his book."

"He wrote a book?"

The sandwich went back down to the table. "Are you serious? He wrote the most controversial—and I think brilliant—book on human evolution to come out in decades. And he must have published hundreds of articles."

"No kidding," John said. "Are you going to eat that pickle?"

She shook her head. "Well, what's he like? He must be a lot older than you."

John bit off half the pickle and shook his head. "No, he's about my age—forty, a little less."

"Forty! That's hard to believe. I always assumed he was one of the grand old men of anthropology. Tell me more." She returned to her sandwich, but her mind obviously was elsewhere.

"Like is he married?"

"That's not a bad place to start."

John finished the pickle. "No, he's not married. Are you planning on leaving the chips over?" She handed him the bag, and he tore it open. "He was married before I knew him, for nine or ten years, and I guess they had some kind of fantastic relationship. She got killed in a car accident three, four years ago, and I don't think he's ever gotten over it. I think he's still in love with her. Nora, I think her name was."

She frowned at her sandwich as if suddenly absorbed in it. "He doesn't go out with women?"

8

John munched a potato chip with a loud crackle. "Do you always show this much interest in the grand old men of anthropology?"

"No, but this is going to be the first one I ever met. Does he go out?"

"Oh, yeah, he likes women, all right, if that's what you mean. Used to go out with this girl in Heidelberg, Janet Feller, but . . . I don't know, like I said, I think he's still in love with his wife."

"What's he like?" Julie asked with undisguised interest. "Is he good-looking?"

"I wouldn't say he's handsome," John said with a shrug, "but what do I know? He's about my size, maybe a little shorter: six-one, six-two. Seems to be in pretty good shape. From what I can tell, the gals seem to like him."

Julie finished her sandwich and crumpled up the waxed paper and threw it into a wastepaper basket near the desk. She took the lid off her Styrofoam cup of coffee and drank. "It's funny, you discuss someone's theories and ideas for ten weeks almost as if you were arguing with him personally, but you never wonder what he looks like, or think of him as human."

John laughed. "Oh, he's human, all right. On the quirky side, in fact."

John Lau's laugh was the kind that made other people join in, and Julie laughed, too. "How so?"

"Well, he might seem a little prickly at first, and he talks like a professor most of the time, and his head's usually in the clouds somewhere. One time I watched him spend twenty minutes looking for a notebook that was tucked under his arm." He laughed again, tilted his head back, and tapped the last crumbs of potato chip into his mouth. "He's a funny guy, kind of a quick temper, but at the same time he's, I don't know, gentle. You'll see."

"He sounds fascinating."

"Yes," John said, nodding, thinking back to other times. "He's the kind of guy who's liable to go bonkers at little things, but in a crisis, when the chips are really down, there's no one I'd rather have around. And I know what I'm talking about."

Julie sipped her coffee quietly, smiling at the faraway look in the agent's eyes. "It sounds like you like him a lot," she said softly.

"Yeah, I like him."

The look left his eyes abruptly, almost with embarrassment. He clapped the potato chip bag into a cumpled ball and tossed it into the basket. "You're not going to leave that doughnut, are you?"

3

FROM THE AIR the lake was beautiful, deep blue in the warm sunlight, and dotted with white sailboats. Their occupants waved as the pilot dropped the little Cessna 210 smoothly toward the water, its engine rackety and echoing. The dense woods that began at the shore and stretched many miles to the northwest were the rain forest, Gideon knew. He studied them curiously, just a little disappointed to find them pleasant and cool-looking, not in the least sinister.

The plane landed on the water not far from what he knew must be Lake Quinault Lodge, a set of big, rambling buildings set comfortably at the back of a huge, lush lawn that sloped down a good two hundred feet to the lakeshore. Turning, the blue-and-white Cessna, rocking gently in its own wake, taxied slowly toward the dock at the foot of the lawn.

He spotted John at once among the two dozen people lounging on the dock. One of the many things he enjoyed about him was how genuinely pleased the big Hawaiian always seemed to see him and there he was, steady and solid-looking in his denim shirt and jeans, grinning happily at Gideon through the airplane window.

When Gideon jumped down from the Cessna's doorway, there were a few moments of handshaking and back-clapping, and finally a powerful hug. Not for the first time, it occurred to him that of all the men he knew, John Lau was the only one he could comfortably and unselfconsciously embrace.

With a final thump on Gideon's shoulder, John turned to a black-haired woman of about thirty in the gray shirt and olive pants of the National Park Service. "This is Julie Tendler. She's the chief ranger. Been a hell of a lot of help."

"Hi, Professor," she said. "I really enjoyed your book. I was an anthro minor," she added by way of explanation.

"I'm glad you liked it," he said with the tolerant smile of a gracious celebrity. Actually, he was delighted. As the author of *A Structuro-Functional Approach to Pleistocene Hominid Phylogeny*, he'd yet to become jaded by the approbation of the masses.

Gideon swung his suit bag over his shoulder and they walked up the sloping lawn to the main hotel building. On the way, John explained about the three missing persons. Two had disappeared six years before on the then new but since closed Matheny trail between the Queets and Quinault rain forests. The third, Claire Hornick, had vanished only a few days ago, about eight miles from there. The search for her had turned up the bones, and that's when the FBI had been called in.

Gideon checked into the lodge and left his bag at the registration desk. They walked across the grand old lobby with its ancient, wicker furniture, old-fashioned and comfortable.

"I haven't seen wicker writing desks in an American hotel for a long time," Gideon said. "Or a parrot in the lobby."

"Yes," Julie said, "it's a great old place."

John held open the door, and Gideon awkwardly bowed Julie through, not at all sure if she would like the gesture. She went through with a pleasant smile, and they stepped out into the town of Quinault. It was a shock. They had entered the hotel building from a spacious, sunny lawn peopled with sunbathers and laughing volleyball players, and with ten square miles of open lake at their backs. When they walked out through the rear entrance, no more than forty feet away, they stepped into a sunless shadowy world of almost solid green, hushed and perceptibly cooler and more moist than the lawn.

11

The "town," invisible from the air, consisted of several buildings out of the nineteenth century along either side of a narrow road. On the right was an old post office and a weathered, rustic general store—"Lake Quinault Merc," the sign said—with a wooden porch complete with an old dog sprawled drowsily on it. On the left was the Quinault Ranger Station, a group of small frame houses. Everything was dwarfed and hemmed in by towering walls of cedar and spruce, so tall and close together that the sky was visible only as a narrow slit high above the road. The road itself gave the illusion of being cut off at either end by more tree walls, and the overall effect was like being at the bottom of a sunken corridor, a narrow, gravelike canyon cut deep into the living mass of trees.

It was in its own way extraordinarily beautiful, but the impact on Gideon, used to the scrub oak and open hillsides of California, was so oppressive that he unconsciously moved his hand to his already open collar to get more air.

"This is fascinating," he said. "I've never been in a rain forest before."

Julie laughed. "Oh, this isn't the rain forest," she said, her eyes looking down the road beyond the barrier of trees. "The rain forest's in there. This is just regular woods."

The ranger station complex was better. The growth had been cut away to provide an open space, probably by some early, claustrophobic chief ranger, and Gideon breathed more easily as he stepped into it.

In the workroom at the rear of the main building, the burials were neatly arranged on a scarred oak table, each one consisting of a pitifully few fragments in front of a numbered paper bag. Four of the groupings sat next to frayed, soiled baskets with red and black designs. On the table, in front of the one chair with arms, were the magnifying glass and calipers that Gideon had requested on the telephone.

Gideon quickly identified five of the six, including all those that had been in baskets, as Indian burials which had been in the ground at least twenty years.

John nodded disappointedly. "That's what Fenster told us."

12

"I don't think there's any doubt about it," Gideon said. "The baskets, the fact that the bodies were cremated, the fact that some of them have been buried a lot longer than others—a hundred years at least, I'd say, for that one there—it all suggests an old, established burial ground."

Julie was frowning. "I don't know. I think I know the history of this rain forest as well as anyone does, and I never heard of any Indians who ever lived here. And I don't remember cremated burials in baskets being very common among North American Indians."

"Maybe not. I'm not an ethnologist, but I know the practice exists, or existed. Some of the central California peoples used to do it."

When Julie continued to frown he said firmly, "Trust me, I'm a world-renowned authority."

John laughed but Julie looked at him curiously. "Joke," Gideon said. "Now, let's have a look at this last one. Fenster thinks this might be one of the hikers?"

"Right, Doc," John said. "You want their descriptions?"

"No, let's do it the usual way. Let me see what I can find out on my own. I wouldn't want to bias my judgment with any preconceived ideas," he explained for Julie's benefit, looking at the small pile of brown bones.

"Quite proper for a world-renowned authority," Julie said. Gideon looked up quickly.

"Joke," she said. "Honest." She smiled, and Gideon realized suddenly that she was very pretty.

He returned his attention to the bones. "There's not much here," he said. "It's been partially burned, and it looks like some animal's gotten in and made off with most of it. Look, you can see where something's been gnawing on the edge of the scapula."

Julie shivered suddenly and apologized. "Sorry, I guess I'm not used to this."

"There's no need for you to be here," John said gently. "If you want—"

"No, I'm intrigued. Don't pay any attention to me. If I faint, just go on without me."

13

Gideon leaned forward, studying the fragments intently: fourth and fifth lumbar vertebrae, held together by a few shreds of brown, dried ligament; third and fourth thoracic vertebrae; left scapula, whole except for some gnawing and breakage along the rim.

He shook his head. "It's going to be hard. There's no way I can tell the race from these, but I'm pretty sure it's male."

John jotted something in his notebook, looking less than hopeful, but Julie was eager.

"How can you tell it's a male?"

"The scapula. See the rough, ridged areas on the extension?" He handed the bone to her. She hesitated momentarily, then took it. "That's where the deltoid and the trapezius muscles . . . Do you remember your anatomy?"

"Not much," Julie said.

"Okay, that's where the large shoulder muscles attach," Gideon said, careful not to sound patronizing. "The ruggedness of the bone shows the muscles were heavy, powerful. A female would have smaller shoulder muscles, and you'd barely see any ridges."

"But what if it was a woman with large muscles?" Julie asked. "Women are a lot more athletic than they used to be."

"Well, if the female heavyweight weight-lifting champion of the world is missing, maybe we've found her, but I don't think so. It's much more than a question of athletics. If a man and a woman exercise the same amount, the man will still have a lot heavier, denser muscles and thicker, rougher bones. A woman would have to exercise a great deal more even to come close."

The corners of Julie's mouth turned down.

"I'm sorry if it offends you," Gideon went on, "but there really are some differences between men and women that are genetically determined, and muscularity happens to be one of them. I'm speaking statistically, of course; there's no way I can be completely certain on this particular bone."

"I'm not sure if I agree," Julie said.

Gideon, slightly annoyed, was about to reply when she suddenly added, "But who am I to disagree with a world-renowned authority?" and broke into another warm smile. She really was extraordinarily attractive, Gideon thought, even beautiful.

"Male," said John flatly, writing. "Okay. Anything else you can tell us?"

He looked so dejected that Gideon laughed. "You mean anything to justify my fee? Yes, I think so." He picked up the scapula and turned it slowly in his large hands. "He's over twenty-three," he said after a while. "All the epiphyses are fused."

Gideon put the bone on the table and leaned close to it, using the magnifying glass like a jeweler's lens. "And he's definitely under forty. "No sigh of atrophic spots."

"Of what spots?" asked John dully, writing.

"Atrophic. As you get into middle age, the supply of blood to the scapula decreases, and the bone atrophies in places." When John winced, he added, "Don't worry, it's harmless."

Gideon turned the bone over several times more, still peering through the magnifying glass. "Ah!" he said, "Look at this. Just the tiniest bit of lipping on the circumferential margin of the glenoid fossa—"

"Doc," said John, "you're going to have to go a little slower or else speak English."

"Don't worry, I'll write it up for you. The important thing is that lipping starts about thirty. I'd say he's twenty-nine, or maybe just turned thirty, considering that the epiphyses look as if they've been fused six or seven years."

John put down his pad and looked squarely at Gideon. "Doc, is this on the level? Eckert was twenty-nine. Did you know that before?"

"I don't play games like that, John, you know that."

"No," said John, "you don't." He wrote some more on his pad.

"Was he muscular, five-ten or six feet, a hundred and ninety pounds?" Gideon asked.

John scrambled through the file. "Height five-eleven," he said with something uncharacteristically like awe in his voice, "weight one eighty-five. I didn't think even you could tell that from a single bone, let alone a shoulder blade."

15

Gideon shrugged offhandedly but glanced at Julie. She seemed, he was gratified to see, as impressed as John. "Just educated guesses," he said. "We can apply some height formulas to the vertebrae and see if we come up with the same thing." He picked up a vertebra. "There's a shadow of osteophytosis here; bears out the age estimate of around thirty. What the heck is *this?*" he said, fingering the strange protuberance.

"Fenster wasn't sure. He thought maybe"—John flipped through his notes—"some sort of bone disease . . . exostosis. . . ."

"I don't think so," Gideon said, excitement rising in his voice. He held the bone in his hand and leaned over it, the magnifying glass practically touching it, his eye an inch behind the glass.

"You look like Sherlock Holmes," Julie said.

"Hmm," Gideon said after a while. "Definitely."

"You *sound* like Sherlock Holmes," she said. "I'm dying of suspense. What is it?"

"It's not a growth," Gideon said, handing the bone to her. "I think it's an arrow point that penetrated the vertebra and broke off, so the tip is still embedded, and that rough projection is the surface of the broken part."

"An arrow point?" John cried, rocking forward in his chair and extending his hand for the vertebra. He picked gently at the projection with his fingertips. "It sure looks like bone to me."

"It *is* bone," Gideon said. "Eckert—if that's who it was—was shot by a bone arrow."

"But people haven't used bone arrows for centuries," Julie said. "Even the most primitive groups in the world use metal points now."

"Yes," said Gideon quietly, "astounding, isn't it? But I really think there isn't any doubt. There's no periosteum."

"Doc—" John began exasperatedly.

Gideon smiled. "All right, I'll speak English." He slid the magnifying glass along the table to John. "The outer layer of bone is the periosteum. It stays on the bone even when it's

16

been buried for hundreds of years; thousands, for that matter. But when you make a bone implement, and shape and smooth it, you invariably scrape it off. If you look carefully, you'll see that outer layer all over the vertebra, except for that projection."

John held the glass and bone out in front of him like a farsighted man trying to read a menu. "I don't—"

"Okay, never mind that," said Gideon. "Look at the bone around the base of the projection. You can see it's crushed *inward*, obviously by the force of the arrow entering the—"

"I see!" John cried. "It's as if . . . it's all . . ."

Julie had risen and looked over his shoulder through the glass. "All mushed in," she said.

"Right," Gideon said. "All mushed in." He took back the bone, grasped the projecting part tightly, and wiggled it.

The point came out at once, noiselessly, without disturbing the crushed rim of bone surrounding it. A faint odor of decay came from the hole in the vertebra. Julie moved back, wrinkling her nose.

"It's a projectile point, all right," Gideon said.

"It sure is," John said. "Goddamn."

Gideon laid the point on the table. It was a triangular piece of ivory-colored bone a little over an inch long, its base rough and jagged. "It was in there deeper than I thought," he said, "about an inch. It almost went clean through."

He placed the point on a white sheet of paper and traced its outline with a pen. Then with dotted lines he extended the shape. "It's hard to say, but I'd guess this is what it must have looked like complete." He had drawn a tapering form about three inches long and an inch and a half wide at its base.

Julie moved closer to the table, squeezing between the two men. Gideon was aware of the nearness of her hip and of her faint, fresh fragrance as she bent over the drawing.

"I've read a lot of Northwest Coast ethnology and archaeology, Dr. Oliver," she said, "and this doesn't look like an arrow. It looks a lot like the kind of spear point they've turned up at the Marmes Rockshelter in eastern Washington."

17

"Does it?" said Gideon, interested. "Yes, it could be a spear. He changed the drawing a little, sketching in a few lines. "That does look better. The wooden shaft would attach there."

"Hold it now," John said. "Are we saying this guy was killed by a spear—a wooden spear with a bone point? That's just a little bizarre, to say the least."

Gideon leaned back in his chair and shrugged.

"So what does that add up to?" John asked. "Was he killed by an Indian?"

"With a bone spear?" Julie said. "You're kidding. The point I was talking about is ten thousand years old. And the local Indians are tribes like the Quileute and the Quinault. They're busy managing their fish hatcheries and motels. With computers. They don't go running around with bone spears."

"Do you know anybody who does?" John asked with a shade of temper. He looked at Gideon. "All right, what's your theory, Doc?"

"Uh-uh," Gideon said. "I'm the anthropologist. I've told you these are the remains of a husky white male about twenty-nine and that this is a bone spear point in his spinal column. You're the one who gets paid to come up with theories. But I agree with Julie; you're on the wrong track if you think the spear necessarily means Indians."

John shoved his chair back and thrust himself out of it. "All right," he said, pacing, huge and bearlike in the small room, "we find a body in an Indian graveyard. He's in there with what you tell me are Indian skeletons buried in Indian baskets. He's got a bone spear that looks just like what the local Indians used to use stuck in him. But," he said, plopping back into his chair, "in no way could it *possibly* be an Indian who killed him. I don't follow the logic."

"Look," Gideon said, "I didn't mean it *couldn't* be an Indian. It could be anyone. I meant don't assume the circumstances point to an Indian."

Julie moved away from his shoulder and swung around to sit on the table, disturbingly near. He could have rested an arm on her thigh without moving from his chair. "I'm not sure about your logic either," she said, looking down at him.

Your logic? He was aware of an absurd letdown feeling. He had expected her support. "What exactly bothers you?" he asked.

"In the first place, how do you know without doing any lab tests that the skeleton hasn't been in the ground twenty years, or a hundred? I know you're not familiar with the soil or the climate. . . ." She paused to let him answer.

"I just know," he said, telling the truth. "You get a feel for it, even if you can't quantify your methods. Color of the bone . . . weight . . . density . . ." He picked up the vertebra. "Five years at least, ten years at most." He turned to John. "Have you ever known me to guess wrong?"

"Lots of times. What about those hand bones in the Reilly case, or the arm bone you said was sharpened when a dog had just chewed it up?"

"Those were different. That humerus *had* been sharpened, only it was a dog that—" He stopped and joined John in easy laughter. John had earned the right to be critical.

He wasn't so sure about Julie, however. "What bothers you in the second place?" he said to her.

She picked up one of the baskets. "These," she said. "I'll check my texts later, but I'm sure these weren't made by any recent Washington Indians. The form is wrong, and the way the decoration is overlaid. The twining itself doesn't look right. At least I don't think so."

Here she might have a point. Gideon knew little about basketry. "You could be right," he said, not sorry about the opportunity to agree with her.

Julie put the basket back on the table. "Besides that, there aren't any Indians who live in the rain forest itself, and there never were, not on a steady enough basis to have graveyards."

"Doc," John said impatiently, "is this point well made? I mean, was it carved by someone who knew what he was doing?"

Gideon took the fragment in both hands, running his fingers

19

along the facets. "It's crude," he said, "but whoever made it had plenty of experience. Why? Were you thinking someone might have been trying to make it look like an Indian killing?"

"Yeah," John said.

"Then why bury the corpse? It was just by luck you found it at all."

John nodded soberly. "I know. I'm just trying to cover all the angles." He looked down at the desk, suddenly uncomfortable. "Look," he said, "I've gone out of my way not to tell you about the Bigfoot tracks they found near the body—"

"Bigfoot!" Gideon said, raising his eyes to the ceiling. "Come on, John, you've got a perfectly solvable crime here with a rational explanation. I'm not even going to *discuss* a creature for which there isn't a sliver of physical evidence—no live specimens, no skeletal material, no fossils, no carcasses, not even a reliable photograph. The very notion that a giant anthropoid could exist unseen . . ." He looked suddenly at John. "What do you mean, you've gone out of your way not to tell me?"

John's eyes twinkled, but his mouth kept its serious line. "I thought you might give me a lecture if I mentioned it."

Gideon laughed. "See? That confirms your good sense. So no more talk of Bigfoot." But then he said, "There were tracks?"

"Yes," John said, "but definitely made yesterday, after we found the first skeleton, so there's no direct connection. The local Sasquatch Society got all excited and made casts, and our people made some to send to headquarters. Fenster wouldn't have anything to do with them. Said they were pranks."

"He's right. Forget about Bigfoot, John. You'll make yourself and the FBI look ridiculous. And I'm sure as hell not going to get involved."

"Look," John said, "I'm not stupid. I think it was a prank, too. But I'm not forgetting about *anything* that might be connected." After a moment he added, "You could at least look at the tracks."

"It wasn't Bigfoot, John, and I'm not spending my time giving credibility to a set of joke footprints."

John was up again, thrashing the air with his hands the way he did when he was excited. "It wasn't an Indian! It wasn't Bigfoot! What was it, your average, everyday John Q. Citizen who walks around with a bone spear and kills people and buries them in the forest? Or maybe Eckert speared himself to death?"

After a lunch of ham sandwiches and chocolate milk from Lake Quinault Merc, Gideon aged and sexed the Indian burials, explaining to Julie and John as he went along: a man in his forties, another man of about eighty, two elderly women, and two infants, possibly twins, who had been buried in one grave and misclassified by Fenster as a single burial. He had identified a horrendous abscess in the upper jaw of the old man as a probable cause of death, but there wasn't enough left of the others to provide any more information.

He put down the magnifying glass and the charred heel bone he'd been holding and rubbed the back of his neck.

"John, I'm not doing you any good. Why don't I just go on back up to Dungeness and get back to my dig?"

"I guess you can if you want to, Doc, but why not relax and spend the night at the lodge? The Bureau'll pick up your tab, and we'll get you on a plane tomorrow."

"The food's quite good at the lodge, if that's any incentive," said Julie, then added, as if she'd been addressing John all along, "Professor Oliver would be a help at the press conference tomorrow."

"In that case, I'll stay," Gideon said, smiling.

Late that afternoon, John had flown back to Seattle, saying that he hoped to be back for the press conference. If not, Gideon was perfectly free to talk as an anthropologist about anything he had found but was not to speak for John or the FBI.

"Also," John said with a smile, "please try not to engage, like, in any elaborate hypothesizing in advance of the facts."

21

Gideon promised he wouldn't, and he and Julie saw John off from the foot of the dock on the sunny blue lake. It seemed perfectly natural, then, to ask her if she were free for dinner, and he nonchalantly did so. She accepted equally matter-of-factly, and they agreed to meet in the lobby of the lodge in an hour and a half.

Gideon did not often think about his appearance; not for the past few years, at any rate. He knew that he was not a conventionally handsome man; his nose, broken twice in college boxing matches, had long ago taken care of that. But he also knew his soft brown eyes combined with that mashed, crooked nose, heavy brow, and cleanly masculine jaw in a look of gentle ruggedness that many women found attractive. Whether the recent appearance of gray at his temples made him more attractive it hadn't occurred to him to wonder.

So why was he wondering now, standing in front of the mirror in the old-fashioned bathroom of his cottage? The reason was Julie, of course. She had reached him somehow, had stirred him in a way he hadn't been stirred in a long time. During an unhurried, relaxing session in the old-fashioned, marvelously comfortable six-foot tub—there was no shower—he had found himself thinking and feeling things he'd almost been ready to put in his past.

He was not on the prowl by any means, not the sort of man whose antennae were always quivering and alert. For nine years he had lived with Nora and had loved her as deeply and unreservedly as a man can love. There had been no one to compare with her when she was alive, and none since she'd been killed three years ago. Still, once in a long while a woman would come along who would rouse him and kindle the old feelings.

At first, when he'd self-consciously begun to date again at thirty-seven, they'd all been intent on "significant emotional relationships"; all he'd been after was some straightforward, uncomplicated sex. More recently, as his own thoughts had begun to turn to significant emotional relationships, the women he seemed to meet just wanted to get laid and be done with it.

He had no idea what Julie was after, doubted that she was after anything from him. She wasn't even the kind of woman he usually found physically attractive, not blond and long-limbed and svelte, as Nora had been. Julie was black-haired, with slightly slanting jet-black eyes that seemed perpetually on the verge of laughter. She was round, and even a little plump—in a definitely pleasing way—and she lacked Nora's cool elegance. Nora had looked wonderfully at home in a museum or a fine restaurant. Julie looked like she belonged in a kibbutz, standing in the sunlight with a hoe in her hand and white shorts on those provocative, curvy hips. He wondered what her legs looked like bare. Probably firm and tan and smooth. God knows they seemed attractive enough in those tight ranger pants.

She was waiting for him when he got to the restaurant, and they ordered martinis before dinner. Gideon told her about the dig he was working on at Dungeness Bay during his fall teaching recess.

"It's a fabulous site. I turned up a scraper and some worked caribou bone inside of a week, and some charcoal, and then finally some human skeletal material—a male and a female—just a few days ago. It's all stratigraphically dated at twelve to thirteen thousand years. That makes it at least as old as the Manis Mastodon site near Sequim, maybe older."

The waitress brought their martinis. "My name is Eleanor," she said, putting them on the table. "Enjoy."

They touched glasses. Julie was smiling. "It's nice to see a man so enthusiastic about his work."

"It's not just the work; it's the site itself and the fact that I'm working it alone. The cave's in the side of a cliff right on the edge of Dungeness Bay, looking across those magnificent straits. The digging itself is mostly a kind of mindless, easy work, you know, more dental pick than spade. And so you poke away and dream, and think, and every now and then you look up and there's that blue water and the gulls. . . ."

Julie was looking at him over the rim of her glass, her black eyes twinkling. "I get the feeling you like being alone."

Gideon frowned slightly. Was he sounding eccentric? Reclusive? "Well, sometimes, maybe, but it's not as remote as I've made it sound. I spend a few evenings a week with an old professor of mine, and the site is right below a main road. When I finish up I just climb a few feet to the top of the cliff and walk across the road to my motel. TV, fridge, all the modern conveniences. If you've never been up that way you ought to come on up. It can't be more than a three-hour drive. I'll show you around."

"Did I just get an invitation to your motel, Professor?"

Gideon laughed. "Tell me something about you. How long have you been with the Park Service?"

She told him she had been a ranger-naturalist for six years, first at Mesa Verde for a summer, then at Lassen, and now in the Olympics for the past two years. She had a master's degree in ecology, with an anthropology minor, and a B.A. in psychology.

Gideon sipped his martini, a good one, sharp and stony and ice-cold, and looked at her as much as listened. She had changed to a tailored beige pants suit that made her eyes and hair even blacker. And she didn't look at all out of place in a fine restaurant, he decided, and would no doubt look splendid in a museum. When she bent her head to drink, her hair fell forward around her face in soft, dark swirls, as in a slow-motion television advertisement. Once, when they both leaned forward over the table, he smelled her hair's clean, woodsy fragrance.

Somehow, she began to talk about her personal life. She'd been married at eighteen in her hometown of Denver, but her young husband had had problems with drugs, and she'd divorced him after a few months. Then she'd gone into the Army and served as an MP in Germany.

"That was an interesting experience. I learned to shoot; got pretty good at judo and karate too."

"I think I'd better withdraw that invitation to my motel," Gideon said.

When the waitress returned for their order, he hadn't yet looked at the menu.

"They're famous for their grilled salmon here, Professor," Julie said.

"She's sure right about that, Professor," the waitress agreed, writing down the order with evident satisfaction when Gideon nodded his agreement.

"Julie," Gideon said, "I'm the last person in the world to refuse a little respect, but I'd prefer 'Gideon' to 'Professor,' if that's all right with you."

"That's fine; I just noticed that John calls you 'Doc,' so I thought you liked that sort of thing."

"I told him long ago to call me by my first name, so he started calling me 'Gid.' 'Doc' is a compromise."

Gideon noted that she didn't ask him any personal questions and knew that John had told her about Nora. That pleased him; it meant that Julie had been interested enough to ask questions.

When the salmon came, along with a bottle of Gamay Beaujolais that Gideon had ordered over Eleanor's injunction that white wine went with fish, it was placed before them worshipfully.

"Enjoy," said Eleanor again, her voice husky with reverence.

The fish was indeed extraordinarily good, with pink, firm flesh that tasted like fine veal.

"It's called blueback salmon." Julie said, "The Quinault Indians have rearing pens on the lake, and they're the only ones who can get them. The lodge has a special contract with them."

"It's superb."

"They catch them with bone-tipped spears," said Julie, blandly chewing.

Gideon put down his fork. "They *what?*"

Julie laughed. "Joke. They use only the most modern methods, I assure you."

"I'm glad to hear it," Gideon said, returning to the fish, but his thoughts had gone back to that triangular point on the workroom table. He sipped the beaujolais abstractedly.

"Uh-oh," Julie said, "I've started him thinking serious

25

things." She drained her glass and held it out to him to be re-filled. "Let's go back to us."

Gideon slowly shook his head. "There's something that bothers me. . . ."

"What?"

"I don't know, but something's wrong. Or not wrong, just not right." He refilled her glass and his own. "The hell with it. Intuition is a sidewise kind of thing, and you can't push it; at least not mine."

They clicked glasses again and made small talk through the rest of the main course. When Gideon asked for the bill, Eleanor told them they couldn't think of leaving without order-ing the house specialty, a creamy chocolate cheesecake, with their coffee.

"If she says 'enjoy' when she brings it, I'll scream," Julie said.

"So help me, I'll kill her myself."

"Enjoy," Eleanor said heartily when she placed the cake be-fore them and was greeted by a burst of laughter that sent her away baffled but beaming.

In the final ruddy afterglow of the day they walked down the deserted, cool lawn to the shore and listened to the gentle, steady lapping of the tiny waves against the gravel.

"You're going to throw a stone in the water," Julie said.

"Why would I want to do that?" It had been just what he was going to do.

"Inborn male trait. Genetic. Haven't you noticed? From the age of three on, no boy or man can pass a body of water with-out tossing in a stone. That's why our lakes are silting up."

"Ah, but I'm no ordinary tosser. I'm a world-class skimmer, silver medal, ought-four Olympics. Give me some room, now."

He sidearmed a pebble out into the darkening lake. Together they counted the soft splashes as it hopped over the water, leaving spreading circles on the smooth surface. "Two, three, four . . . five."

"A new world's record," Gideon said, "and you were there."

"Let me try," Julie said. "Here goes."

"You're holding it too high. You have to do it underhand."

"Oh, yeah?" She threw the stone. There was a heavy plunk. "One," they said.

"See?"

Julie shook her head. "Nope. I think it's something men can do and women can't, that's all."

"You might be right, actually. Women do throw differently than men; they have different shoulder girdles. In a male, the top of the sternum is on a level with the third thoracic vertebra—" He stopped when Julie laughed. "John's right, you see," he said, smiling. "I do tend to give lectures."

"I like it," she said. "You're a professor. That's the way you're supposed to be. Are you absentminded too?"

"Well, actually, you know, that depends more or less on the nature of . . . What was the question again?"

She laughed again, and they stood silent for a while, listening to the water and smelling the clean breeze coming off the lake. Gideon began to think about putting his arm around her. Did people still do that on first dates? Or did they run right off to bed, and only put their arms over each other's shoulders when they were better acquainted?

"Chilly?" he asked when he saw her shiver. "Would you like to get a nightcap at the bar?"

"I don't like bars very much."

"I don't either," he said with sincerity. "I have some Scotch in my cottage, though, right across the lawn."

She looked at him for a long second. "I think maybe the bar would be better this time."

As they turned from the lake, she smiled and took his arm. "I need a chance to practice up on my karate."

After the soft, cool lakefront, the bar was a shock, full of happy, noisy people, mostly in their fifties and sixties. Even the walls were crowded: elk, antelope, and deer heads peered down from every flat space with lustrous, ruminant eyes. There was a monstrous salmon over the bar and even a small bear, seemingly frozen in midstep with one foot raised as it was padding over the top of the upright piano.

They found a free table in a corner and sat down. The laughter and closeness had made them suddenly shy with each other, and they were still searching for something to talk about when Gideon's brandy and Julie's Grand Marnier came.

"I'm going to practice, you know," Julie said. "I intend to beat your rock-skimming record, even if my vertebrae are funny."

"It's not that they're funny," Gideon said brightly, working hard to reawaken the conversation, "it's just that their relationship to the sternum . . ." He put down his brandy snifter abruptly. "Holy cow, do you know where your seventh thoracic vertebra *is*?"

"I'm not sure. Have I lost it?"

"No, I'm serious," he said. "It's just about the middle of the back, at the thickest part of the rib cage."

"That's fascinating, but I have the feeling I'm missing something."

"Julie, the seventh thoracic—the one the spear point was in—it's here. . . ." He groped over his right shoulder with his left hand, and under his left arm with his right hand, but he couldn't reach it. "Let me palpate yours," he said, leaning toward her.

"Professor Oliver! Is that legal in a public place?"

"Damn it, Julie—"

"Yes, sir," she said quickly, putting down the liqueur and turning so he could reach her back.

His sure fingers quickly found the familiar prominence of the lowest cervical vertebra at the base of her neck, then the first thoracic, and the second. After that the back muscles made the spines harder to feel, but he worked his way carefully down, counting aloud, until he pressed the seventh.

"There!"

"Ouch."

"You see, it's right in the middle of your thorax."

He took his hand from her spine and leaned back in his chair. "In order for a spear to penetrate the front of the seventh thoracic vertebra, it would have to enter here." He placed his middle finger in the center of his chest.

28

"That would smart, all right."

"Not for long. I'd be dead at once. But that's not what I'm thinking of," he said, his eyes thoughtful.

She pushed his brandy across the table to him and waited for him to go on, her own eyes more serious now.

"Look," he said, his hand at his chest again, "that spear would have had to go through the thickest part of the sternum and probably cut through a couple of sternocostal ligaments. And that would have been after severing the pectoralis tendons."

He sipped his brandy without tasting it. His eyes looked inward, seeing the chest cavity behind his hand. "Then it would have gone through the middle of the heart, clean through the whole thing—and the heart is one hell of a tough hunk of muscle. And then after that—we won't even consider the veins and nerves and esophagus—it penetrated nearly an inch into a living vertebra."

"That's a lot of work for a bone spear point to do," she said.

He nodded. "And remember, Eckert was a big guy, with thick bones and muscles. Julie, I don't see how anyone could throw a spear with that much force. A razor-sharp, perfectly balanced metal spear, maybe, but not that crude bone point."

"How about if it was an arrow after all? Would it have more power if it had been shot from a bow?"

"Yes, but it's too big for an arrow point. The shaft would have to be five feet long, and thick, to balance it."

"What about a crossbow?"

Gideon brightened momentarily, then shook his head. "That might give it the necessary force, but I think the point's too big for a crossbow, too. But I don't know anything about them; we can ask John."

"Ugh," Julie said, and shivered suddenly.

"What is it?"

"I just had an image of somebody sneaking through that dark rain forest with a crossbow, stalking human beings."

Her hand lay on the table at the base of her glass. He covered her hand with his. "Yes, that's creepy," he said. "But if you rule out the crossbow, the alternatives are even creepier."

"Like what?"

"Like somebody getting Eckert down on his back and then using a mallet to pound a spear through his heart. That might do it."

"Boy, when you say creepy, you mean creepy. Why would anyone do that? I mean, aside from the possibility that Eckert was a vampire." When he didn't smile, she went on: "Gideon, do you think it was one of those weird cults? Or are you joking?"

He patted her hand. "No, I'm not joking, but I don't really think that's what happened. The trouble is," he said, and paused to finish his brandy, "the trouble is, the only other conclusion I can come up with is even more weird."

He sat silent and staring at the empty glass on the table through two long, deep breaths.

"Dr. Oliver," Julie said finally, "has anyone ever told you that you can sometimes be just a teeny weeny bit irritatingly slow in coming to your point?"

"Frequently," he said with a smile. "I'm just trying to figure out a way of saying it so that I don't sound like a character in a 1930s horror movie."

He put his hands flat on the table and looked directly at her. "All right, Frau Bürgermeister, the conclusion that I am forced to reach is that Eckert was killed by someone—some*thing*—with superhuman strength."

Julie's eyes were wide. Someone behind Gideon struck a match, and they shone briefly in the dim light, like a cat's. "Gideon, you're not suggesting, not implying . . . ?"

"Bigfoot? Absolutely not. Superhuman doesn't necessarily mean supernatural, Julie. Bigfoot doesn't exist; it can't."

"But then what did kill him?"

Gideon slowly shook his head. "It beats the hell out of me."

4

GIDEON WAS IN a good mood. He had, as usual, slept well, had risen about six, and taken a tonic early-morning walk along the misty footpaths on the hillside across the road from the lodge. Then, invigorated but damp and cold, he'd eaten a big breakfast of ham and eggs in the dining room and had sat over two cups of coffee, contentedly gazing across the placid lake.

Now, relaxed, full, and pleasantly sleepy, he slumped comfortably on a weatherbeaten wooden lawn chair, long legs stretched out and crossed at the ankles. The press conference had been going on for half an hour, and Julie, in the chair next to him, had so far handled most of the questions.

She was explaining in cool, professional tones to the three reporters that one of the skeletons found two days earlier had been tentatively identified as Eckert's and that a bone spear was the probably instrument of death. Gideon poured himself more coffee from the silver server that had been brought out to the lawn from the dining room and leaned back again in his chair, drifting tranquilly and almost dozing. The questions and answers droned on; the golden morning sunlight was warm on his cheeks.

He opened his eyes suddenly to find the reporters looking brightly at him, pens poised.

"Uh," he said, "I'm afraid I missed the question."

"Well, now, I guess us country cousins have put the professor to sleep." The speaker was the oldest of the reporters, a heavyset, redheaded man of fifty who looked as if he might have been a hotshot cub reporter thirty years before, with porkpie hat, bow tie, and appealing grin. The bow tie was still in place; the grin, too, but time had worn it into more of a sly smirk than a smile.

"Sorry," Gideon said, "I guess I was thinking of something else. If you'd repeat the question I'd be glad to answer it, Mr. . . ."

"Hood's my name and newspaperin's my game, like I said before. My friends call me Nate. I tell you, Gideon, I don't know much about bones and things, but it sure seems to me that it'd take one hell of a lot of power to put a bone spear through that poor fella's breastbone. . . . Is that its right name?"

"Sternum."

"Mmm, sternum, sternum. My, my." He sipped his coffee and crossed his thick legs, straining the double-knit fabric of his trousers and revealing in unpleasant detail the contours of a plump thigh. "Well, through his *ster*-num then, and through his heart and everything else in there, and still stick way down deep in his backbone."

"Vertebra. Seventh thoracic."

"Right, right. *Número* seven. Anyway, the thing I keep wondering about is, you'd sure have to be one strong *hombre* to do that, wouldn't you?"

"That's good thinking, Mr. Hood. You're quite right. The average person couldn't do it. It would take extraordinary strength, superhuman strength, to drive that spear—that bone spear—in so deeply."

"What about Bigfoot?" The question came from one of the others, a gangling, nervous girl of twenty who had introduced herself tersely as Walker of the *Globe*.

Gideon smiled. "I suppose Bigfoot could have done it, assuming that he's—what is it supposed to be, eight or nine feet tall, and built like a gorilla? But I think a lot of things would militate against drawing that conclusion, not the least of which is the fact that he almost certainly doesn't exist."

"But—" the girl began.

"But *something* killed him," Hood interrupted. "Just what kind of thing *is* running around Quinault Valley? I mean, superhuman strength, carrying a bone spear . . . ?"

Julie looked concerned and opened her mouth, but Gideon spoke first: "You said that, Mr. Hood, not I. I don't know what killed Mr. Eckert, or rather *who* killed him, and I hope the article you write reflects that."

"*If* I write an article. You're not giving us much to write about."

Walker of the *Globe* raised a three-inch nub of pencil in a childish hand with chewed, grubby fingernails. "Just what is the FBI doing to—"

This time Julie cut in. "I think we've covered everything we're able to. I'm sorry Mr. Lau isn't here to give you the FBI perspective, but I'll let you know as soon as there's anything to tell you."

When the reporters had left, Gideon poured two more cups of coffee from the silver pot. "That wasn't too bad," he said. "My first press conference, did you know?"

"I'd never have guessed."

"What do you mean? I thought I did pretty well. How'd you like the way I handled that sleazy Hood character? I know what he was trying to do."

"Oh, great, wonderful. I'm going to love reading the papers."

"Come on, Julie. What did I do wrong? Aside from falling asleep."

She refused to elaborate, so they sipped their coffee in companionable silence, enjoying the sunlight and the sounds of hotel guests beginning to straggle down toward the lake for a day's play.

"Gideon," Julie said after a while, "what do you think *did* kill him?"

"*Who*, not what."

"All right, who?"

"I can think of a few possibilities. First, that this was a ritual execution or a sacrifice. A cult, perhaps—the sort of thing we mentioned last night: stake driven through the heart and so forth."

"That's horrible. Do you really think so?"

Gideon ran his finger around the rim of the empty cup. "Pretty doubtful. I've never heard of it happening before. Not that I know anything about cult murders. Or want to know."

"What are the other possibilities?"

"Well, that there might be a small band of Indians, primitive Indians, living in the rain forest—"

"I checked in my *Ethnography of the Northwest Coast* after dinner last night. Indians have never lived in the rain forest itself."

Gideon shrugged abstractedly, watching a noisy, laughing group of teenagers playing volleyball nearby, boys against girls. "Far be it from me," he said, "to quarrel with *Ethnography of the Northwest Coast*, but if they haven't lived there they've certainly died there. Those basket burials, at least the ones I could determine race on, were American Indian to the core. And the baskets certainly look Amerind, even if they're not local."

"Maybe . . . you know, you're not the first one to suggest this. There was a graduate student from Alabama or Mississippi—Dennis Blackpath—who spent a couple of summers poking around Quinault researching his dissertation."

"Blackpath? That sounds like he's an Indian himself."

"I think he is—or part Indian, anyhow. He had a theory that there was a lost Indian tribe in the rain forest."

"He did? Why didn't you mention that before?"

"Well, this was six or seven years ago—before my time. The only reason I know about it is that he's become kind of a joke to the other rangers over the years. I guess he was a first-class crackpot. He never found anything, of course."

"Still," Gideon said, "if he had some evidence . . ."

"Gideon," she said, leaning intently forward, "if there were a band of Indians wandering around in there, I'd know it. They'd have been seen, or left signs; there'd be rumors." She shook her head. "No, I just don't see how it can be."

"I know," Gideon said glumly. "It isn't very credible, is it?"

"Besides, what about that business of the superhuman strength?"

"What about it?"

"Indians aren't any stronger than anyone else," she said. "Or are they?"

"No, of course not."

34

"So, Indians or not, you're still left with the question of how the spear penetrated so deeply."

"Yes," he said. "I mean no. John's left with it. My part in this is finished. Would you like me to get us some more coffee?"

"No, thanks. Will you get angry if I ask you something?"

"Probably. How do I know until you ask?"

Julie laughed, a bright, easy laugh that made Gideon feel they were friends. "My God, I didn't even ask it, and he's already cross."

"That," said Gideon, "is because some deeply perceptive part of my subconscious tells me it's going to be about Bigfoot."

"Well, after all, 'superhuman strength' is *your* term—"

"To my growing regret."

"—and you don't have any plausible theories of your own. Look, John's due any minute. Couldn't we all go and have a look at those footprints? Aren't you even a teeny bit curious?"

There was a shout from the volleyball court, and the ball bounded squishily over the grass toward them. Gideon caught it in one hand, stood up, and batted it back with his fist, all in one movement, clearing the net some seventy feet away.

"Hey, great shot, mister!" shouted a tall, yellow-haired girl with long, brown legs. "Did you guys see that?"

"Big goddamn deal," muttered one of the boys loudly enough for Gideon to hear.

"Yeah, big goddamn deal," Julie said, smiling up at him. "Don't look so smug, you show-off. It's not talent, it's just that *macho* shoulder girdle."

Standing there in the sunshine, looking down at her with the clean morning breeze riffling his hair and the lively sting of the volleyball still on his knuckles, Gideon was oddly happy. He reached for her hand and hauled her easily out of the chair, feeling powerful and in control.

"Okay,' he said, laughing and holding both her hands, "let's go see the monster footprints."

* * *

35

They drove east on South Shore Road among giant fir, hemlock, and spruce draped with mosses and spotted with lichens. Within a few miles the lake narrowed into the Upper Quinault River, and the paved road gave away to gravel and then to rutted dirt. The cab of the Park Service pickup truck was small for the three of them, and Gideon sat in the middle, jouncing and uncomfortably constricted, between Julie in the driver's seat and John on the right. Julie drove fast and well, obviously at home at the wheel and in the forest.

Gideon had gotten over his initial reaction to the woods. The towering, increasingly dark forest with its filtered light now seemed majestic and beautiful.

"I take it," he said to Julie, "that *this* is the real rain forest?"

"It is," she said with proprietary pride. "What do you think of it?"

"Too damn dark," John muttered out the window.

"It's beautiful," Gideon said simply.

Julie smiled at him, clearly pleased.

"Technically, what makes it a rain forest?" he asked her.

"Rains all the goddamn time, that's what," grumbled John, still looking out the window. "It's even worse than Seattle."

"Actually," Julie said, "it hardly rains at all from July to October. All the rain falls in the winter."

"How much rain does it get in a year?" Gideon asked, then quickly said, "Too goddamn much," in time with John's growl.

They all laughed. Julie said, "Ten or fifteen feet a year; about a hundred forty-five inches." She waited for Gideon's obligatory low whistle and went on. "Strictly speaking, it's not a rain forest. The term technically applies to tropical forests with broadleaf trees and woody vines and clay soil. These trees are evergreen, and the soil is fantastically rich. You can dig through two or three feet of humus with your fingers. But it's temperate and wet, and it has a pretty solid roof of treetops, and lots of ferns and flowers and mosses on the ground, and most botanists would agree nowadays that that qualifies it as a rain forest—the only one in the Northern Hemisphere, and the only coniferous one in the world."

36

"I am suitably impressed," Gideon said.

"Too much like Hawaii," said John. "Everything's so damn wet and soggy it falls apart if you touch it."

"John," said Gideon, "you must be the only person in the world—certainly the only native—who hates Hawaii."

"Too damn wet," John said again. "I wish they'd assign me to Tucson."

After half an hour's drive, they crossed over the river on a surprisingly modern bridge and followed a sign toward the North Fork Ranger Station. Julie swung the truck suddenly to the left shoulder of the road—until then, the shoulder had not been wide enough to park on—and stopped.

"Here we are," she said. "It's up on that ridge."

They walked up the shallow incline on a narrow trail with frequent switchbacks. Gideon, who had poor woods sense, lost sight of the truck and the road in thirty seconds. Within two minutes, he had no idea of which direction it lay in. The trail was well cut and easy to walk on, however, and the fragrances and varied greens of the rain forest absorbed him.

They left the trail after twenty minutes, climbed a fifteen-foot slope, and stood in a small clearing. The trail was swallowed up at once; they might have been miles from the nearest path. Before them, a twenty-by-twenty-foot area had been stripped of undergrowth and pockmarked with deep trenches cut in right-angled patterns.

"Looks like a dig," Gideon said. "This is where they found the bodies?"

"Right," said John, "and here are the tracks." He went to the far edge of the clearing, with Gideon and Julie following, all three working their way carefully among the trenches. "The tracks apparently came from over there," John continued, "skirted the edge of the clearing, and then left through here."

"They're pretty well trampled over, aren't they?" Gideon said, frowning.

"Yeah, with the Sasquatch Society people and our own men making casts, I guess there isn't much left."

Julie walked a few feet into the undergrowth in the direction

37

from which the tracks had come. "Unless it's been messed up since yesterday, there should be at least one good print. . . . Here it is."

Cut crisply into the soft duff of the forest floor was a gigantic, splay-toed footprint, roughly human in form, but much elongated.

Gideon knelt and pulled out a tape measure.

"Eighteen and a quarter inches," Julie said, "by eight at its widest point."

Gideon quickly confirmed the measurements, then lay prone on the spongy, fragrant earth, supporting himself on his elbows and peering at the footprint, his nose a foot away from it. After a minute he got back to his knees and brushed himself off, still looking at the track.

"Sorry, folks," he said. "Believe me, I'd love to say this looks like it's from a live creature." He looked up at John and shook his head. "It's a fake."

He expected an argument, but the big man merely dropped to his own knees to see better. "How can you tell?" he asked quietly.

"There's no sign of a stride, no dynamic. With a basically human foot like this, you'd expect a basically human stride that starts when the heel strikes the ground, runs down the lateral edge of the foot, swings to the ball, and then ends with a toe-off." He rose to his feet and gestured at the track. "But this print was put down all at once, flat, and then picked up heel first in a clumsy attempt to imitate a stride. I imagine a horse or deer would leave that sort of print, but of course I don't know much about tracks—"

John, still on his knees, looked up. "You *what?*"

"More accurately, I don't know *anything* about tracks. I couldn't tell a bear print from a rabbit's."

"Well, Jesus Christ, how can you be so godawful sure that this isn't real?"

"It's not a matter of footprints at all. It's a question of the biomechanics of locomotion—"

John was on his feet, his hands chopping the air. "Oh, boy,

Doc, whenever you start talking like that I *know* you don't know what you're talking about."

"That's not true at all," Gideon said testily. "I can't help it if you can't follow perfectly direct scientific language for—"

"Now, boys," Julie said, sitting on a fallen log and beginning to take off her shoes, "I *do* know something about tracks, and I think Gideon has a point. But let's test this empirically."

Her feet were strong and brown, as Gideon thought they would be, with square little toes, and wide at the base. "Ooh," she said, "this feels good; you guys ought to take your shoes off." She wiggled her toes. "Okay, what should I do?"

"Go across to the other side of the clearing, then walk back across it as normally as you can," Gideon said.

She did so and marched right up to Gideon. The top of her head was a little above his chin. "Now," he said, "next to that right footprint you left over there, stamp down your right foot hard."

They stood together looking at the prints. It was hardly necessary to explain anything, but Gideon explained anyway. "You will note," he said professorially, "that the single footprint stamped into the ground is clear and sharply delineated all around the edges. But look at the tracks made while walking. Only the heel and toe portions have any depth to them; the outside margins, while generally visible, are indistinct and shallow. The inside margins, between the ball of the foot and the heel, haven't left any imprint." He looked at Julie and leered, twirling an imaginary moustache. "You have lovely arches, m'dear, lovely."

"Thank you," she said.

"Most important," Gideon went on, "the walking tracks have little ridges of earth just behind the toes. Those are thrown up when the toes push off on each step. Equally diagnostic, the toes make the deepest impression, the heel a shallower one, and the sole the shallowest of all. Whereas the stamped-in print—"

"Okay, okay, Doc," John said with resigned good humor, "you're right. It's a fake."

"It's obvious, really," said Julie.

"Sure," Gideon muttered, "as Watson was always telling Holmes—*a posteriori*."

On the way back down the trail, a gray-white, lichen-spotted bone gleaming in the pearly light caught Gideon's eye. He bent and picked it up.

"Probably an elk," Julie said. "There are plenty of them here."

"Probably," said Gideon. "It's a femur from one of the Cervidae."

The three had continued walking while he turned the bone in his hand.

"What's special about it?" John asked.

"I'm not sure anything is. It's just . . ." He stopped, continuing to turn the bone, and the others stopped with him. "See how it's split, with this big dent right here at the start of the split?"

They nodded, and Julie fingered the dent.

"That's just what bones look like in ancient-man sites where they've been broken open with a stone chopper to get at the marrow. I've turned up a couple like this at the dig I'm working on."

"Couldn't another animal have done it?" Julie asked. "Or a bullet? Or a fall?"

Gideon looked at the bone for another long second, and flung it over his shoulder into the woods. "You're absolutely right. Even world-renowned authorities have one-track minds."

They continued down the trail, and emerged so suddenly onto the road that Gideon almost walked into the truck.

5

GIDEON LAY ON his stomach in the dirt, at the back of the low, shallow cave, cramped and aching, his knees and elbows scraped raw. He had been wedged in like that for hours, choked and half blinded by the showers of pebbles and dust every movement brought down. His hair was heavy with dirt, his nostrils caked with it, his teeth on edge with it.

He was happy as a clam.

He lay the tiny pick and brush next to the newly uncovered humerus and inched his big frame backward on his elbows, bringing down a rain of pebbles. At the entrance, where the cave widened, he sat up and stretched, wincing as joints creaked and muscles burned.

He found the last of the apple juice he'd had with lunch and drank a great gulp from the bottle. It had warmed in the sunlight, but it washed away the dust in his throat. Aching and content, he sat back against the cliff face and looked at the lovely scene below. It would have been far less pleasant thirteen thousand years ago.

The cave dwellers who'd lived there would not have been thirty feet above a small, pretty beach of dark pebbles, but miles from the water's edge, facing a huge, gray expanse of desolate land scoured flat by the retreating Cordilleran glacier. Treeless it would have been, and swampy, and full of kettle lakes holding the slowly melting, stagnant ice that the glacier had left behind. Far in the distance they would have seen the ribbon of invading seawater that was the Strait of Juan de Fuca aborning. On the very horizon would have been the trailing edge of the immense ice sheet itself, black with churned-up rocks and earth, grinding its way back into what is now British Columbia.

There was no ice sheet now. Where its grim edge had been was the green, soft outline of Vancouver Island. And between Vancouver and the algae-covered beach just below him was only the thin, white curve of Dungeness Spit a thousand feet offshore, and twenty miles of water. Juan de Fuca Strait—named by an eighteenth-century English captain for a sixteenth-century Greek sailor traveling incognito on a Spanish vessel—had swelled and flowed over the glacier-scarred land

41

until it formed a deep, mighty channel, from Vancouver to the Olympic Peninsula, and from the Pacific to Puget Sound.

He finished the last of the apple juice and stood up on the narrow ledge, looking with pleasure at the placid water, glasslike except for the sporadic, silvery splashes of leaping salmon, always where one didn't expect them. Overhead, sea gulls and elegant, black-headed Caspian terns cried and planed in great, flat circles.

Gideon sighed happily. There was still almost a month of this before heading back to the teaching routine at Northern Cal. And tomorrow morning he'd be driving back down to Lake Quinault, not to look into some musty, ancient murder, but to see Julie. If the investigation were still going on, they'd drive elsewhere to be away from it; to the beach, perhaps to Kalaloch or La Push.

With three easy, powerful strides he clambered up the old, warped planking that he had dragged up to serve as a ramp to the clifftop. As always, the scene at the top startled him momentarily. It was a constant source of surprise that ten feet above this marvelous, seemingly isolated site in the side of a beach cliff was Dungeness with its wide, carefully tended lawns and flowerbeds, its big homes and sedate cottage motels.

He walked across Marine Drive directly onto the close-cropped lawn of Bayview Cottages, five tidy, gray-shingled little houses with white trim which looked as if they might have been transported whole from the coast of Maine. All were identical except for little rustic signs over the porches. "Sea Gull Cottage," said Gideon's.

Inside, he picked up the telephone and dialed a Sequim number.

"Hello, Bertha," he said. "Is Abe there?"

A few seconds later, an old man's voice, thin but full of energy, said, "Hello, Gideon, this is you?"

Gideon smiled. Abe Goldstein had been born in a ghetto near Minsk and had fled to the United States at the age of seventeen, speaking no English, having no money, and possessing no marketable skills. He had peddled thread and ribbons from a

42

pushcart on Pitkin Avenue in Brooklyn and gone to night school to learn English. In six years he had graduated from the City College of New York, and four years later, in 1934, he had a Ph.D. in anthropology from Columbia University. For twenty years he'd taught at Columbia, then gone to the University of Wisconsin for another twenty, where he'd been Gideon's professor. He'd finished his teaching career with a few distinguished years at the University of Washington.

Almost sixty years in America, most of it spent as an eminent scholar of worldwide repute, and he still spoke like an immigrant ribbon peddler. Most of the time, anyway; the accent varied noticeably. More than one academic adversary had suggested it was a studied eccentricity, and Gideon, no adversary, was inclined to agree. If ever there was a studied eccentric, it was Abraham Irving Goldstein.

"Yes, Abe," he said, "this is me."

"So how is the dig?"

"So how should it be?"

"Of an old man you shouldn't make fun. So tell me."

"I had a great day, Abe. That's why I called. Uncovered a juvenile humerus today, eleven, twelve years old, from stratum four. So it looks like it was a family habitat. Also a piece of wood; I'm not sure what. Rectangular, two, three inches wide, with a hole at one end. About a foot long, unless we only have part of it. It's pretty rotten—needs to be set in plaster of Paris *in situ.*"

"Wonderful. So."

Gideon waited. The "so" said that something besides the dig was on Abe's mind.

"Listen, Gideon, you didn't happen to see yesterday's *Chronicle?*"

"No, what's in it?"

"All about you is what's in it. You want to hear?"

"I don't know. You've got me worried. You sound a little too happy about it."

Abe's delighted cackle, strong and hearty, came over the wire, and Gideon, smiling to himself, poured some Teacher's

43

into a jelly glass from the cupboard. He couldn't reach ice or water without putting down the telephone, so he stood there sipping it neat, one elbow on the television set atop the cupboard.

"What's it about, Abe? That interview in Quinault?"

"You bet it is. Give a listen. First the headline. You ready?" There was some theatrical throat clearing, then: "Quote. Unknown Creature Stalks Quinault. Could Be Bigfoot, Says Noted Skeleton Detective Gideon Oliver. End quote."

"Oh, boy," Gideon said and sighed, sinking into a plastic armchair with the drink and the telephone.

"Gideon, tell me, what's a skeleton detective, something new? This I never heard of."

"Come on, Abe, let's hear the rest." He kept his voice irked to please Abe, but he was more amused than annoyed. He understood now what Julie had been talking about.

"Believe me, even better it gets. But look, what are you doing tonight? Why don't you come over to Twilight Harbor Estates? You can read it yourself, and Bertha's got already a pot roast on the stove. We'll drink a bottle beer, have a nice glass tea. And then . . ."

That singsong "and then" meant that something besides pot roast was cooking. Not that there would be a pot roast or bottle of beer at Professor Emeritus Abraham Goldstein's house. The dialect remained, but the street peddler's tastes were long gone.

"And then what, Abe?"

"*Nu,* so come on over, you'll see. What else better you got to do? Come on, make happy an old man's heart."

Gideon laughed. The accent was growing more atrocious by the second. "Okay," he said, "but I have to clean up first. May I bring something?"

"A bottle of red wine would be fine, a Cabernet, but California, not Washington. French I wouldn't ask."

"What happened to the bottle beer and the glass tea?"

"For me, good enough, but you're a guest; I got to treat you right. Hurry up, it's depressing here at the old folks' home."

* * *

Abe lived neither at Twilight Harbor Estates nor at an old people's home. He lived in Sun Meadow, a peaceful, wooded community of sumptuous homes grouped around a golf course on which he never played. Sun Meadow, as the name implied, lay in the famed rain shadow of the Olympics. Storms moving in from the Pacific would drop most of their moisture on the windward slope of the mountain range, leaving only about fifteen inches a year to fall in the "banana belt" on the other side. Thirty-five miles away the annual rainfall might be fifteen feet.

Abe complained frequently that there was too little excitement and too many sun-seeking old people (most of whom were decades younger than he), but Gideon knew that Abe had found his earthly paradise there in the green, soft hills between Sequim and Dungeness.

Abe met him at the door. "Welcome to Restful Acres," he said. "Come in the study." He led the way, his soft old slippers whispering over the gleaming hardwood floor. With a sigh he eased himself into one of two leather armchairs in front of a wall filled with photographs of an unbelievably young Abraham Goldstein peering at a skull in Kenya, surrounded by shy Pygmies in the Congo, crawling out of an Aleutian igloo, and arm-in-arm with a grinning, frizzled-haired Melanesian with a bone through his nose and Abe's own pith helmet perched atop his head.

At seventy-five, the old man in the chair had aged better than most. He was arthritic and terribly frail now, but he hadn't put on weight and was easily recognizable as the young man in the photographs. The kinky mat of black hair had turned white without thinning, and Abe wore it in an outrageous, flamboyant Afro. The eyes were still playful and sprightly, if anything enhanced by the papery wrinkles that nearly buried them.

"Mix yourself a drink," he said, "and one for me, too."

"What would you like," Gideon asked, "a glass seltzer? A cup prune juice?"

"Don't be funny. Give me a Chivas, but light. The old liver ain't what it was."

45

Gideon mixed two Scotch-and-waters and sat down next to Abe. Then he picked up the copy of the *Chronicle* on the coffee table and followed Abe's jabbing finger to the article on the second page.

UNKNOWN CREATURE STALKS QUINAULT. COULD BE BIGFOOT, SAYS NOTED SKELETON DETECTIVE GIDEON OLIVER
by Nathaniel Hood

QUINAULT—Experts say that a charred skeleton found buried in the Quinault Valley is that of Norris Eckert, twenty-nine, one of two hikers who disappeared there in 1976. Physical anthropologist Gideon Oliver, a highly paid consultant to the FBI, said that Eckert had apparently been killed by a large bone spear point which was found still imbedded in the skeleton's backbone, at the seventh cervical vertebra. "It would take superhuman strength to drive that bone point in so deeply," the California scientist said. When questioned about what sort of creature might have such strength, Oliver said, "I suppose Bigfoot could have done it," and further described the creature as "eight or nine feet tall and built like a gorilla."

Eckert's remains were discovered during the continuing search for Claire Hornick, eighteen, of Tacoma, reported missing in the same area last week.

Gideon folded the paper and put it back on the low table. Abe picked it up and pretended to read it again, shaking his head and clucking. "Such a thing," he said. "Eight or nine feet tall, hah? *Oy, oy, oy.*" He was practically singing. "Like a gorilla, yet." He laughed outright. "God forbid, you really said this?"

"Well, they got the vertebra wrong, as you know. It was T-7, not C-7. And I'm afraid they were very much mistaken about the 'highly paid.' Other than that, they were pretty accurate, I'm sorry to say. I'm going to have a heck of a time living this down at Northern Cal."

Abe patted his knee. "Live and learn," he said. "Come on, time to eat. Bertha said six o'clock.".

Bertha was Abe's unmarried, fifty-year-old daughter, who had lived all her life in the shadow of her brilliant father. She had gotten an M.A. in anthropology and had taught for a while in a community college but had long ago settled with apparent complacency into the role of his housekeeper. She was a superb cook and had prepared a luscious dinner of *boeuf à la mode* (pot roast after all, but what a pot roast!) with broiled tomatoes and buttered, homemade noodles.

As usual, talk of anthropology ceased over the meal, and the three of them chatted like the old friends they were of past times and old acquaintances. Bertha and Abe frequently used Yiddish expressions which Abe would laboriously, and for the most part unnecessarily, explain to Gideon.

As soon as Bertha cleared the dishes and went to get coffee, Abe said, "Listen, I want to talk to you about this Bigfoot business."

"Abe," Gideon said, "I was quoted out of context; you know that. I don't really—"

"I know, I know." His thin hand fluttered dismissively. "You know a Professor Chace from Berkeley?"

"An anthropologist? No."

"You heard of Roy Linger?"

Gideon shook his head.

"You never heard of Roy Linger?"

"Abe, if you have a point to make, I wish—"

"All right, hold your horses, don't get excited. This Roy Linger is a famous explorer, a hunter, a rich man. In textiles or something—"

"Your old line."

Abe looked confused for a moment, then laughed delightedly, slapping his hand on the table. "You're right. Maybe his father had the next pushcart! Anyway, this Linger, he's very active in the Sasquatch Society; always making expeditions to go off in the mountains to find Bigfoot."

"Has he had any luck?" Gideon asked dryly.

Abe waved his finger under Gideon's nose. "Don't be so smart, mister. You're a young man yet; you got a lot to learn.

47

Listen, this E. L. Chace from Berkeley, he's supposed to be the number one expert on Bigfoot; he's all the time talking in some seminar, or on the television. Wrote a couple of books. You sure you never heard of him?"

Bertha came in with the coffee but stood politely in the doorway, holding the tray while her father continued.

"So this Professor Chace, yesterday he gave a lecture in Seattle, and he's staying tonight with his old friend Mr. Roy Linger in Port Townsend. And guess what? He reads that wonderful article about you, and he wants to meet you. So this Mr. Roy Linger calls the university to see if they know where you are, and they refer him to me, and so on and so forth."

"I hope," Gideon said, "that you're not about to tell me that you've invited him here. Abe, I really don't want to meet the number one expert on Bigfoot."

"Certainly not. Of course not." He looked over his shoulder. "Bertha, don't just stand there. Bring in the coffee."

She poured the coffee, a rich, black Italian roast, into tiny green and white cups that Gideon had once sent as gifts from Sicily. Abe sucked in half a cupful with a smack of the lips.

"Certainly not," he said again. "Would I invite him here without asking you first? Hah?"

"I apologize," Gideon said somewhat dubiously, sniffing the coffee and taking a small sip. "I jumped to conclusions."

"You certainly did." Abe swallowed the rest of his coffee. "No. I told him we would go there. . . . Bertha, what time is it?"

She twisted to look behind her at the wall clock he could have seen merely by looking up. "Eight-thirty."

"In three quarters of an hour."

"Go where?" Gideon said.

"To Port Townsend, to Linger's house. For after-dinner brandies. Very fancy."

Gideon put down his coffee cup and rotated it slowly, between thumb and forefinger, in its saucer. "Abe, you don't give any credence to the Bigfoot stories, do you?"

"No, but I don't rule it out either. It seems crazy to me, but maybe I don't know everything."

"I did check those prints near Quinault, you know. They were obvious fakes, very amateurish."

"And if you found some fake human footprints, that proves there's no such thing as human beings?"

"I know, but there's so much junk written about Bigfoot, so much charlatanism and plain bad science. . . . I just don't want to get involved in it."

"Look," Abe said gently, "a man who's written books about it, a professor at a big university, I'm willing to give him a little of my time. Maybe I'll learn something."

Gideon smiled and turned to Bertha. "How old is this man now?"

"Seventy-five years young last July."

"Don't patronize, goddamnit," Abe said testily.

"Seventy-five and still giving me lessons in open-mindedness."

"That goes for you too," Abe snapped. "You're coming or you're not coming?"

"Okay, let's go," said Gideon, still smiling. "But I'm warning you, I'm going to take some convincing."

Abe brightened immediately. "Fair enough. Come, give a listen, keep an open mind. Unless you got some other answers?"

"Answers?"

"To how this Eckert guy got a spear stuck through his T-7. If not a nine-foot gorilla, what was it? Bertha, where's my black shoes with the buckles that don't need shoelaces?"

6

ROY LINGER AND Port Townsend were made for each other; a pair of handsome, elegant anachronisms only faintly gone to seed. The town, especially the part on the hill, would

49

not have been out of place a hundred years before. The houses were all Victorian, most of them modest, but many with French mansard roofs, gabled cupolas, and widows' walks that looked far out over Admiralty Inlet and Port Townsend Bay.

Linger himself was pure F. Rider Haggard, an extraordinarily good-looking, silver-haired man in bush jacket and cream-colored ascot.

"Professor Goldstein?" he said in a polished Bostonian accent. He pronounced it the German way: *Goldshtine.* "Professor Oliver? How good of you to come."

He led them through a long entryway, the walls of which were covered with mounted heads of tigers, leopards, deer, ibex, and animals Gideon couldn't name. Below each head was a small gold plaque. Gideon managed to read one, under an open-mouthed tiger's head, as they walked by: *Bihar, May 7, 1957, 440 lbs.*

The living room, down two carpeted steps, was completely modern, with a huge, rectangular fieldstone fireplace in the middle, rising twenty feet to the canted ceiling. The carpet was a pale rose, most of the furniture white.

Linger paused, smiling, at the entrance. "I'd like you to meet my good friend Professor Earl Chace."

In a deeply upholstered white couch sat a large, beefy, smiling man in a three-piece peach-colored suit that might have been chosen to go with the rose and white and gray of the room.

"A pink suit?" Abe murmured in Gideon's ear. "Already I don't like him."

Chace strode forward to greet them, hand extended. "Professor Goldstein?" (He said *Goldsteen.*) "Professor Oliver? I'm truly glad to meet you, truly privileged."

He had very white teeth, a great many of them, and abundant black hair that was slicked back, except for full sideburns down to the corners of his jaw and a single, curling lock that tumbled boyishly over his forehead. A big, strong grip with a palm so clean and dry that it rustled when he shook hands, a redolence of musky cologne, and a palpably oleaginous aura

50

made him seem half country singer, half country preacher, and not at all Berkeley professor. When he shook hands he revealed a large expanse of smooth, lilac-colored French cuff with a diamond-spangled cuff link that matched a heavy gold ring on his pinkie.

Already I don't like him either, Gideon thought, as they seated themselves in the white sofa grouping.

"We were having some Courvoisier," Linger said. "Eighteen sixty-five. Remarkable stuff. Would you care to join us?"

He went to a fieldstone bar built into a corner of the room and poured four generous measures from an old bottle. While the others were turned in his direction, Gideon saw Chace quickly pick up one of the two snifters on the coffee table and toss off most of it, choking slightly before it all got down. Linger brought them their cognacs and then noticed with a small frown the two glasses on the coffee table. He took them to the bar and poured their contents down the drain.

It might well have been meant to impress—the cognac had to be wildly expensive—but his action seemed to come naturally to him. So, for that matter, had Chace's.

In near-unison, they all raised their glasses, swirled the dark, golden liquid, sniffed it appreciatively, drank, and said "Aah."

Linger elegantly crossed one trouser leg of powder blue over the other, being careful first to hitch up the material. He cupped the belly of the glass between his first and second fingers and continued to swirl the contents.

"Gentlemen, I want to thank you for coming. As . . . yes, Earl?"

Chace had politely raised his forefinger and waited for Linger's attention. "Roy," he said, "I think we ought to start taping now."

"Oh, yes. Would you mind," he said to Gideon and Abe, "if we tape-recorded our conversation this evening?"

"I'm not sure if I do or not," Gideon said, faintly uneasy. "Why do you want to tape it?"

It was Chace who answered, when Linger deferred to him with a nod. "It's for our own protection. There are people out there who twist our words for their own ends, who have their own sinister purposes. There are those who are just out for the money, who don't—"

"What Professor Chace means," Linger said, "is that the Sasquatch Society, having been involved in more than one unfortunate controversy, now makes it a point to record all pertinent discussions. With your permission, of course?"

"Sure," said Abe. "It's okay by me."

"I think I'd rather you didn't," Gideon said.

Chace spoke after a moment of silence. "Would you mind explaining why?" he said, his eyes fixed on his glass.

Gideon minded. He was offended by the implication behind the taping and annoyed by Chace's manner. "Yes, I'd mind," he said curtly.

Chace's cheeks flushed an angry purple, but Linger cut smoothly in. "Fine. No need to tape if you'd rather not." He uncrossed his legs, then recrossed them the other way around. "Now, as I'm sure you know, I've spent most of my life in the attempt to further man's knowledge, and I like to think that, in my small way, I've succeeded." He paused, looking down into the swirling brandy.

"You sure have, Roy," Chace said, "and we all appreciate it."

Linger continued, "I believe that this evening presents an unparalleled opportunity to share and increase our understanding of one of the most fascinating and mysterious creatures known to science."

Gideon shifted in his chair. Linger was as oily as Chace once he got going. This would not be the first time Abe's enthusiastic eclecticism had gotten them into an uncomfortable situation.

With the placid assurance of the rich and powerful that he would not be interrupted, Linger slowly sipped his brandy, then let his eyes rest on the ancient maps on the wall across from him, as if gathering inspiration. "In this room tonight," he said, "we have three of the finest scientific minds of our times: the dean of American anthropology, the world's leading

52

authority on giant anthropoid behavior and morphology, and one of the foremost younger anthropologists of his day."

"Thank you, Roy," Chace said.

Gideon said nothing.

"You got maybe a little seltzer in the icebox to go with this?" said the dean of American anthropology, holding out his glass. "Gives me heartburn."

With the merest tic of irritation at his chiseled lips, Linger took Abe's glass to the bar, added soda water from a cut-glass siphon, and returned with it.

"Now, gentlemen," he said, sitting down and crossing his legs as meticulously as before, "the quest for accurate and unimpeachable data on the last of the great anthropoids, the being we call Bigfoot or Sasquatch—"

Gideon could sit still no longer. "Mr. Linger, pardon me, but I'm not quite sure just what this meeting is about."

It was Chace who leaned forward, his big-boned elbows on his thighs, the snifter cupped in both hands, in a posture of warm sincerity that showed he forgave Gideon his gauche performance over the tape recorder. "That's my doing, Professor. I read about your interview in Quinault, and I knew you were on a dig up this way, so I asked Roy—Mr. Linger—if he'd have the kindness to bring us together. It's an unanticipated honor" —he bowed toward Abe—"to meet the eminent Professor Goldstein as well."

He leaned back and crossed his legs, not delicately like Linger, but in an expansive, masculine way, right ankle on left knee. "Now, the Sasquatch Society is always delighted to find a reputable scientist with whom we can begin a meaningful dialogue. As I'm sure we all know all too well, the halls of academe are sometimes just a little bigoted about certain things."

"I've found them pretty open-minded," Gideon said.

"Ah-ha-ha," said Chace. "Now, as you may know, the Sasquatch Society sponsors a massive educational program of seminars and institutes, and we are always looking for highly regarded academics to serve on panels and so forth."

"Thanks," Gideon said. "I don't think I'd be interested."

"We'd pay your expenses, of course, and there'd be compensation, substantial by academic standards, for your participation."

"Professor Chace, I don't believe that Bigfoot exists."

"But you were quoted as saying—"

"I was quoted out of context."

"Surely," Linger said suavely, "you don't mean that you would refuse to accept legitimate evidence because it's contrary to your views?"

"Legitimate evidence, no. But I've never seen any."

"Professor," said Linger, "were you quoted accurately on the matter of superhuman strength having been required to drive that spear point in?"

"Well, yes, that was accurate."

"Then what do *you* think killed that unfortunate man?"

If the question kept coming up this often, he was going to have to find an answer. "I don't know," he muttered lamely. He was anxious to leave. It was unlikely that the evening was going to improve, and the sooner it was over, the better. He looked over at Abe, but the old man was clearly enjoying himself, sitting up as straight and interested as an eager puppy.

Chace took a large swallow of the brandy and said, "Professor, I don't see how you can say there's no legitimate evidence. Have you ever seen the Rosten-Chapman film? That's indisputable." He raised his glass and grinned. "In my poor opinion."

Not in Gideon's. He had seen it—with Abe, as a matter of fact—ten years before, at the Milwaukee national conference of the American Society for Physical Anthropology. He could still recall his disappointment with the much-talked-about film. The focus had been poor, the action jerky. All that could be seen was a blurry, dark figure, more or less apelike, walking away from the camera—with what seemed to the assembled anthropologists to be an extremely exaggerated stride, less compatible with general anthropoid locomotion than with a poor actor's interpretation of a giant ape's manner of walking.

"We've seen it," Abe said with a cheery smile. "Indisputable it ain't."

Linger laughed heartily, and Abe beamed at him.

Chace was very serious. "All right, even if you don't accept the film—and you have that right—you can't just wish away the thousands of years of verified, responsible sightings of similar species like the yeti."

"I'm afraid," Gideon said, "that the Abominable Snowman doesn't seem to me any better verified—"

"It's not just the Abominable Snowman—which, incidentally, isn't abominable at all; the term is a misinterpretation of a Sherpa word meaning manlike wild thing." Obviously, Chace was getting into a familiar speech. "No, it's much bigger than that. There's the *wudenwasa* seen and reported by the Anglo-Saxons; the Fomorians that inhabited Ireland when the Celts invaded it; and the hairy men of Broceliande in Brittany. What about Grendel? Knowledge of these beings goes back to *Beowulf.*"

"So does knowledge of griffins, and devils, and goats that fly."

Chace laughed. "I guess we differ on the reliability of myth."

I guess we do, Gideon thought.

"But what about scientists? Modern scientists with unimpeachable credentials? What about Ivan Sanderson? Bayanov? Bourtsev? Kravitz, right here at Washington State? How do you respond to them?"

Gideon could respond, all right, but he wasn't interested in an argument. He shrugged. "All I can do is look at the data and draw my own conclusions."

"Professor Chace," Abe said, "I'm a little curious. What does Sherry Washburn think about your theories? Or Howell?"

"I beg your pardon?"

"You don't know Washburn? . . . You're not with the University of California?"

"Yes, I am."

Abe's eyes narrowed. "Sherwood Washburn is—"

Chace laughed easily. "Oh, I see. Are they on the biology faculty? Well—"

"Anthropology," Gideon said.

"Yes, well, I'm in supervisory development."

"Supervisory development?" said Abe. "This is a university department?"

Chace seemed to find that very funny. "No, goodness me, I'm not technically on the faculty, you see. I teach evening courses in Extension—public speaking for managers, office organization, that kind of thing. Just do it to keep my skills up."

"You're not a professor, then?" Gideon asked.

Chace slapped his thigh and chuckled with the air of a man who was above overly fastidious distinctions of academic rank. "Never said I was."

No, and never denied it either, Gideon thought.

"You got a Ph.D.?" Abe asked bluntly.

Chace's face became solemn. "I have a D.B.A., a doctorate of business administration. My formal education is in marketing and public relations."

Gideon looked at his watch. "Mr. Linger, I've certainly enjoyed this evening, but I'm afraid I have to be up early tomorrow—"

Chace put down his glass with a thump. His expression had changed from solemn to earnest. He leaned tensely forward. "Gideon—may I call you Gideon?—I'm not one of your kooks, or one of these UFO nuts, or someone out to make big bucks. I'm a scientist like yourself, even if I'm self-taught, and I don't go off half cocked. But I'm sitting here telling you"—his first two fingers began tapping on the coffee table, keeping time with his words—"that I *know* Bigfoot exists." His fingers curled into a fist, and he banged on the table. "I *know* it!"

"Dr. Chace," Gideon said, "neither contemporary nor fossil evidence support you. No one has ever found an ape bone on this continent. The only primates that have ever lived in North America are people."

Abe corrected him at once. "And what about the Eocene prosimians? They weren't primates?"

Gideon deferred. "All right, but they were gone by the middle Oligocene, thirty million years ago. Bigfoot's still supposed to be around. Does anyone have even a single tooth? One bone? One conclusive photograph?"

"Don't get mad at me," Abe said, his hands outspread. "I only asked a question."

Linger smiled and tilted his handsome, silvered head to the side. "But *isn't* there evidence?" he said, addressing them all. "I've seen a thousand-year-old scalp in a Tibetan lamasery— more than a thousand years old, they say—that no scientist in the world has been able to identify."

Gideon leaned forward. "If you give a decently sized piece of skin, in good condition, human or otherwise, to a laboratory, they'll be able to tell you what it is very quickly. But once it's tanned, or rotted, or simply desiccated from the passage of time, it becomes unidentifiable. The thing is, you have to remember there's a big difference between finding an unidentifiable piece of skin and saying it's from an unidentified species."

"The yeti's beside the point anyway," Chace said. "It's a different species altogether." He turned toward Gideon, his face set, seemingly on the edge of anger. "I have in my files," he said slowly, "verified and certified by me, personally"—he waited for a challenge—"hundreds of cases in which Bigfoot sightings or unmistakable Bigfoot tracks have been positively identified."

"Yes," said Gideon, "I saw some of those unmistakable tracks myself near Quinault a few days ago."

Chace brushed the comment aside with a wave of his hand. "Pranks. Kids probably, amateurish, as I'm sure you know. I've already seen the casts and rejected them. I'm not one of your fanatics, Professor. I don't accept everything people tell me. When I certify something, it's *real*. And I'm telling you I've seen eighty clear, fresh sets of prints with my own eyes, in Washington and British Columbia alone." He leaned back and waited for Gideon's reaction.

"Olas Murie once made a simple observation," Gideon said. "He pointed out that where tracks are abundant, the animals that make them are abundant." Chace looked warily at him, not sure where he was heading. Gideon continued, "You say you've seen all those Bigfoot tracks—eighty?"

Chace nodded. "Eighty-two, and another ten probables I didn't certify."

"Well," Gideon said, "how many bear tracks have you seen? I mean clear, fresh, unmistakable ones. Or mountain lion? How is it that a presumably rare creature can leave so many tracks? Are they more common than bears?"

"Maybe they are. We don't have an accurate count, but we know there are many populations of them."

"You keep saying you know," Gideon said, "not you think."

"We know. The Bigfeet are there, watching us, hiding from us. No question about it."

"Then why," Gideon said, "hasn't anyone ever found a bone, a carcass? Don't they die and leave remains? Why hasn't a dog ever dragged a piece of a Bigfoot home with him?"

Chace sat quietly a while, then sighed. "It's like I told you, Roy. They'll deny the evidence even when it's right in front of them if it doesn't fit their theories."

"What do you mean, *they?*" Abe said cheerfully to the room at large. "I'm denying something? I'm just sitting here listening." He spoke good-humoredly to Chace: "Who's denying?"

Chace looked darkly at Abe for a long time, then noisily expelled air through his nostrils: an unambiguous snort of derision. The skin under Gideon's eyes grew taut; for the first time he was angry, angry at this shifty con man who derided Abraham Goldstein. Before he could speak, however, Abe went calmly on, still smiling:

"All the same," he said, "it's a funny thing. . . . Where's the kids?"

Chace looked at Linger and shook his head slowly back and forth. Linger glanced at Gideon with a small, polite smile of commiseration. Gideon hadn't followed the question either, but he'd long ago given up wondering if Abe's mind ever wandered. It didn't.

"The kids," Abe repeated patiently. "Aren't there any Bigfoot kids? All the tracks I ever heard of, they're sixteen, eighteen inches long. All the Bigfoots anybody ever sees, they're great big guys that scare the pants off everybody. No one ever sees a little baby Bigfoot? A medium-size teenager, even, say six feet high? How come?"

Gideon had never thought about it; it was a good question.

Chace didn't agree. "I don't see much point in continuing this," he said. "You've obviously closed your minds. There's nothing I can say that would—"

"It's not a question of *say*," Gideon said, "it's a question of *show*. It's evidence that's needed, not argument."

"I have in my home," Chace said slowly, with infinite patience—he was straining the limits of his tolerance to give it one more try—"a glass-walled box in a climate-controlled vault. In that box sits nearly two pounds of fecal matter. I can show you letters from the University of Michigan, the University of Arizona, and Cal Poly, all of which say that those feces cannot be identified as belonging to any scientifically known form of life." He paused to let the weight of his words sink in. "They were found in 1974 in a cave. . . ." When Gideon wearily closed his eyes and shook his head, he stopped. "You don't believe me?"

"Oh, I believe you," Gideon said wearily, "but I'm sure you know quite well that once feces have dried, a lab analysis usually can't do more than identify the digested or undigested contents—grass, hairs, bits of bone. Determining species from old fecal matter is impossible except indirectly, through dietary analysis."

"Goddamnit!" Chace exploded. "There *is* evidence, plenty of evidence! There *are* bones, tools . . . whole frozen bodies that have been sent to museums and colleges. They disappear! There have been hundreds of specimens that disappeared in museums, hundreds!"

Chace was on his feet, shouting and waving his arms. "You goddamn so-called scientists look at it for five minutes and you brand it a fake—" His rage choked him, and he turned his back on the others.

It was an argument Gideon had heard before but one which always astounded him: the strange belief that the scientists and academicians of the world had formed a sinister conspiracy to suppress knowledge of Bigfoot, or UFO's, or snaky monsters that lurked in lakes. As if there were a scientist anywhere who wouldn't give his right arm, both arms, to come up with definitive evidence of any of them.

"Well," said Gideon, "I think maybe we're beginning to repeat ourselves." He stood up, and Linger arose instantly, still gracious. "Thanks for your hospitality, Mr. Linger. I think we'd better be getting back; I have to be up early." He turned to Chace and forced himself to smile. "Dr. Chace, if you do come up with hard evidence, I assure you I'd be more than glad to look at it."

"Oh, no," said Chace, not bothering to turn around. "No, no. If I find me a Bigfoot you so-called scientists are gonna be the last ones to ever get your hands on it. I haven't been killing myself all these years so some cloud-nine Ph.D. with clean fingernails gets all the glory."

"All right," said Gideon, shifting down to turn from Hill Street onto Highway 20, "I came, I listened, I kept an open mind—to a reasonable point. Do I now have your approval to discard the Bigfoot-as-killer hypothesis?"

"You sure do," Abe said. "What a *plosher* that guy was. That means a phony, a blowhard."

"I wouldn't have guessed."

"*Goniff*," Abe mumbled under his breath.

"Crook," Gideon said.

"Crook, you got it. Boy, am I tired. I'm going to grab a little nap." He lowered his chin to his chest, blew out his cheeks, and began at once to snore, or rather to make the small, periodic clucking noises which Gideon knew to be his snores.

Gideon had left Linger's house disgruntled and annoyed, but the deserted, sweeping bends of the road had relaxed him, and the occasional glimpses through the trees of Discovery Bay, glinting like pewter in the moonlight, had lulled him into a soft reverie. If nothing else, that absurd discussion had killed the notion of Bigfoot as a murder suspect. It was a pleasure to put the lid on that particular box, even if he had no other hypotheses. But then, he didn't need a hypothesis, he reminded himself. Murder hypotheses were John Lau's problem. Gideon had done what he'd been asked to do: a skeletal analysis. And he'd delivered good value. The only thing at Lake Quinault that still interested him was a very live, most unskeletal Julie Tendler. And he would be pursuing his investigations in that regard in a very few hours.

Abe clucked away, swaying peacefully from side to side as the car swung smoothly around the big curves that meandered through the endless black forests. Even when they got to Highway 101, with its brightly lit patches and with huge trucks roaring wildly by them, he slept on. In the neat little town of Sequim, where Highway 101 became East Washington Street, Gideon slowed, unsure of where the turnoff to Sun Meadow was.

Abe began to twist and snuffle. "Right turn on Sequim Avenue," he said with his eyes closed. "A Gulf station on the corner." He opened his eyes. "Next block."

As Gideon made the turn, Abe stretched and sighed contentedly. "Listen," Abe said, "could I ask you a question?"

"Could I stop you?"

"What are you being, funny?"

"What do you mean, funny?"

They were both smiling. "Tell me," Gideon said, "why do you people always answer questions with questions?"

"Why shouldn't we?" It was a very old joke, but it always made them laugh. "You got something against the Socratic method?"

"Should I have?" Gideon asked.

Abe leaned forward and patted Gideon's arm. "Enough already. Who are you supposed to be, Henny Youngman? Look, you want to hear my question or not?"

"Why not?"

"No, this is serious. And it's the same old question: If it took this superhuman strength—"

"Let's say extraordinary," Gideon said.

"—extraordinary strength to kill this Eckert, poor guy, who killed him?"

"I'm starting to think I was wrong," Gideon said. "Maybe a fairly strong person could have done it. John Lau's having some tests run. They're throwing spears into pig carcasses or some such thing."

"And what conclusion do you think they'll come to?"

"I think they'll conclude it took superhuman strength." Gideon was quiet a moment. "Abe, I guess I'm up a tree on this. I just don't have any hypotheses."

"Well," Abe said happily, "I got one. I figured it out while you were driving. You probably thought I was sleeping, right?"

"Just because you snored for a solid half hour? Of course not."

"No, I was thinking. And finally I said to myself, what a *schlemiel* I am. *Schlemiel*, that means—"

"I know. So why are you a *schlemiel*?"

"Because anybody who calls himself an anthropologist, it should take him five seconds to figure it out. We're *both schlemiels*. Look, remember you called me this afternoon about the dig?"

Gideon nodded.

"And what did you say you found?"

"The distal end of a juvenile humerus."

"And what else?"

Gideon was puzzled. "Nothing. A piece of wood. An arrow straightener, maybe."

Abe waved off the idea as ridiculous. "No, no. Whoever heard of an arrow straightener like that? Look, it had a hole at one end, right? The kind of hole that maybe once had a peg stuck in it?"

"I suppose so."

"And if it did have a peg in it, what would you guess it was?"

Gideon didn't see why Abe was harping on a twelve-thousand-year-old artifact. "I don't know, Abe," he said impatiently, a rare way for him to talk to the old man.

Abe took no offense. "So," he said cheerfully, "guess."

"An atlatl?"

"Finally," Abe said, "the light dawns."

"I don't—" Gideon began, and then the light did dawn. "Atlatl!" he exclaimed. "Of course! An atlatl! My God, I've been—"

"A *schlemiel*," Abe said. He settled back against the seat. "Now that I've solved your case for you, Professor Skeleton Detective, I'm going to catch forty winks. Wake me up when we get to Phlegmatic Haven." In an instant he was asleep again. Or thinking.

Gideon's mind was buzzing. An atlatl. A spear thrower. How could he possibly have failed to make the connection? The atlatl was one of the most primitive of weapons, a step above the hand-thrown spear, a step below the bow and arrow. It had been common among prehistoric hunters all over the world.

Its use took skill, but the principle was simple: The atlatl added an extra joint to the arm, and more length, in much the same way as did the sort of slingshot one whirled around one's head. The spear was laid on the atlatl, its butt against the peg. Both objects were held in the hand and the spear was flung from the atlatl, more or less catapulted from it.

The result was a projectile that could be thrown with many times the force that could be achieved without it. The Spanish conquistadors of Aztec Mexico had found to their considerable discomfort that an atlatl-propelled spear could pierce metal armor. And not five miles from where they were at that moment, at the Manis site, an atlatl-launched spear point had been found deep in a vertebra of a twelve-thousand-year-old mastodon. Certainly there was no doubt about its ability to penetrate the seventh thoracic vertebra of a mere human being.

Gideon frowned as he turned off the road at the big, wooden Sun Meadow sign and drove down the dark entry drive. A doe stepped lightly from behind a pine tree, her eyes beaming back the headlights. She froze momentarily, then bounded across the road in two arcing leaps to disappear into the foliage, her graceful, raised rump remaining as an afterimage. Gideon barely noticed her. Twelve thousand years. And the atlatl he'd found this morning, if that's what it was, was even older. As far as he knew, the atlatl had been extinct in North America for hundreds of years. Until March 1976.

Abe gave a final cluck, cleared his throat, and opened his eyes as Gideon braked to a stop in front of his compact modern home. "Already?" he said. "How about some chess?"

"Chess? It's practically midnight."

"Well," Abe said, his voice cracking pitifully, "an old man like me never knows how much time he's got. He's got to take his enjoyment when he can. But maybe you're right."

When Gideon helped him out of the car, Abe sighed and groaned. "I guess an old man can't expect you young people should want to spend an hour with him," he said mournfully, "even if there isn't much time left."

Gideon laughed, but he was dismayed to find his hand completely encircling Abe's upper arm. Through the sleeve of the coat it felt like a dry wooden stick sheathed in loose, papery leather. "Okay," he said, "let's play some chess. Maybe you can beat me for once."

Bertha had waited up for them and shuffled off in furry slippers to make some tea. They sat down at the chess table in the den.

"Bertha!" Abe bawled suddenly as Gideon held out his hands, a pawn concealed in each. "Gideon wants another bite to eat!"

"No, really—" Gideon said.

"Quiet, you're a growing boy. So, you agree it was an atlatl?"

"I'm sure it was."

"You *think* it was. Don't be so sure."

"But—"

Abe waggled his hand at him. "All right, let's assume it was. Now, the next question: Who goes around using an atlatl in 1982? Who killed this guy?"

"It was 1976."

"Oh, that's entirely different. All right, 1976."

Gideon extended his hands again. "I thought you wanted to play chess."

"You can't talk and play chess at the same time?"

Abe chose the left hand. "All the time I get black," he said. "That's how come you always win."

"Take white if you like."

"To beat you I don't need any favors. So what do you think? Who killed him?"

"Well," Gideon said, "there's the atlatl and the fact that he was buried in a hundred-year-old Indian cemetery—"

"So therefore it was Indians who killed him?" asked Abe, a cheerful devil's advocate. "What kind of logic do you call this?"

Gideon pushed his king's pawn up two squares.

Abe frowned at the conventional opening as if he'd never seen it before. "There's a law that only Indians can use atlatls? A Caucasian or an Eskimo couldn't have buried him in an Indian cemetery?" Abe moved his own king's pawn out to face Gideon's and looked up. "What's to smile at? Is it such a terrible move?"

"No, I'm smiling because you're telling me exactly what I told John Lau last week when he was so sure it was Indians."

"But now you think so too?"

"Let's just say it's emerging as the most probable hypothesis."

Abe laughed. "Let's just say you think so too. Boy, you cloud-nine Ph.D.'s!"

"Okay," Gideon said, grinning, "let's say I think so too. Look, you say *anybody* could have buried him in that cemetery, but, as far as we know, there wasn't anybody who *knew*—except the Indians themselves, of course—that there was a cemetery in there at all. The federal archaeologists never heard of the cemetery *or* an Indian group, and neither did the universities."

Bertha padded in with a glass of hot milk and honey for Abe, and tea with coffee cake for Gideon.

"Just the tea for me, thanks, Bertha," Gideon said.

"Don't look at me," Abe said to Bertha. "He changed his mind."

Bertha fussed over her father for a few minutes while he grumbled and told her he wanted a stiff bourbon, not baby food. She pooh-poohed him, patted him a final time, and left.

Abe sipped his hot milk. "I actually like this stuff, you know? But don't tell Bertha." He put down the glass. "I got another question: If there are Indians in there, how come nobody but you knows it?"

"All I can think of is that they've kept themselves hidden," Gideon said weakly. Abstractedly he swung his king's bishop off to the right, where it focused on the opposing king's bishop's pawn. "And since the cemetery's been in use at least a century, they must have been hiding all that time. What do you think? Is it possible?"

Abe frowned at the chess board. "Always with that damn bishop. This time you're not going to catch me." With the back of a finger he pushed his king's rook's pawn up one square. "Ha. Now let me see you come in with that knight, Mr. Wise Guy." He settled back, pleased with himself.

Gideon smiled. For all his brilliance, Abe had never gotten the hang of chess.

"Look at him, so sure of himself," Abe said. "I got a few tricks up my sleeve, wait and see." He took another sip of milk. "Look, Gideon, they'd have to be invisible, just about. That place, that Olympic rain forest, it's pretty remote in there, but it's still America. You got hikers, surveyors, botanists, shmotanists, everybody. But in a hundred years nobody ever saw them? It's pretty hard to believe."

"It's happened before, Abe."

The old man was silent a while and serious, his tongue probing the inside of his cheek. "The Yahi, you mean. Ishi."

7

ISHI. THE MOST romantic name in the annals of American anthropology. Ishi, the Wild Man, who had staggered naked and starving into the little California town of Oroville one summer morning in 1911 and collapsed, terrified, in the corral of a slaughterhouse. Ishi, the last of his people, who had grown to adulthood on the isolated slopes of Mount Lassen. For decades white men had believed the Yahi extinct, killed off by settlers and gold prospectors in the 1850s and 1860s. But a small band had lived on in the most remote forests, barely self-sufficient and constantly dwindling. By December of 1910 there were only two left, and when the old woman died in December, her son Ishi lived in awful solitude through the winter and then finally stumbled blindly down from the hills, hopeless and desolate beyond imagining, for in all the world he was the only one who spoke his beautiful Yahi, who knew the Yahi ways. In all the world no one else would ever remember his mother or sister or his own young manhood. And when he died, all of it would be as if it never was.

But he didn't die. The astounded Oroville sheriff, finding him cowering in the dirt, covered him with an old shirt and put the exhausted, near-dead Indian in the jailhouse. Word quickly spread, and within a few days the great anthropologist Alfred Kroeber had come to him in the jail and sat patiently and kindly with him and learned a few Yahi words and even made Ishi laugh when he mispronounced them.

The rest of the story was no less incredible. Kroeber took Ishi back to San Francisco and found a place for him to live—the University of California Anthropology Museum on Parnassus Heights. There Ishi maintained simple quarters and earned money for his needs—he wasted no time developing a taste for sugar and tea—by giving popular demonstrations of point-carving and arrow-making to an appreciative public.

In the four years before he died of tuberculosis, Ishi developed a deep, genuinely reciprocated friendship with the brilliant Kroeber. During their long conversations and their trips back to the Yahi country, Kroeber learned as much about Ishi's early life as one man can acquire from another. He learned how the little band of Yahi, certain they would be killed if the white man ever found them, had walked from stone to stone so they wouldn't leave footprints and had walked under and not through the chaparral, traveling for miles on all fours. He learned how they had lain perfectly still when whites were nearby, sometimes from morning until dark, and how they had lived in tiny, camouflaged huts impossible to see at fifty paces, shielding their fires with tall rings of bark.

And for forty years, no one had even vaguely suspected they were there.

Ishi's name was enough to end Abe's resistance. "It's possible, it's possible," he said, his eyes glowing. "Why not? A little band of Indians in the rain forest. What better place to hide? Not luxurious, but they wouldn't freeze either, and they'd have plenty to eat. Oy, Gideon, think what we could learn—a Stone Age people, maybe—what a thing it would be!"

"What a thing, indeed," Gideon said. "But . . . they're almost *too* primitive—bone spears, atlatls. Even the Yahi were more advanced, and certainly the Northwest Coast Indians were way ahead of that even a hundred years ago. So who *are* these people?"

"Well, remember, they've got to be a small band, like the Yahi were—five, six, a dozen people. Even if they walk on rocks you can't hide a hundred people."

"True, and the cemetery is small. Not many people for a hundred-year occupation, assuming that's their only burial ground."

"Right. And when you get a group that small and that isolated," Abe said, "you get what I would call the cultural-drift phenomenon."

"And what would I call it?"

"You wouldn't call it nothing because I just named it, but it's got to be true. Like genetic drift, where you got only one guy with blue-eyed genes. He gets killed, and good-bye blue eyes in *that* gene pool. Look, you got one guy, say he's the bowmaker, the only one who knows how. One day he falls off a cliff, and poof"—he snapped his fingers inexpertly—"good-bye bow technology. You just lost five thousand years of cultural evolution."

Gideon thought about it and nodded. "And you're more isolated and scared than ever. You see the jets go over, you hear the automobiles, maybe see them sometimes, and you retreat farther and farther, where you're safe, where those strange beings can't kill you or eat you or whatever they think is going to happen."

"And if someone gets too close, you kill him? Like Eckert?"

Gideon had almost forgotten. "Yes. I think so."

Abe finished the last of his milk and licked his lips. "And you're going in the rain forest and find them."

"When did I say that?"

"You don't got to say it. You think I don't know you?"

He was right, of course. "Abe, think what it'd be like to go in there and *talk* to them!"

"Yes, sure, only they kill people who get close, remember?"

"Well, yes, but I'm an anthropologist, not a casual drop-in. I'd research the language, I'd—"

"Very nice, only what language? You don't know who they are, you don't know what they speak. Look, are we playing chess, or aren't we?"

Gideon picked up his queen, hesitated, and waved it vaguely about. "Well, I didn't say I was going in tomorrow. I have the Dungeness dig to finish, for one thing. Then I have a lot of research to do before I try it. I was thinking of next summer." He put the queen down in front of Abe's advanced pawn.

"Already the queen?" Abe said. "On the third move?"

Gideon pushed his chair back from the chess table. "I think I'd better get going, Abe. I have to be up early."

Abe looked up from the board in surprise. "In the middle of the game?"

Gideon grinned at him. "Checkmate."

Abe stared at the board in rueful confirmation. "In three lousy moves," he said bitterly.

"Child's play," Gideon said, smiling. "I try that on you about once a year. It always works, and you always say you'll remember to watch for it next time."

"Next time I'll remember." He laughed and patted Gideon on the back of the hand. "Gideon, you're a physical anthropologist, not a cultural anthropologist. I don't say you don't know ten times as much as any of them, but why not leave it to the trained ethnologists? Report it to the university. Let them take it from there."

"But the university says there can't be any Indians in there. I'm not sure I could convince them otherwise."

"You're not sure you *want* to, you mean."

"Maybe I'm not," Gideon said.

Abe took a deep breath and let it out in a shuddering sigh. "Ah, in your shoes I wouldn't be either. Boy oh boy, I wish I was ten years younger. I'd go with you. But this damned arthritis . . ."

"I wish it too, Abe, with all my heart," Gideon said.

The jingling of the telephone was fading to an echo as Gideon opened the door to Sea Gull Cottage, and the caller had hung up by the time he got to it. He stood there a little worried—it was 1:20 a.m.—waiting for it to ring again. It didn't.

"I *know* you're going to ring again if I get into the shower," he said aloud, glaring at it. He brushed his teeth slowly and packed his bag for the weekend, waiting all the time for the ring. After fifteen minutes, he gave up, took off his clothes, and stepped under the shower.

The telephone rang.

"Doc, where the hell have you been?"

"John? What's up? Where are you calling from?"

"Lake Quinault. I'm at the lodge. Julie told me you were

70

coming down tomorrow, and I wanted to catch you before you started out. There's—"

"Wait, let me get a towel."

He came back to the telephone, rubbing vigorously. It was cold in the cottage, and he'd forgotten to turn on the electric wall heater. "Okay, I'm back."

"Doc, can you bring your tools down with you? We've kept on digging around that cemetery, and we've turned up another body—a partial skeleton, that is. It looks like Hartman."

"Who the hell is Hartman?"

"Hey, what are you getting mad about?"

"I'm getting mad because, one, you got me out of the shower and I'm freezing, and two, because it's going to be a beautiful day tomorrow and Julie and I were going to take off for Kalaloch Beach as soon as I got to Quinault, but you're going to ask me to work all day in a dusty workshop on some dumb skeleton, and I'm going to rant and rave and say no, but eventually I'll do it out of a ridiculous sense of friendship or service or something equally absurd." He gasped for breath. "That's why I'm getting mad!"

John laughed, the delighted, childlike burble that always broke down Gideon's defenses. "I thought you liked working with bones."

"I *do* like working with bones. I *love* working with bones. There are just some things I like even more." Gideon sighed. "All right, who's Hartman?"

"He's the other guy who disappeared."

"I thought that was a girl. Claire Hornick."

"No, I mean six years ago, the same time as Eckert. Hornick disappeared last week. She's still disappeared."

"What makes you think it's not another Indian burial, an old one?"

"Well, we've tentatively identified it through dental records, but I'd sure appreciate it if you'd have a look anyway."

"Okay," Gideon said, "okay. I'll see you about nine. Uh,

71

John? . . . I've been talking the case over with an old professor of mine. . . ."

John listened quietly for ten minutes while Gideon told him about the discussion with Abe, interrupting only to ask for an explanation of atlatls. After Gideon had finished, the line remained silent.

"John? Are you there?"

"I'm here. I'm just in shock."

"Well, after all," Gideon said magnanimously, "you were the one who first suggested Indians—"

"I know. That's what I'm in shock about. I never won an argument with you before. You're actually telling me *I* was right and you were wrong? I can't believe it!"

"Come on, John," Gideon said, laughing, "I'm not that unreasonable. Sometimes even *you* make sense—to a certain degree, of course, and in your own way."

"Thanks a lot. I wish I could say I deserved such fantastic compliments. But," he said, his voice dropping to a lower, grimmer register, "I'm afraid this new body doesn't do much for your theory."

"What theory?"

"That wild Indians are running around bumping off people with Stone Age spears. Doc, this guy was shot."

"Shot? With a gun?"

There was a pause, and Gideon knew John was nodding soberly. "Yeah, with a gun. He's got a neat little round hole drilled clean through the side of his skull."

8

"HMM," GIDEON SAID, almost as soon as he had sat down and looked at the ivory-colored skull on the worktable. "Huh."

John had his chair tipped back against the wall, and his

hands were clasped lazily at his belt line. "I don't like that 'hmm, huh' stuff," he said. "It always means you're about to screw up my case. Not that I have a case."

"He wasn't shot, John," Gideon said quietly.

The front legs of John's chair came down on the linoleum tile. "Not shot . . . !" He gestured expressively at the circular hole in the left side of the skull.

"Not shot. In the first place, look at the placement. High up on the coronal suture, almost at bregma. Isn't it pretty unusual for someone to be shot so high up on the head?"

"No, as a matter of fact."

"Really?"

"Sure," John said, obviously relishing the unaccustomed role of instructor. "It's a fairly common placement in suicides."

"And what would he have used to leave a hole that big? An elephant gun?"

"Doc," John said easily, "no offense, but aren't you a little out of your league with this forensic pathology stuff? Little bullets can make big holes."

"Maybe," Gideon said, "but when they make big holes they make big *sloppy* holes, not neat round ones like that. And consider this: To drill a hole that cleanly, a bullet would have to be traveling at a heck of a velocity, wouldn't it?"

"So? That's what bullets do. Say fifteen hundred feet a second—three thousand if you assume it was a rifle. Muzzle velocity, of course." John was still teaching and enjoying it.

"Then where's the exit hole?"

John chewed the inside of his cheek. He was beginning to waver. "Lodged in the brain, probably, then fell out later."

"A projectile that big, going that fast? It would have plowed through the brain like so much vanilla pudding and exploded the forward right side of the skull on the way out—here at the temporal or the sphenoid; both very fragile, thin bones."

"Unless," John said, "it had a soft tip. Then it could have stayed inside."

"But—"

"I know. It wouldn't have made such a neat hole." John

leaned back in his chair and folded his arms, looking glum. "Okay, Doc, I give up. You're right. Let's hear your theory, but try to keep it to words I can understand, okay?"

"This was a trephining, not a shooting."

"Oh, one of those."

"It's also called trepanning. The cutting out of a disc of bone from the vault of the skull. A lot of primitive peoples have practiced it, including American Indians. For that matter, it's still a common surgical technique."

John took the skull carefully in both hands and peered at the hole. "And that's what this is? Trephining?"

Gideon nodded. "See those annular grooves encircling the aperture?"

John shook his head in exasperation. "These scratches around the hole?"

"Yes, they scraped round and round with something sharp until they got to the inner table and the disc of bone separated."

"Ugh." He looked suddenly at Gideon. "Did they do it when he was alive or dead?"

"Could be either. Sometimes it was done as a treatment for headaches or insanity, sometimes to get a piece of a dead enemy to wear as an amulet. There's a twentieth-century group in New Ireland that did it just for fashion. They—"

"For Christ's sake, Doc, I mean *this* guy."

"I don't know." He took the skull from John and moved his fingertips slowly over the area surrounding the clean-rimmed hole. "Or maybe I *do* know. The differential healing of this fracture and the absence of septic osteitis suggest—"

"Wait a minute," John said and sighed, rising and going to the coffee pot at the back of the room. "If you're going to give a lecture, I'm going to need some fortification. You want some coffee?"

"I'll have some coffee," Gideon said, "but I'm not going to give a lecture. I'm simply going to demonstrate the art of scientific detection in a simple manner—simple enough," he said, looking loftily at John, "for even the most unformed of minds to comprehend."

"Oh, brother," John said, "I better have two sugars." He returned to the table with two mugs cupped easily in one big hand, placed one of the mugs in front of Gideon, and sat down.

"In the first place," Gideon said, "do you see this crack coming out of the upper part of the hole?"

"This squiggly line?"

"No, that's the coronal suture, the division between the frontal and parietal bones. No . . . this thin crack here, that runs up to the top, just behind the suture."

"Yeah," John said, fingering the almost-invisible fissure. "I noticed that before. I figured either it cracked when the hole was made, or after it was in the ground. Pressure from the earth or something. That happens, doesn't it?"

"All the time, but I don't think it did in this case. In fact, I know it didn't." He sipped his coffee, choosing his words. "Now: That barely visible fracture is more significant than this big round hole. There are three things to be learned from it. First, that it—and the blow that caused it—occurred not after he was dead, but while he was still alive. Second, that the blow didn't kill him outright, and possibly not at all, but that he lived a week or so afterward. And third, that the fracture definitely preceded the trephining—and the trephining probably *did* cause his death."

He paused, well launched in his best professorial style. In response, John's mild truculence had evaporated, as it usually did, into a respectful, only slightly skeptical attentiveness.

"Run your finger over the crack, from side to side, near the edge of the round hole," Gideon said.

John did so and frowned. "The bone feels kind of concave—dented. How can you dent bone?"

"Easily. Living bone is relatively soft. It bends, splits, dents. But dead bone quickly loses its elasticity and becomes brittle. Therefore—"

"He probably got cracked on the head when he was alive."

"Right." Gideon said. "By something heavy enough to cause

the fracture and blunt enough to cause the concavity. The exact locus of the blow was undoubtedly a little lower down, at the site of the trephining."

John took a notebook from the pocket of his denim shirt and jotted something down. "Okay, that's point one," he said. "The fracture occurred while he was alive. Now, how can you tell he didn't die on the spot?"

"If you look at the crack closely—here, use the magnifying glass—you'll see that the edges aren't really sharp. They're slightly rounded because there's been some resorption of the bone. And at the very top of it there's a thin, very slightly raised bead of bone that joins the two edges together. See it? It's a little lighter than the rest of the skull."

"I see it," said John with interest. "That shows it's started to heal, right? Which wouldn't have happened if he died right away."

"Righto. That's point two."

"All right," John said approvingly, "but you said you could also tell that he didn't live more than a week longer. How can you . . . ? Ah," he said, tapping his forehead, "if he'd lived very long, it would be *all* healed, right?"

"Right. Stick with me; I'll make a detective out of you yet. All right, here comes the third conclusion—that the trephining came after the blow on the head and probably killed him immediately." Gideon slid the skull a little closer to John. "Now, this is going to take a small leap of faith, you understand."

"No, it won't. I'm ahead of you. The crack has started to close up, but the hole shows no sign of healing at all. So he must have died as soon as it was made." John beamed. "How'm I doing, Doc?"

" 'A' on logic, 'F' on conclusions. A narrow fracture begins to show healing within a few days, but a larger perforation, like this hole, takes longer. In fact, it never actually heals in the sense of closing up; it just rounds the edges. But even that wouldn't begin to show for a while. So even with the lack of visible healing, he could easily have lived another few weeks."

"So how do you know he didn't?"

"I mentioned septic osteitis a few minutes ago." Gideon waved his hand as John began to write again. "Don't worry, I'll write it up for you. Septic osteitis is simply inflammation of the bone due to infection. If it had occurred, you'd see a roughening, a pitting of the bone all around the hole. But it's smooth. So, no infection."

"Okay," John said dubiously, "but I don't see—"

"As a matter of fact, primitive trephining—with a sharpened mussel shell, say, or a piece of flint—almost always did cause a severe, often fatal infection of the bone. But not here. Therefore, I think we can assume it caused Hartman's death."

John opened his mouth to speak, looked confused, and closed it again. "Come again?" he finally blurted. "It didn't infect, and so therefore it *did* cause his death?"

"Right," Gideon said, smiling at John's expression.

"This must be the place where we make the leap of faith," John said.

Gideon laughed. "Look, if Hartman had lived, we can assume—say, with ninety percent probability—that the bone would have become infected within a few days. But once bone is dead, it doesn't infect. This bone didn't infect. *Ergo*; the operation killed him right then, or a day or two later at most."

Gideon sat back in his chair and drank some coffee, but John leaned forward. "Wait a minute, not so fast. I'll go along with you up to a point: Hartman couldn't have lived long after the trephining, okay—that is, okay with a ninety percent probability. But that doesn't mean the trephining *killed* him. That's just a guess. There's a big difference between correlation and cause-and-effect." He grinned. "Want to know who I learned that from?"

"It's a guess, all right," Gideon said, "but when all you have is dry bones, some educated guesswork is part of the game." He patted the skull. "Here you have a guy who's dead. Obviously. You examine his remains and you see that, probably on the same day he died, he had a big hole gouged out of his head in an appallingly primitive manner. I'd say you're on reasonably firm ground proposing something more than a chance relationship between the hole and the death."

"Yeah, but it's still guesswork. It's not proof."

"Pardon me," Gideon said with some asperity. "I'm simply trying to make reasoned inferences from extremely limited data. If that isn't good enough—"

"Take it easy, take it easy. God, you're as bad as Fenster." He laughed suddenly, a childlike peal that crinkled the skin around his eyes into a thousand good-humored folds. "I'm not as used to these leaps of faith as you are. Can I ask a question without getting thrown out of class?"

Gideon smiled. "What?"

"If there's no healing and no septic whatever-it-is, how do you know he wasn't already dead when the hole was made? Didn't you say people used to make amulets out of the piece of bone?"

Gideon tilted the skull so the light slanted across the parietal. "Do you see that hairline crack coming out of the bottom of the hole?"

"I think so," said John, leaning over the skull. "And isn't this another one, a healed one?" he said, fingering a slender white line that ran an inch into the frontal bone from the anterior border of the hole.

"It is. Three cracks altogether, radiating from the center of the piece of bone that was removed. Doesn't that suggest that the original blow to the head pretty well splintered the bone there? It would have made a pretty lousy amulet."

"Whew," said John. "So what does it all add up to?"

"My guess—"

"Your reasoned inference?"

"That's what I said . . . is that Hartman was hit on the head with something blunt, something like a hammer or the back of a hatchet, resulting in a depressed fracture of the left parietal. When he didn't mend properly—perhaps he never regained consciousness—they tried to relieve the pressure by trephining to remove the sunken fragments of bone. That didn't work and probably set him back, and he died."

"Who's 'they'?"

"The Indians. I can't see anyone else doing that kind of surgery."

"I don't know," John said. "I'm still not used to this Indians idea. I mean, you were telling me just a few days ago—you and Julie both—it couldn't be Indians, it's ridiculous to think it's Indians, it's anybody *but* Indians."

"Well, you get fresh data, you change your hypothesis."

John looked doubtful. "So the new hypothesis is that these phantom Indians that nobody but you believes in hit Hartman on the head with a war club or something and then changed their minds and nursed him for a week and then tried to cure him by cutting a piece out of his head, and that finally did him in?"

Gideon shrugged. "That's what it looks like to me."

"Well, what the hell kind of dumb theory is that?" John shouted, his hands outspread.

"Inferential reasoning," Gideon said with a smile, "will only get you so far." He began to gather his tools and put them in his attaché case. "Now, having given you the better part of my morning, only to be shouted at and abused, I am going to drag Julie away from whatever administrative trivia she's performing, and we are going to go engage in some richly deserved recreation."

John slumped back into his chair. "Why do I keep calling you in?" he said, shaking his head. "Things are always nice and simple until you stick your finger into them."

"Ah, but they come clear in the end, don't they?"

"Yeah," John said, smiling, "they do. Usually. Up to now. Have fun, Doc. I'll just slave away on this while you're out playing in the sunshine."

"Excellent idea," said Gideon.

Julie was at Fall Creek campground, a quarter of a mile away. The camp was packed with people, and Gideon was concerned about finding her in the crowd. Every site seemed to be taken, and the paths bustled with people heading off to the woods.

There were plenty of serious hikers: sturdy, chunky girls and lean, hard boys with clumpy, ankle-height shoes and towering, bedroll-topped backpacks on metal frames. These Gideon might have expected to find, had he thought about it, at a small campground on the edge of Mount Olympus's low, western flank. But there were others: fat, pasty city men in Bermuda shorts, youngsters on skates and skateboards, and cross mothers with pouty children.

And there were still others, not many, but a distinctly recognizable breed all the same: sinewy, grim men in their forties and fifties, loners with lank hair and creased cowboy's faces, eyes narrowed against the smoke from cigarettes dangling at the corners of their mouths.

"Gideon!"

Julie was behind him and looked competent and pretty in her ranger uniform. She laughed with obvious pleasure as soon as he turned, and he laughed, too. "Hi," he said. "How's business?"

"Booming," she said, holding out both hands.

Gideon clasped her hands and held them a moment. "It certainly is. It's mobbed here."

"Oh, yes, the campgrounds are crawling with people, and you practically have to wait in line to get on a hiking trail."

"Why? What's going on?"

Julie looked at him oddly, her head tilted to one side. " 'What's going on?' he says. A good question."

"That means something, apparently, but I'm afraid the significance eludes me."

"Well, Dr. Oliver, I believe that every thrill-seeker from the seven western states is here." She smiled at him. "It seems they read a certain professor's article about Bigfoot being—"

Gideon laughed uncertainly. "You're not serious. . . ."

"The story got picked up—and considerably elaborated upon—by a bunch of other newspapers. It was even in the Sunday magazines. You really didn't know?"

"They *elaborated* on the story?" For the first time, Gideon was becoming genuinely concerned about his reputation. He

80

stepped aside for a fat woman in a housedress who was pushing a grumbling, dyspeptic baby in a stroller.

"Oh, yes," Julie said sweetly. "The only thing they all got right was the spelling of your name. One of the magazines even got a picture of you from somewhere. You looked awful. You had a beard."

"That was five years ago at least. I always thought I looked rather good in it." His tone was playfully cross, but, absurdly, he was hurt. Nora had always liked his beard. He had shaved it off to go for a job interview with UNESCO, only to find that two of the three members of the interview panel had beards of their own. He hadn't gotten the position and somehow had never found the fortitude to go through that first scraggly month of beard-growing again.

"No," Julie said. "I like you the way you are now." She reached out and gently touched the side of his jaw. At once his petulance vanished.

Julie must have seen the change in his eyes. "Boy," she said softly, "you really are a pushover, aren't you?"

Before he could think of anything to say, something bumped into him from behind, and a little girl's voice, shrill with mock terror, cried, "Watch out! Everybody watch out! Here comes Bigfoot Kevin!"

Behind her, stomping down the campground's one-way-only circular road, came a giggling boy of eight, swaying from side to side with a stiff-legged, clumping gait, arms outstretched—every child's image of a monster since the first horror movie.

"Why don't we get out of the traffic lanes?" Gideon said.

They threaded their way among campsites cluttered with clotheslines strung between majestic pines, and around TV-antennaed recreational vehicles and dusty pickup trucks with racked rifles in the backs of the cabs—those would belong to the lean, grim men, Gideon thought. At the lakefront there were few people and no commotion. They sat on a log a few feet from the water, enjoying the minute, silky sound of the tiny waves. Gideon picked up a handful of gravel and began

81

flipping pebbles into the water. Julie watched him quietly for a while.

"It isn't," she said, "just your article—"

"I wish you'd stop calling it *my* article. I was framed, as you know only too well."

Julie laughed. "Led on, perhaps. Taken advantage of, maybe, but not framed. You did it unto yourself, I'm afraid. But aside from the Bigfoot hubbub, the Quinault Valley is back in the news as Disappearance Valley again, and it's brought a lot of people out of the woodwork. We've had reports of two flying saucer landings, one of them complete with—don't laugh—little green men. We've had ten Bigfoot sightings, including a group of five hundred of them on the lawn at Lake Quinault Lodge at dawn . . . all this in addition to seven broken limbs and thousands of cuts and bruises. We're practically out of Band-Aids."

"Sounds awful," Gideon said.

"That isn't the worst of it. The Hornick family—that's the girl who disappeared last week—has offered a fifty-thousand-dollar reward for finding her, or her abductors, or her killers. And there's some Texas millionaire who's gone on national TV and renewed an offer of a hundred thousand dollars for a Bigfoot, dead or alive."

"Whew," said Gideon. "That accounts for the people with the guns. What a mess."

"Indeed it is. And if someone actually *finds* a Bigfoot, it'll be even worse. Not that there are any," she added quickly.

"Of course there aren't," Gideon said. "And we don't, thank God, need to hypothesize anymore about superhuman strength." He told her about Abe's deduction concerning the atlatl and about their conclusions.

"An Indian group," she mused, "hiding in there. Just like the Yahi. Ishi all over again. Wouldn't that be fascinating?"

"It would be fascinating if we had some concrete proof, but it's little more than speculation at this point."

Julie poked at the gravel with the toe of her boot. "Well, as it happens, I just might be of help there. I think one of the reports of a so-called Bigfoot campsite might interest you."

"You jest. I'd be happy if I never heard of Bigfoot again."

"But they found a bone spear there. They brought it back. I've seen it."

"A bone spear?" Gideon paused in the act of tossing a pebble. "Like the one that was in Eckert?"

Julie nodded. "I think so. The people who found it are in Site 32. I told them who you are, and they'd be glad to show it to you."

Marcia Zander was one of the sturdy, chunky girls, an experienced hiker. Louis Zander was softer and chubbier, with a downy moustache, a blank, slightly sullen expression, and a cloudlet of marijuana fumes about him. The two sat on the wooden bench on one side of the table, while Julie and Gideon sat on the other. The long, bone-pointed spear lay down the center of the table, looking disconcertingly crude in the bright morning sun. Gideon stared at it, and the others looked at him, waiting for him to speak.

"Let's see what we have here," Gideon said to start his observational processes going. "It's a little under six feet, I'd say."

Louis Zander nodded vacantly. "Right, man."

"It's five feet, ten inches," Marcia Zander said earnestly. "I measured it against my shoe." Her short, straight blond hair fell over her eyes as she leaned forward. She brushed it impatiently away, only to have it come down again. "Does anyone have a bobby pin?" she asked. No one did.

The shaft of the spear was obviously made from a tree limb that had been painstakingly smoothed and straightened. One end had been carefully thinned and split, and between the two prongs of the resulting fork, in the manner of prehistoric peoples everywhere, a rough bone blade, much like the one in the vertebra, but whole, had been lashed.

"You're the local ethnology expert," Gideon said to Julie. "Does it look like anything from around here?"

She shook her head. "It's a little like some of the old Makah points, but they live way up north and always have, around Cape Flattery. What it looks most like," she said doubtfully, "is . . . well, one of those Middle Paleolithic points you see in the textbooks, from Germany or France." She looked quickly at Gideon, as if expecting correction.

"It does, doesn't it?" he said mildly.

"But those are forty thousand years old!"

"Curiouser and curiouser," Gideon said. He peered more closely at the head. "The binding is nearly rotted through. Look at it, will you? No one bought that in a store. It's sinew; deer or elk, scraped thin and smooth. Between someone's teeth, probably."

Louis Zander seemed to shake himself awake. "Well, so, is that a Bigfoot spear or not?"

Gideon looked at him closely, but the boy seemed to be in what must have passed in him for a state of earnestness. "I don't think so. I wouldn't give much credence," he added gratuitously, "to any of the tales going around about Bigfoot."

"Huh?" said Louis Zander, letting his mouth hang unpleasantly open for considerably longer than was required, while his dull eyes blinked twice. "I thought you were the Bigfoot expert." He turned to Julie with a look of stolid accusation. "I thought he was the big-deal Bigfoot expert."

"All right, kids," Julie said brightly, "do you suppose you could show us where you found this, on a topo map?"

"Bigfoot expert," Gideon muttered as they walked back along the road to the ranger station. "Thanks very much."

"Well, I had to tell them something to get them to stick around long enough to show you the spear."

"What were they doing way out there, anyway?"

"Actually, it isn't way out there. They found it on Pyrites Creek, not even a mile from the trail—as the crow flies, that is. For people, it's well over a thousand-foot climb. More like mountain climbing than hiking."

"Then how did the Zanders get there? He didn't seem like the mountain-climbing type?"

"They'd gotten lost coming back from Chimney Peak and were following Pyrites Creek downstream. They hoped it would get them to the trail eventually, which it did."

They stepped to the side of the road, out of the way of one of the dusty pickup trucks, complete with rifle and grim, lean driver.

"Bigfoot hunter," Gideon said.

"Or bounty hunter. Either way, they make me nervous." As they continued to walk again, Julie went on: "They smelled smoke from somewhere, and one of them spotted a path leading up from the creek."

"A path?"

"They said it was like an animal path, just a wearing away of the brush. They barely noticed it themselves. They went up it, hoping to get directions from somebody. They climbed way up—almost gave it up—but finally found a big ledge near the top. They found their smoke, too, just a dead campfire, with a few warm coals. But no people. They waited around for an hour and left."

"And that was where they found the spear?"

"Yes, in some bushes near the ledge."

Gideon walked along pensively for a while, his hands thrust into his back pockets. "Julie," he said, "would you take a rain check on Kalaloch? I'd really like to see that ledge."

"I thought you might. You think it's where your Indians live?"

He looked at her, smiling. "You mean you think there *are* Indians now? Notwithstanding *Ethnography of the Northwest Coast*?"

"I'm beginning to think so. But you have almost ten miles of trail to get there, and a rough climb at the end of it. You can't get in and out in a day, especially when you start this late."

"I'll camp out overnight, then. It'd be fun; like spending a night in a haunted forest. No. I can't do that; no sleeping bag."

"That's not the problem. We have all kinds of gear you can borrow."

"What's the problem, then?"

"The problem is, you'd get lost."

He stopped walking and drew himself up. "Miss Tendler, I have managed to survive very well in the trackless sands of the Sonoran Desert, the Arctic wastelands of Baffin Island, even the Boston subways—all without getting lost, or hardly. I'm sure I can make it in a national park."

"Yeah, you'd get lost," she said soberly. "You'd need a guide."

"Julie," he said, standing in the middle of the road with his hands on his hips, "with a topographic map and a river to follow, I assure you I'm competent. . . . You wouldn't care to go along with me, would you?"

"I'd love it," she said happily.

9

AT THE RANGER station, John lukewarmly endorsed the idea. "Yeah, you never know. You might find something interesting. Incidentally, did you know they've been finding those bone points around here for years? They're nothing new."

"They're not?" Julie said. "How is it that I didn't know?"

John shrugged. "One of my agents, Julian Minor, heard a couple of old guys talking about them at the market in Amanda Park. He told them who he was, and one of them took him home and showed him his collection. Three of them. Found one over fifty years ago. Plus a lot of other stuff."

"Indian stuff?" Gideon asked.

"Yeah. Baskets, that kind of thing. I wish I could go to the ledge with you," he said halfheartedly, "but I can't spare a couple of days. I'll send an agent along with you, though."

"What for?" Julie asked quickly. "Protection?"

"That's right, protection," John said, blustering and concerned. "A bunch of people have been killed in there, you know."

"Two people," Julie said. "And that was six years ago. Claire Hornick is still missing. Look, John, we haven't sealed the place off to ordinary weekend hikers, and we don't send a bodyguard in with them, do we? So why us?"

John appealed to Gideon. "What do you think, Doc?"

What he thought was that he didn't want some grumpy, griping agent horning in on his night under the stars with Julie. "I think she's right," he said. "There are thousands of hikers in the park all the time, and as far as we know there have been two murders in the last six years. Those are better odds than I get in San Francisco."

"Damn it, let's not play games. You spent all morning with a guy with a big, ugly hole in his head. There's something skulking around in there with a Stone Age spear and murder on its mind. And superhuman strength, from what you tell us. Or an atlatl, which is just as bad."

"John," Julie cut in, "I have a sidearm, and I know how to use it, and I mean to carry it. We'll be all right."

"Yeah," John said, the fight draining out of him, "but—"

"She also has me. Don't worry about it, I'll protect her."

"Protect *me*?" Julie said. "I'm going to have to hold his hand the entire time to make sure he doesn't get lost."

"That," said Gideon with a grin, "is far and away the best offer I've had all day."

"Be right back," Julie said, giving his hand a preliminary squeeze. "I want to change into civvies. Then I'll bring the truck around."

After two miles on the trail, the crowds began to thin out. After three, they were alone. They walked steadily but gradually uphill, beneath giant limbs that blocked the sunlight a hundred and fifty feet above them, through translucent and ethereal archways of club moss that hung from the branches in exquisite, two-dimensional crescents and vaults. Indeed, it was like a haunted forest, Gideon thought, in which they'd shrunk to Lilliputian size. The ferns and herbs and flowers and mosses that covered the forest floor were all familiar, but grown to monstrous proportions. He half expected to see a house cat the size of an elephant poke its nose around a tree and leer at them.

They walked quietly for the most part, listening sometimes to the singing of far-off wrens and thrushes, but mostly absorbed in the dreamy, heavy silence that seemed to hang like a fog over them. Even their steps made no sound on the spongy trail. It had been a long while since Gideon had had a pack on his back, but he quickly fell into a hiker's steady, swinging stride. The incredible foliage and immense trunks enchanted him now, and he was comfortable and relaxed, enjoying the odd illusion that he was not walking, but floating through a green and dappled ocean, far below the surface, where the water was dark but pure and gloomily transparent.

After two hours . . . three? . . . four? . . . the pack began to weigh on him, his feet to drag. Julie seemed as fresh as ever.

"How are you doing?" she asked cheerfully as they paused at a rough wooden bridge.

"I'm doing fine," he said. "Great. I could do this all day. It's fantastic." *Say you're tired*, he willed her ferociously, *so I can take this miserable pack off my back and rest for a while.*

"That's fine," she said, "because here's where it starts getting hard. We don't cross this bridge. Here's where we leave the trail. This is Pyrites Creek. We follow it up the hill."

He swung his eyes to the left, up the nearly vertical waterfalls. "Hill?" he said weakly. "Good God, I hope we don't have to go up any mountains."

Julie laughed. "If you think you've had it, there's no reason why we can't camp here and call it a day."

"Not on your life," he said grimly. "On we go." Hopefully he added, "Unless you're really tired?"

"Oh, no. I could do this all day. Let's go."

To climb the next half mile took them an hour of rugged scrambling. Sometimes they had to pull themselves up by grasping branches or exposed roots. When they came to a small cove made by a gravel shelf about ten feet wide at one of the creek's few level spots, Gideon flung his pack to the ground.

"That's it. As fresh as I am," he said, gasping, "I have no right to subject you to this pace. Let's take a breather."

Julie sat heavily down. "Foof," she said. "I thought you'd never quit."

For five minutes they lay back and caught their breath, looking at the tops of the trees waving against the bright sky and listening to the tumbling water. Julie pulled the map from her pack and studied it. "Gideon," she said, "I think we're there. The ledge ought to be across the creek, about halfway up the other side."

Gideon got to his elbows and stared. "Halfway up *that*?"

"What would you say," Julie asked, "to stopping here for the night and going up there in the morning? We could leave our packs down here."

"I would say yes, by all means, yes. It's nearly six anyway. And," he said, suddenly realizing it, "I'm starving. We wouldn't have any powdered *escalope de veau* in those shiny little packets we've been lugging around, would we? Or a few freeze-dried *quenelles*?"

"It's beef stroganoff. And don't laugh. It's not bad, considering."

It was awful, but they gobbled it down happily, leaning over the camp stove for warmth when the sun dropped behind the peaks at their backs and plunged the cove into shadow. Afterwards, they made a tiny campfire and drank several cups of hot cocoa out of tin mugs, using water from the creek, and talked and laughed for several hours.

There was a little awkwardness and uncertainty when it came time to bed down, but they agreed, after a dignified and objective discussion, that precocious sexual relations might damage a burgeoning friendship. They would, therefore, as mature and rational adults, sleep in their separate sleeping bags.

But there was nothing wrong with putting those sleeping bags side by side and holding hands, and it was thus that they drifted to sleep after talking another hour. Julie fell asleep first, and Gideon watched her for a while, hungry for her but happy, too, with the way things had gone.

The first premonition came in the depth of the night. Awakened by some imperceptible movement, some soft, furtive sound, Gideon opened his eyes suddenly. He was lying on his back, holding his breath, and straining to listen. The air was fragrant and luminous, the huge plants sharply defined and frighteningly still. Next to him, Julie lay in her sleeping bag, her breath slow and steady. She had turned away from him onto her side so that now he could see only her black hair, stirring gently in the soft breeze.

There was the sound again. Not just the river burbling over the stones, but another sound, a sinister, dry whispering, a faint, drawn-out whirring that seemed everywhere, closing in on them with a terrible, hushed intensity. Still half asleep, he had almost leaped up shouting when he saw what it was.

He fell back then, relaxed and feeling foolish, and watched the pine needles float down. From the highest branches they came, pulled loose by a passing puff of wind far above and drifting to earth in a pale, twinkling rain, glinting silver as they passed in and out of shafts of moonlight. And they rustled minutely as they came. He closed his eyes as they neared the ground and let them fall like flakes of snow on his cheeks and eyelids.

A headline in thick black print ran across his mind: *Professor Panicked by Attack of Pine Needles.* He must be feeling very edgy indeed. He laughed softly but knew as he did that it was forced. There was a crawling tightness at the back of his neck which told him he was still tense; there was something else. . . .

He had never had the feeling before, so it took a while before he recognized it and still longer until he owned up to what it was. Once, in fact, he had spent half an hour trying to prove to a stubbornly unconvinceable John Lau that there could be no possible validity to it, that it was a silly superstition without an ounce of empirical support. Nevertheless, silly or not, there was no question that he felt he was being watched; he *knew* he was being watched. He could feel the very points in his neck where the eyes bored in.

As inconspicuously as he could, he turned slowly to survey the scene around them. They were in a small cove made by a gravel shelf about ten feet wide, on the outside of a bend in the creek, their feet toward the water, their heads at the base of a hillside covered with ferns and giving root to great spruces and firs. Dark as it was, things stood out in the moonlight with a hard-edged, flat-planed clarity. Nothing moved, nothing sounded except Julie's breathing and the faint hiss of the water over the pebbles. But somebody was there, on the mountainside, watching him, studying him, somebody—Gideon refused to even think "something"—*somebody* stood silent in the shadows of the somber, moss-laden trees, waiting to . . . what?

He looked at the trees for a long time and listened but he heard nothing, saw nothing, and after a while the feeling gradually passed. It must have been a dream that had set him off, or the delicate fall of the pine needles on his face, or the mere fact of lying in the dark and fantastic rain forest. He yawned and looked around once more, then nestled down, sleepy again, into the warm sleeping bag.

Julie's back was still toward him, and he watched as the quiet eddies of air softly set the dark ringlets of her hair trembling, ringlets sculpted like those on the ancient stone busts of Assyrian kings.

Feeling positively degenerate but unable to resist the urge, he reached across the gravel between them and gently cupped the dense mass of hair. Some of it, not heavy at all but weightless and cool, fell over his hand, and he shivered as it brushed the backs of his fingers. He briefly considered waking her, thought better of it, and quietly pulled his hand back. When he put it under his cheek he could smell her hair's fragrance, already familiar.

There was another gust of wind far above, another rustle, and another twinkling rain of pine needles. Julie moved, turned on her back, wrinkled her slightly convex nose—a movement that Gideon had always found attractive in a pretty girl—and brushed the needles from her face. He saw her eyes open.

"The moon's so bright," she said.

"Uh-huh."

"It's like . . . do you know that picture, Rousseau, I think, where that Arab is sleeping under the moon, with these gigantic flowers—"

" 'The Sleeping Gypsy.' "

"And that strange, still lion is watching him. . . . Doesn't it look like that here?"

It did, and Gideon said so, strange, and still, and surreal.

"Rousseau wasn't a surrealist," Julie said, "he was a primitive."

"Don't be pedantic."

"Gideon, do you have the feeling," she said, and he knew perfectly well what was coming, "that something's watching us?"

"No."

"Well, I do."

"Julie, don't be silly. The idea of knowing when you're being watched is based on the invalid idea that some kind of energy flows from the observer to the observed object. The most elementary principles of vision make it clear that light travels the other way around, from the stimulus—"

"Did someone say something about being pedantic?"

"Okay, in simple, nonevaluative terms: It's stupid. You're being ridiculous."

"Yes, sir." A long silence. She turned to face him. "But I feel it."

"Julie, the absurdity of it is empirically demonstrable, and there—"

"I liked it when you touched my hair."

"—were several experiments in the late sixties. . . . What?"

"I liked your hand on my hair."

"I . . . didn't mean to wake you. I'm sorry." Like hell he was.

She lay on her side, looking at him, her eyes enormous. The wind whispered in the tops of the trees again, and another gleaming rain of pine needles fell. Gideon brushed some from her cheek. Her face was warm.

"Gideon," she said, "you know that conversation we had about being adult and not letting animal passions interfere with a burgeoning, mature relationship?"

"Mmm."

"Did I really say that?"

"I think maybe *I* did. It sounds more like my style."

"Mmm. Dumb, huh?"

"Boy, dumb is right," he said. "I mean, like, I *know* dumb, and that's what that was. Dumb."

She raised her arm, lifting the top of her sleeping bag. He could barely hear her whisper, "Come to me."

Unmindful of the cold, he threw back the cover of his own bag and went, kneeling on the sharp gravel and bending to kiss her. He could hear his heart pounding, feel his chest vibrate with the hammering, but the kiss was chaste and almost austere, a gentle, tranquil touching of lips while their bodies held apart. They moved their heads slowly back and forth, so that their lips brushed softly. Her hand lay lightly on the back of his neck; his fingers traced the line of her cheek.

In another moment, each with a small cry, they were in an embrace of furious intensity, their mouths seeking each other's lips, throats, eyelids, ears; kissing, nuzzling, licking, inhaling. Urgent and clumsy, they tore at each other's clothing. Gideon pulled her body roughly to his. It was over in a few seconds, and they rolled apart, gasping.

After a while she spoke in a tiny voice: "Oh, my goodness, was that really me? How embarrassing."

Gideon took a deep, slow breath and let it out. "Wow. Talk about animal passions. I'm afraid I got carried away."

"Yes. Wasn't it terrific?" She giggled, and he thought: This is serious. Even her giggling sounds wonderful. Watch out, Oliver.

"Terrific," he said.

They turned to each other and embraced, more gently this time.

"Mmm," she said, nestling against his chest, "hairy devil, aren't you? That's nice. Very appropriate for a physical anthropologist." She ran her hand down his side to his knees, then slowly up his body and over his chest. "I must say, Dr. Oliver, for a grand old man of anthropology, you are built."

"Thank you, I think. You're quite well preserved yourself." With his face buried in her hair, he slowly stroked her smooth back from shoulder to waist and cupped her ample, firm buttocks in both hands.

"Ah, Julie, you feel marvelous: solid and soft and sexy and female."

She lay without moving, purring quietly as his hands roved over her, caressing, rubbing, gently kneading. "Gideon," she said, her voice muffled by his chest, "this feels so lovely, but I'm falling asleep. I can't help it. Do you mind terribly much?"

"Shh, no. Go to sleep. Why should I mind?"

"Don't you want to despoil me again, you beast?"

"*Despoil* you—?"

"Well, violate me, then?"

"No, I don't even want to ravish you. Well, maybe a little."

Her hands worked down over the hair on his belly and grasped and held him. "What's this then?"

"A mere, mindless, purely physical reflex. Pay no attention." He kissed her hair. "Really, I'm happy, believe me. Anyway, I can ravish you better when you're asleep."

"You're sure you don't mind?" she said, barely awake, her cheek warm against his chest, her breasts pressed to his side.

"Shh, sleep."

He shifted slightly to let her snuggle in more comfortably and lifted one of her breasts for the pleasure of letting its warm, soft weight come down on his ribs again. Breathing in the fragrance of her hair and putting one hand protectively on her shoulder, the other one possessively on her thigh, he settled himself for sleep.

"Hey," he said suddenly, "why are you wearing perfume? Who wears perfume in a sleeping bag? You were expecting this, weren't you, you hypocrite?"

"Well," she murmured sleepily, her lips moving deliciously against his chest, "a girl never knows."

They woke later and made love again, but slowly this time, laughing, and whispering, and learning each others' pleasures. When they were done they slept again, only now it was Gideon who lay in Julie's arms, his face between her breasts.

In the coldest part of the night, just before dawn, Gideon woke once more, cramped and confined in Julie's narrow sleeping bag. He climbed out, shivering and grumbling, to try to fit the two bags together.

"Put some clothes on," Julie said thickly. "It must be forty degrees."

He slipped quickly into his shirt and jeans and tried some more, unsuccessfully. They finally settled for simply moving the bags together and leaving them open along the connecting sides. When they finally settled down again, Julie warmed him in her arms, then gave him a motherly little pat on the behind, turned away onto her left side, and wriggled her own posterior into his lap so that they lay spoon-in-spoon fashion.

She reached around and patted him again, on the hip this time, and sighed. "Isn't this nice, Gideon, dear?"

"Ah, God, Julie . . . it's nice." He blinked in confusion. He had almost blurted out, "I love you."

She found his right hand and moved it to her breast, gently molding his fingers around the yielding flesh. Then, after she seemed to be asleep, she lifted his hand, kissed the back of it, rubbed her cheek against it, and placed it again around her breast.

"Why are you wearing clothes?" she asked sleepily.

"You told me to put them on. Do you want me to take them off?"

"Well, certainly." But when he began to move, she clamped his arm down with her own, keeping his hand on her breast. "No. Too comfortable. Want to stay just like this. Besides . . ."

"Besides what?"

"Besides, it feels so decadent being naked next to a fully

dressed man. I feel like a harem girl." She giggled softly and began to breathe slowly and deeply.

"Julie . . ." he whispered. He'd nearly said it again: I love you.

"Hmm?" she said from a million miles away. Then she laughed again, sighed, worked her buttocks still more securely against him, and quieted.

Gideon lay there, his mind inflamed and perplexed. Did he love her? Not likely. Love as he knew it—and he knew it—came maybe once in a lifetime, and he had had his once; an overflowing, never-to-be equaled once.

A cool, predawn wind with a touch of moisture carried the scent of pine bark and sent strands of Julie's hair drifting over his face. It was the *dear* that had done it—homely, old-fashioned word. Nora had called him *dear* sometimes. Or had she? My God, were the memories already dimming?

But they weren't *already*. It was three years, three long years in which no one had called him *dear* and—of this he was certain—in which he had never once said or wanted to say to anyone, "I love you."

He moved his left arm slightly to ease the pressure of her body on it. Julie adjusted automatically, as if they'd been sleeping together for years. She caressed the hand on her breast, loudly kissed the empty air, and in a sleep-furred voice murmured, "Gideon."

His throat tightened and hot tears sprang unexpectedly to his eyes. He took his hand from her breast to enwrap her more fully in his arms and bent his head forward so his lips were against the downy, sleep-fragrant nape of her neck. "I love you," he whispered tentatively to the soft flesh.

That wasn't bad at all. No queasy fluttering in his chest, no deeper, twisting knot of guilt. It felt good, in fact, to say it after all this time. Premature, of course—he'd just met her—but good.

He tried it out again. "I love you," he murmured, his mouth still against her. "I think," he added sensibly, then snuggled closer to her warmth and fell asleep.

10

WITH A TWIG, Gideon prodded at the powdery gray charcoal in the circular fire pit and watched it emit a few dusty wisps.

"Well, something was certainly here not too long ago." He bit his lip. "Someone. Not for at least a day or two, but since the last rain. Otherwise the charcoal would be matted down."

"A very woodsmanlike observation," Julie said.

Gideon gestured at the two-foot slabs of bark that stood on end around the pit, forming a three-quarter circle. "What do you make of these?"

"Heat reflectors?"

"Could be. Could also be a screen to hide the glow. Notice how the opening faces the back of the ledge, away from the valley. From below, you'd never know there was a fire going up here."

"From below, you'd never know there was *anything* up here."

She was right. From their camp they had raked this mountainside with binoculars but had been unable to find the ledge. Yet from here there was a clear, broad view over Pyrites Canyon. The gravel bar on which they'd camped was in plain sight almost directly below, on the other side of the stream. The orange backpacks they'd left behind were clearly visible—just as visible, Gideon thought, as they themselves would have been in last night's pellucid moonlight.

The ledge was obviously deserted and apparently abandoned, but Gideon was jumpy and vaguely apprehensive. Even in the daylight, with birds singing vigorously, he had continued to feel under scrutiny. Julie did, too. He could see it in the way her eyes darted at little snaps and creaks from the woods.

The ledge, about seventy feet long and thirty feet wide, was screened and camouflaged by trees that grew on it and on the slope beneath. Above, a forested, nearly vertical bluff rose two hundred feet. Below, the barely discernible path that had led them to the ledge, as it had led the Zanders, dropped steeply toward the river far below.

Part of his uneasiness, Gideon knew, stemmed from the weather. The temperature had dropped, and there was a high, pearly overcast, as heavy and solid as a stone roof. Underneath that, somber, iron-gray clouds were moving in from the west to pile and swirl against the mountains. Yet there was no wind. The air seemed viscous and torpid, dank and raw. Julie said the rainy season was on the way.

As they approached the eastern end of the ledge, Julie wrinkled her nose and frowned.

"Yes, I smell it too," Gideon said. "And I know the stories. Bigfoot lairs are always supposed to be pervaded by an awful stink. Or is that the Abominable Snowman?"

"No, that's Bigfoot; a pungent, unidentifiable stench. That's what made the Zanders think of Bigfoot."

"It's pungent, all right, but I wouldn't call it unidentifiable. It smells like a latrine that's been stopped up for a week."

That was very much what it was: a circular depression at the very end of the ledge that had obviously seen a lot of use as a toilet pit.

"Either they had an army up here for a few nights," Gideon said, "or this ledge has been inhabited for a long time."

"Can we move back upwind, please?" Julie asked.

When they were a few feet away she spoke, frowning. "It's awful that anyone would live this way: an open toilet—"

He looked at her in surprise. "Everyone lived like this until a couple of hundred years ago. There are plenty of people who still do. The toilet's on the very end of the ledge, so the wind would almost always carry the stench away. Really, it's better than indiscriminately fouling the forest or the river. And they've been scooping earth over the feces so they'd degrade quickly."

"Yes, but this isn't a hundred years ago, and there aren't any primitive people living in the rain forest." She shook her head. "That is, there aren't supposed to be."

Gideon raised his eyebrows, "There wasn't supposed to be *anyone* living in the rain forest."

"That's right," she said, "but somebody obviously lives here. What's this?"

They had come upon a smaller fire ring only about twenty feet from the first, also shielded with slabs of bark toward the open side of the ledge. Gideon knelt to poke at the cold charcoal.

"Two fire pits?" Julie said. "What would be the point of that? Two separate groups?"

"I don't think so. See how there's a layer of sand under the charcoal?" He scrabbled in the pit with a twig. "And then another layer of charcoal? I bet there's another layer under that, of" —he dug some more—"of sand. See?" He sat back on his heels. "Know what this is?"

She shook her head. "Some kind of kiln? For firing pots? Baking bread?"

"You're close. It's a kiln, all right, but it's for making stone tools. Right out of the Lower Paleolithic."

"You can make stone tools in a kiln?"

He laughed. "No, but you can heat-treat the rocks before you make them. There are certain kinds of rocks—coarse-textured ones like jasper—that need heat-treating before you can do a good job of flaking them. It's very delicate. Glassier stones like obsidian and agate don't need it."

"So you're telling me somebody has been making stone tools here in 1982?"

"I sure am. Look."

She got down on her knees to watch him turn over the earth just outside the rim of the pit. "The ground's full of little flakes of rock," she said.

"Yes, the pieces that get chipped away when you're making a stone implement."

"But," Julie said, frowning, "if they can make stone tools

why make those horrible bone spears? Aren't stone points better?"

"Infinitely better, if you're skilled at making them. But making stone points is different from making stone hammers, say. It requires some difficult techniques—percussion chipping, then striking off the core blades, then pressure-flaking. It's not easy. Bone points, on the other hand, you can more or less make by carving and abrading; no specialized knowledge necessary."

She sat back on her haunches, her arms around her knees. Her voice was dreamy. "You're saying, then, that whoever lived here is able to make crude stone tools but not fine ones. What would that make them equivalent to—Mesolithic people?"

"I hadn't thought of it that way, but that's right."

"And the Mesolithic ended in Europe, what, fifty thousand years ago?"

"Thirty-five thousand, say."

"All right, thirty-five thousand. Thirty-five thousand years! Gideon, you're not saying these Indians, if that's what they are, have been lost here for thirty-five thousand years?"

"No, of course not. Here in the New World the Indians had Mesolithic technologies, so to speak, until the Spaniards arrived in the sixteenth century. And in a lot of tribes, practically up to the twentieth century. No, what I'm suggesting is that some Indian group came here maybe a hundred years ago and has been here ever since." He shook his head suddenly. "It *is* on the fantastic side, isn't it?"

"It really is. Look, why does it have to be an Indian group? Why couldn't it be a bunch of hermits, or hippies maybe, who want to live a simple, more primitive life?"

He got up and brushed himself off, and brushed Julie off as well. "No. How would they know about heat-treating rocks?"

"They could have read about it in a book."

"Did you ever read about it in a book?"

"I never even heard of it."

100

"And you're an anthro minor, so there you are. No, I think these are genuinely primitive people."

"But where would they actually live, sleep? Just out in the open?"

"I doubt it. There must be a shelter. Let's look around some more."

In fifteen minutes of prowling among the trees they found the first hut. They had walked by it several times before they realized it was not a natural tangle of dead branches but a structure of lashed-together poles thatched with brush and capable of holding three or four people.

It took a while for Gideon to find the entrance, a low, covered opening through which he had to crawl. Inside it was dusky, but some light came through a smoke hole in the domed roof and through the interstices between the branches. It was just tall enough for him to stand slightly stooped. The hut was empty, but there were signs of human habitation. There was a small fire pit in the center, and the walls were black and greasy from many fires, and redolent of smoke. On the floor were a few fish bones. The floor itself was of earth, with many footprints, all naked—and none eighteen inches long.

The whole was drearily depressing, and he was happy to crawl back out into the daylight. There was a second, smaller hut, which received a cursory examination and turned up no additional information.

They made a final examination of the area around a large fire pit and found one more object of interest, man-made and man-used. It lay lodged between two of the bark slabs—an eight-inch stick about the thickness of an arrow shaft, broken at one end and tapering to a blunt point that was charred and worn down.

"Is it a fire drill?" Julie asked.

"Yes, the lower part of it. Do you know how it works?"

"Not exactly. Do you rub it against another stick?"

Gideon smiled. "No. Regardless of what any Boy Scouts may tell you, one cannot make sparks by rubbing two sticks together. You need to concentrate the friction in a very small spot. You take another piece of wood, a slab, and you bore a socket just large enough to fit this burned end of the drill. Then you gouge a channel from the socket to the edge of the slab. In the channel you place tinder. . . . Why are you laughing?"

"I love it when you shift into your professorial mode. You get so serious. Not at all the sort of person who would fool around with a lady park ranger in a sleeping bag. But please continue."

"Just because I did it doesn't make me the *sort* of person who does it," he said, laughing, "but I'll skip the rest of the lecture. The point I was going to make, which is important, is that it's very hard to do. Even when you know how, it takes a lot of muscle and determination. I've demonstrated it before classes several times, and I'm always smoking before the tinder is."

"I understand, but why is that important?"

"It's important because it clinches the fact that these are genuinely primitive people. If I were just playing at returning to the Stone Age, or simply dropping out, the one concession I'd make to civilization would be matches. And if I didn't have them when I left, I'd sure come back and get some after trying out this thing once or twice."

He turned the drill slowly in his hands. "Indians. For sure."

She frowned. "I still don't understand why it has to be *Indians*. All right, forget the twentieth-century dropout idea, but why couldn't they be some primitive Caucasians who have been living here, maybe for a hundred years?"

"Uh-uh. By the time the first Europeans set foot in Washington, in the eighteenth century, their technology was already way beyond this."

Julie nodded. "You're right, of course." She shook her head slowly back and forth. "The idea that there might still be people here living in the Stone Age, hiding, watching us . . ." She shivered. "Gideon, can we go back now?"

He put an arm around her shoulder and squeezed. "Ready to get back to the twentieth century?" he said smiling.

"Desperately."

He tilted her chin up and kissed her softly on the lips. "Me, oo. Let's go."

It took them only four hours to walk back to the trailhead, and an hour later, with Gideon driving, they pulled into the anger compound at Quinault.

"I don't know about you," Julie said, stretching as she climbed down from the cab, "but I need a hot shower before I do anything else."

"Me, too," Gideon said. He went to the back of the truck and hauled out the backpacks. "Maybe I can get a room at the odge. I sure don't want to drive back to Dungeness tonight."

"Are you joking? You'd have to book a month in advance, what with the crowds."

"Gee, that's too bad," Gideon said mournfully. "I could really use a shower."

Julie laughed. "All right, you don't have to look so sad. You can use mine. On the condition that you behave."

"Of course I'll behave. What do you take me for?"

In an hour, clean, happy, and utterly relaxed after a long, shared, soapy interlude under the shower head, they sat in bathrobes in the living room of the old, forest-green frame house that went with the job of chief ranger.

"See?" Julie said, handing him her empty glass. "Isn't civilization wonderful?"

Gideon poured a second dry sherry for each of them. "Rahther," he said. He knelt as he brought her her drink, and softly kissed her. "I say, old girl, frightfully considerate of you to suggest I might spend the night here."

"On the condition you conduct yourself in a gentlemanly manner."

"You certainly set a lot of conditions," he said, slipping his hand into her robe to caress her breast.

"God," she said, "aren't you ever satisfied?"

"I *am* satisfied. I couldn't be more satisfied." He put his other hand into her robe and embraced her with both arms. "I'm just being friendly."

Julie put down her glass to hold his face in both hands. "Mmm, I feel friendly, too. But I haven't called into the office yet to let them know I'm back. I think I'd better do that."

"That's supposed to motivate me to let go?"

"And the sooner we dress, the sooner we get some dinner."

"The restaurant doesn't open for another hour."

"And we've just killed the last of the sherry. If you want some more, we need to go over to the lodge."

"That's different." Gideon kissed her and promptly stood up. "You call your office and I'll dress. Or would you like me to help you into your clothes while you're on the phone? It'd save time."

"No, thanks. I don't think it would work, somehow."

The elderly woman at the wicker writing desk looked up from her letter and peered irritatedly over the tops of her reading glasses.

"Be quiet, you children," she said, her voice quivering with annoyance. "Go outside and play."

But the two little boys, falling over themselves in their excitement, dropping their quarters and scrambling after them under chairs, ran unheeding down the elegant old lobby of Lake Quinault Lodge to the far wall, where a table with an electronic game imbedded in its top stood anachronistically among the potted plants and fine old 1920s furniture. Once there, they dropped into the chairs with blissful, adult sighs, inserted their coins, and fell at once into deep trances over the screen, which emitted twitters, splutters, and beeps that could be heard all over the sedate lobby. On its perch the parrot muttered and complained.

Gideon smiled at Julie. "Well, you wanted the twentieth century. Welcome to it."

"I love it," she said, laughing and snuggling farther into her chair, her legs tucked beneath her.

Gideon sipped his amontillado and leaned back, enjoying the crackling fire in the huge brick fireplace. His wicker chair creaked dryly when he moved, a clean, leathery, masculine sound that went well with the sherry.

The woman at the writing desk, unable to bear the noise of the game table any longer, swept up her papers with a snort and marched out. On her way she stopped briefly near Gideon and Julie, her writing materials gathered against a formidable bosom.

"They shouldn't allow those things in here," she said.

"I agree with you," Gideon said. When she was gone he turned to Julie. "Did she mean the machines or the kids?"

"I don't know," she said, laughing. "Both, probably."

"Well, I agree with her."

"Gideon," Julie said after they had both looked into the fire again for a while, "I've been wondering why those Indians would have left anything as valuable as a spear behind for the Zanders to find. It must take a long time to make one."

"They were probably surprised and left in a hurry. Anyway, I don't imagine that time management is a particular problem for them. Besides, the binding was rotten and the shaft was split. Those are what take all the time, you know. The point's nothing."

"No, I didn't know. There's a lot they don't teach you in school. Do you think they've deserted the place now?"

"I think so. The Zanders may have been the first people to stumble on that ledge. And now us. They've probably gone even farther from the trails and the people."

"That would mean going higher into the mountains. It's going to be awfully wet and cold up there." She moved her head slowly back and forth, letting her lips brush the rim of the glass. "What a horrible life they must have. Shouldn't we be trying to find them?"

"I'm not sure if we should or we shouldn't," he said, debating with himself as well as with her. "Looking at the historical record, it's hard to make a case for primitive people's lives being much improved by contact with the outside world. They don't have immunities to common diseases, their mores can't stand the shock, their values get screwed up. What would we do with them, anyway? Put shoes and socks on them and send them to junior college? Put them on a reservation?"

"I know all that," she said impatiently, "but this is a tiny, frightened band of people cowering out there in the woods, living in leaky huts in a rain forest, for God's sake. And if they really move higher they'll be in the snow! We could at least get some clothing to them, and food, and tell them they don't have anything to be afraid of."

"Except the FBI. Don't forget, your wee, timorous, cowering band has committed at least two murders, if we're right. Probably three."

"You don't really think they'd be taken to jail . . . put on trial . . . ?"

"I don't see what choice the FBI would have. If they could find them."

"So we just leave them there?"

Gideon hadn't meant to mislead her. "No, I want to find them, too, but it has to be done right. I want time to do some research, to think through the implications for them and for us, to get ready. I'd like to go next spring, after the rainy season."

"You? Do you mean alone? In the rain forest? Just you?"

"Your confidence is heartwarming."

"It's just that, anthropologist or not, you're basically a . . . a city person," she said, laughing. "You'd have gotten lost twenty times without me yesterday. I'm going with you."

The hell you are, he thought. Not with wild men running around with spears. Not now. Yesterday you were just another nice girl. Today you're . . . more. "We'll see," he said. "Maybe."

"Definitely. Now that I've found you, I'm not about to lose you." She looked suddenly at him. "That sounded possessive," she said soberly. "I'm not that way. I was only joking."

Sorry to hear that, Gideon thought. He had liked the sound of it. He could see that she had, too. He said nothing, but smiled at her, and they finished their sherries in an easy, companionable silence, gazing into the fire.

They walked into the dining room hand-in-hand and were

conspiratorially asked by the hostess if they wanted a private booth. Julie said yes and Gideon said no, and they all laughed. They took a table at the window. In the cold, ashen light, the lawn was gray, the lake almost black. It was comfortable to be in the warm, clean dining room, awaiting a hot meal prepared by someone else. What would it be like to spend a gray, chilly winter out there in a hut of twigs?

A relish tray of raw vegetables was plumped heartily before them. "My name is Eleanor," the waitress proclaimed without recognizing them. "Enjoy."

In the morning they breakfasted in the window nook of Julie's kitchen, looking out on a day that was colder and more drearily overcast than the one before. They munched hot bran muffins with butter and jelly, and drank steaming coffee, and felt very cozy and protected.

"Winter's coming," Julie said dreamily. "It's the time of year I start wishing I was a bear about to hibernate."

"I thought you liked the wet weather."

"Oh, I didn't really mean hibernate. I meant I'd like to hole up in a nice, snug house like this one, and have fires in the fireplace, and eat hot soup out of mugs, and listen to music, and have some lovely male animal at my beck and call."

"To light the fires, and make the soup, and turn on the phonograph?"

"And other duties as assigned. Kiss, please."

"Is that illustrative of other duties, or is it a request?"

"A request. Demand."

"Yes, ma'am." Gideon slid along the cushion of the window seat and kissed her gently. "Umm," he said, "delicious. You taste like apricot jelly."

Julie laughed and put her arms around him. "I can't tell whether you're amorous or hungry."

"Are they incompatible?"

"Well, would you like to go back to bed, or would you rather have another bran muffin?"

107

Gideon frowned, thinking hard. "Do I get jelly with the bran muffin?"

"You're awful," Juie said, pushing him away. "I'm not even going to respond to that." She resettled herself. "Gideon, I've been thinking. You really can't wait until next spring."

"Why not? They've managed to get along in there for a century."

"Maybe, but there's never been a fifty-thousand-dollar bounty on them, or a hundred-thousand-dollar reward. The woods have never been so full of crackpots with guns. Someone's bound to find them, maybe shoot them. And don't forget about the FBI. John will be here tomorrow, and he'll want to go right out and check the ledge."

"You're right," Gideon said. "They won't be at the ledge anymore, but the FBI's likely to come up with a lead on where they went. Do they still use bloodhounds?"

"I don't know. I think maybe they do."

"You know, as good a person as John is, he has to go in regarding them primarily as murder suspects. That's some way to introduce them to civilization, isn't it?"

"So what's to be done?"

"There's nothing we *can* do. I don't know where they are, and if I did, I couldn't communicate. And if I could, what would I say? 'Greetings from Great White Father. You are going to prison.' Maybe nobody'll find them, and maybe by next year I'll have learned some more."

"Maybe and maybe. Not too satisfactory a resolution, is it?"

Gideon agreed, but before he could reply, the telephone rang and Julie went to answer it. At the kitchen doorway she turned and muttered, "You'll figure something out. And whenever you go, I'm going with you."

"Hello," she said into the mouthpiece. Then she paused and darted a sidewise look at him, a little uncomfortably, he thought. "Uh, well, no, I don't exactly know where he is, but I can probably find him. I'll let him know."

She came back from the kitchen. "For you."

He smiled. "Don't tell me you're a little shy about letting

108

people know I'm here at seven-thirty in the morning?" He was sorry, as he said it, for the flip, sleazy sound of it.

"No," she said angrily, and two spots of color appeared on her cheeks. "He just caught me by surprise. And I didn't know how *you'd* feel if people knew you were here. You *are* on the stuffy side, you know."

"I am?" he said, surprised. That he was a little stuffy, he knew. That Julie knew it was a bit of a shock.

"Well, sometimes, yes. How *would* you feel, anyway?"

"About people knowing I'm here? Julie, you must be kidding. I'm proud of it. I'd like it if everyone knew."

"Well," she said, still looking angry, "I wasn't sure." She giggled suddenly. "I think I need another kiss, and a hug, too. I guess I'm feeling insecure."

He rose and took her in his arms, squeezing until she yelped. "Enough!" she cried. "I'm secure, I'm secure!" He kissed her and felt her throat tremble, and trembled himself. Again he almost told her he loved her, and again a niggling prudence held him back. "What was the call about?" he asked.

"Oh. Two things. First, a couple of teenagers from Hoquiam admitted faking those Bigfoot tracks."

"No surprise there. And second?"

She took her head from his shoulder. "Gideon, they've found another body. They think so, anyway."

11

WHAT THEY THOUGHT was a body had been fished from Pyrites Creek only about a mile downstream from the ledge. It lay on a rubber mat in the workroom, a gummy, greasy mass of brownish-black tissue, formless and tattered, with bones sticking through, like a gobbet from the lion cage at the zoo. Julie had taken one look at it and fled. Gideon wished he could do the same. There was a great deal of difference between the impersonal, dry bones of archaeology and this hideous thing.

"We'd appreciate your help, Doctor. Can you tell if it's human?" Julian Minor was John's assistant, a middle-aged black in a dark suit and tie, with rimless glasses, neat, grizzled hair, and a tidy, complacent chubbiness that gave him the air of a self-satisfied accountant.

Gideon nodded. "Yes, it's a human pelvic girdle, but I can't tell any more than that until we get the bones cleaned."

"You mean remove the soft tissue?" the agent said with a delicate scowl. "I don't know if I'm authorized to let you do that."

Let's hope not, Gideon thought.

"But I'll call Seattle and inquire," Minor said.

He dialed, muttered a few secretive syllables into the telephone, nodded three times, said, "Very well then," and hung up. "Mr. Lau says go ahead, but you're to save the soft tissue for the pathologist."

"Okay," Gideon said with a sigh. "We'll need some chemicals, though." Which would, with any luck, turn out to be unavailable.

No luck. When he went to Julie with the list she called in a young, redheaded ranger who prepared exhibits of birds and animals for the Hoh Information Center and who had everything needed. The young man was patently aggrieved when Minor told him he could not sit in on the operation.

In twenty minutes Gideon and Minor were back in the workroom at the far end of the table from the grisly chunk of flesh. In front of Gideon were dissection tools, rubber gloves, and measuring cups and containers of various sizes. He prepared a solution of water, sodium carbonate, and bleaching powder in a large dented pot and set it aside. "That's antiformin," he said. "We'll boil the flesh off the bones with it." A slightly different mixture was poured into a stone jar.

"But what about saving the tissue?"

"I'll cut away everything I can first, and we'll preserve it. Now," he said grimly, "to the dirty work."

He chose a heavy-duty scalpel, a rugged pair of forceps, a

probe, and a pair of scissors. Then he talced his hands, slipped on a new pair of rubber gloves, went to the shapeless thing at the other end of the table, and began to work.

After years of dealing with human remains, Gideon still maintained a remarkable squeamishness. Through long practice he had developed the trick of not quite focusing his eyes on what he was doing at such moments, at least no more than was necessary to keep his own fingers out of the way of the scalpel. He employed the technique now.

Minor sat primly at the other end of the table some ten feet distant, watching him cut away the dark shreds of flesh and put them in the jar.

"The fact that it's only a pelvis . . ." Minor said. "Was mutilation involved?"

"No sign of it. The body's been in the water a while. I think it was just pulled apart by the current and the rocks."

"I see," Minor said. "May we assume that the remains are those of an individual of the, ah, Negroid race?"

"Negroid?" said Gideon, puzzled. "No, why?"

"The color of the skin is quite dark. Or isn't that the skin?"

"Some of it's skin, some of it's muscle, and other, tissue. *Gluteus maximus*, mostly, and some of the other flexors and extensors; a little *fascia lata*. The soft inside stuff and the external genitalia are gone, decomposed or eaten by the fishes."

Minor's lips twitched downward. Gideon didn't blame him. With the forceps he teased out a black ribbon of flesh. "This still has some skin on it," he said, "and you can see it's black, but once decomposition has begun, the color isn't any guide to race. Caucasian skin turns brown or black a lot of the time, and black skin is likely to turn whitish-gray."

"I see," said Minor, slightly whitish-gray himself.

"You're welcome." With his own stomach churning, Gideon stripped off the greasy gloves and stood up. "Now comes your part," he said.

"My part?" Minor blinked, and his hand went reflexively to the knot of his tie. "I don't take your meaning."

"The solution in the pot needs to be stirred every thirty minutes for about three hours. Then mix this into it." He held up a bottle of sodium hydroxide in fifteen percent solution. "Then, if I'm not back yet, put the pot on the burner, heat it to a low simmer, and put in the pelvis. Take it out in a hour—but I'll be back before then."

"My understanding," Minor said, not at all pleased, "was that you would be responsible for all the technical details."

Gideon shrugged. "If you'd rather not do it, you can ask the kid with the beard. I'm sure he'd be delighted."

"I think I can manage," Minor said. "I take it this is some sort of caustic solution."

"Yes, using one's finger to do the stirring is not recommended."

Minor did not seem to find this amusing. Neither did Gideon. He was anxious to get out of the workroom, into the open air. "In the meantime," he said, "I thought I'd run over to Amanda Park and see the man who has the bone spear points."

Minor brightened. "Old Mr. Pringle? That shouldn't take you any three hours. Amanda Park is only a couple of miles away. His house is a bit off the beaten path, but I can give you directions. It'll take you fifteen minutes to get there."

It took him two hours. "Off the beaten path" was an understatement, and Gideon got hopelessly lost on back roads more than once before he stumbled on the place. When he finally pulled up at the side of the road next to the worn, birdhouse-shaped mailbox, he was ready to admit that Julie had a point about his being a city person. He got out of the car and stood looking at the ramshackle old bungalow of dingy white with faded green trim. On a gray day, with no other houses around, and made tiny by the thick forest, it was a forlorn sight. Only after a few seconds did he become aware that a very old man was sitting hunched in a corner of the porch, deep in the gloomy shade of a corroded tin roof.

Sleeping, or perhaps senile, Gideon thought. He walked to the house with a smile but with a distinct sinking of the heart.

112

For an anthropologist he was peculiarly loath—nearly obsessively so—to intrude on others' privacy.

"Mr. Pringle?" he said quietly when he reached the porch.

The head came up and Gideon saw that the man wore a knit, dark blue watch cap pulled tightly down over a long, lean-fleshed head. He was even older than Gideon had thought, more than ninety, with waxed-paper skin stretched painfully over a large-boned skeletal face, and purplish-brown discolorations on his cheeks. Astigmatic and winking, he looked emptily about, everywhere but at Gideon.

Senile, Gideon thought, his heart sinking further. "Mr. Pringle?" He spoke gently. If the old man were frightened or failed to comprehend, he would go. "My name is Gideon Oliver. . . ."

"Ah, there you are," said the man in a thin, cheerful voice, fixing a pair of astonishingly lucid blue eyes on him. "The old eyes are getting a bit queer these days. Not what they used to be."

Gideon saw, as if by the light of those luminous eyes, that he had a tiny white moustache, pencil-thin and meticulously trimmed, midway between his long nose and thin gray lips, with plenty of pale skin showing all around it. Cheered by the sight of that absurdly sprightly ornament on the ancient face, Gideon smiled. "Mr. Minor of the FBI told me about your collection. I wondered if you might show it to me."

The man's eyes lit up even more. "With the greatest of pleasure," he said, and began to rise, gripping a cane with one hand and the shaky arm of his folding chair with the other. He was, Gideon realized, a very tall, rawboned man, and he had a lot of difficulty getting out of the chair. Taking his arm to help him to an unsteady balance, Gideon was struck by the freshly laundered smell of his woolen shirt. There was nothing slovenly about him.

The old man laughed. "Got going too fast. Wouldn't have had any trouble if I'd gotten myself organized first."

The front door opened into the kitchen, and Pringle shuffled slowly onto the ancient linoleum, concentrating heavily on his balance, carefully predetermining each spot on which the thick rubber tip of his cane would come down.

"Forgive the hat," he said over his shoulder. "Had an operation or two, and the surgeon did a little excavating up there. Are you with the FBI, too, Mr. Oliver?" His large hand groped for support at the old, white-painted chairs, the table, anything within reach.

"No, I'm an anthropologist."

"Anthropologist? Well, I'm really delighted. May I offer you a cup of tea?"

"No, thank you," Gideon said, not even wanting to think about watching him try to manipulate kettle and cups at the old-fashioned gas range.

The living room was fusty and stale, with brown, flowered linoleum nearly as worn as that in the kitchen, but the collection was neatly housed in three clean, glass-fronted cases of mahogany. There were bottles and belt buckles and old nails, but there were also a great many Indian artifacts.

Gideon examined the three bone spear points at length. All were cut with the same technique and in the same shape as the two he'd already seen.

"Do you remember when you found these, Mr. Pringle?"

"The one you're holding in 1950. That one, in 1934 or 1935. And this . . . let's see, it was my first summer here. I was twenty-five, so that would make it 1913," he said without any apparent pause for calculating.

"And all from around here?"

Pringle nodded. "The one you've got was way up along the east fork of the Quinault—of course, there wasn't much of a trail then—and a little ways up one of the creeks that run down from Chimney Peak."

"Pyrites Creek?"

Pringle was surprised. "Why, yes, that's right, about a mile up, on the east bank."

Nineteen thirty-four. Did that mean the ledge had been inhabited for nearly fifty years? It seemed probable. At *least* fifty years. "And the other points?"

"The other old one also came from around Chimney Peak,

but the one in 1950, that was near Finley Creek. Here, let me show you on the map."

"That's not necessary," Gideon said quickly as Pringle began to gather his gangling, tottery legs under him.

"No, no, it's quite all right. It's a question of preparation and organization, you see." Midway through preparing and organizing, when he had gotten his lanky frame to the edge of the chair and was about to make the final effort, he looked at Gideon with those surprising, brilliant eyes and smiled. "My," he said, "everything takes a long time when you're old."

When Pringle had meticulously pointed out the precise locations, Gideon said, "You know, nobody seems to believe there are Indians in the rain forest, Mr. Pringle. How would you account for the points?"

"Of course there are Indians. When I first came out, it was common knowledge. They'd come out at night and steal things from the cabins. Naturally, that was before it became a national park. All the cabins are gone now. But in those days, lots of people saw them. I saw them myself."

"You saw them?"

"Certainly. I talked to them, too, or at least we made noises at each other. Are you sure you wouldn't like a cup of tea after all? It's an interesting story, I believe."

12

THERE WAS ALREADY water in the kettle, and Pringle, moving slowly and carefully, put it up to boil and produced from a cupboard a tin of Earl Grey tea bags. They sat at a kitchen table with a surface that was spongy from many paintings, the last one green, and pushed aside a pile of newspapers to make room for themselves.

"I generally use one bag for two cups," Pringle said. "Is that all right? The cups are quite clean."

"That's fine," said Gideon. There were, he saw, only two bags left.

Pringle paused with his long fingers in the tin. "If you want a whole tea bag, just say so. No trouble at all."

"No, this is fine. I don't like it too strong." He tasted the watery tea. "This is delicious."

"Do you like it, really?" Pringle asked. "It's the bergamot that gives it the flavor, you know." He drank some with ponderous care, steadying the cup in both enormous, knobby hands, and reaching for it with his lips as it neared his mouth. Then he put the cup down, sighed, and closed his eyes. With the clear, cornflower-blue irises hidden, the face was suddenly cadaverous, a death mask.

"It would have been 1913," he said suddenly in his quavery tone, with his eyes still closed. "I was pretty young."

*It was late April of a long, **wet winter**, and Big Herb Pringle was twenty-five then, six-feet-six, two hundred forty pounds, a powerful, red-haired ox of a man who didn't have to worry about dribbling when he drank his tea. He'd already established himself as a schoolteacher in Olympia, and three years before, he and his father had built the hunting cabin on Canoe Creek with their own hands, cutting the trees down, shaping the logs, all of it.*

It must have been a weekend, because that was about the only time Herb was able to get away from Olympia. He was coming back with some squirrel on his belt and his rifle on his shoulder when he heard a noise from the cabin, and he stepped quickly into the trees to watch.

Three Indians climbed out of the cabin's single window, one after another. When Herb stepped from behind a tree with his rifle, they stopped, thunderstruck, and then docilely lined up against the cabin, shaking and looking at the ground.

There was an old man who had taken a shabby coat and a rusty, worn-out saw blade from the cabin, a filthy woman who might have been twenty or fifty wearing two of his old jumpers and just about nothing else, and a boy of no more than eight with a horribly crippled left foot.

"Luther Yacker did that," Pringle said, suddenly opening his bright eyes. "The year before. He'd shot at a woman and a child rifling his cabin one night. There were three or four cabins built on the creek, you see, and I remember I grabbed my rifle and ran over when I heard the shooting. The woman was lying there dead. Luther was all excited and telling Billy Mann and Si Keeler about it." Pringle sat pursing his lips and blinking at the table. "I can remember just what he said. He said he'd hit the papoose, too, and the little bastard was going to have a hard time finding all his toes. He was really excited, trying to find the bloodstains with a lantern so he could show us.

"And," Pringle said, finally raising his eyes to Gideon's face, "all they'd taken was a couple of hard-boiled eggs. The woman still had them in her hand."

All three of the terrified Indians who were flattened against Herb Pringle's cabin were scrawny and dressed in rags or in the old clothes they'd gotten from inside. Except for the saw blade, they'd taken nothing but clothing. They'd left the food untouched because it was all in cans and they probably didn't know how to get at it or what it was.

The old man shoved the woman forward and she made motions as if she were nursing a baby. Then she fell on her face on the ground and just lay there crying. Herb indicated with gestures that they could keep their pitiful loot and offered them the squirrels as well, but they were afraid to come and take them. They were afraid to leave, too, and just cowered there, so Herb had to send them on their way by shouting and waving his arms to frighten them off.

"Did they say anything that you remember?" Gideon asked.

"Oh, yes, there was a bit of jabbering when I waved at them. The woman kept crying and shouting, '*cara!*'—like the Italian word—and all three of them were yelling, '*sin-yah!*' or some such."

Gideon took a small notebook from his pocket and jotted it down. "That's quite a story, Mr. Pringle."

"Oh, there's more," Pringle said.

They had finally run off, the little boy scrabbling sideways like a crab. Herb never saw them again, but when he went up to the cabin one weekend in the fall of that year, he saw that someone had been in it again. He was a little put out, feeling that he had dealt fairly with the Indians.

When he went in he saw that nothing had been taken. Instead, two Indian baskets had been left on the floor in front of the fireplace.

A large yellow tear ran crookedly down Pringle's face. "Another problem with getting old," he said. "You cry awfully easily." He sipped his tea and smiled wanly. "I haven't thought about those Indians in a very long time. It *is* a nice story, isn't it?"

Nice, yes, but was it any more than a story? Pringle was very old, and he was talking about a time sixty-nine years ago. "I don't imagine you still have the baskets?" he said.

"Oh, yes, *surely.*" Pringle was peaceably offended. "They were gifts. I wouldn't give anything like that away. They're the ones on the top shelf of the case to the left."

Gideon went into the living room and looked at the baskets. They were similar to the ones from the graveyard. He made a quick sketch of the decorations: black rectangles arranged like steps and running from top to bottom in diagonal rows.

He came back frowning. "I've seen baskets like those before, Mr. Pringle. From what I understand, the local Indians don't make them."

"No, that's right. I had another fellow come out to look at them, oh, seven or eight years ago—fellow named Blackpath—"

"Dennis Blackpath? An anthropology student doing research?"

"Yes, I believe he was. He said they were California baskets. I forget the name of the tribe. He said they must have been traded for."

Traded for? With whom? How could a tiny, isolated, starving band of Indians trade with people who lived hundreds of miles away, beyond several formidable mountain ranges? Still, it wasn't impossible. He made a mental note to look in *American*

Doctoral Dissertations the next time he was at the Cal library to see if Blackpath had ever written that dissertation. Maybe he wasn't the crackpot Julie said he'd been.

Standing, Gideon finished his tea. "Mr. Pringle, I'd like to thank you for your hospitality. You have a fine collection."

"Oh, I've enjoyed talking with you," Pringle said, and looked as if he had. A tinge of pink was visible through the gray of his cheeks. "Are you sure you wouldn't like another cup of tea? I'm afraid I don't have anything sweet to go with it right now, but I'm sure I could locate some toast and a little jam." He said this with an air of courteous bewilderment, as if there were usually piles of sweets, and if Gideon had arrived an hour earlier or later the table would have been overflowing with cookies and pastries.

"No, thanks," Gideon said, "I really have to go. Let me pour yours, though."

"Why, thank you. Thank you very much." He reached for the tin, then stopped, his hand in the air. "That last tea bag was rather strong, don't you think? I'll just see," he said lightly, "if we can't get another cup out of it."

Gideon's eyes were irritated. The Formalin, no doubt; he should have gone to an office somewhere to type, instead of using the old portable in the workroom. He rubbed his eyes gently, stretched, pulled the sheet from the typewriter, and set the completed report on the table in front of him.

To: Julian Minor, Special Agent, FBI
From: Gideon P. Oliver
Subject: Examination of skeletal remains found in Pyrites Creek, Olympic National Park, conducted September 14, 1982
Summary

The skeletal remains presented to me appear to be those of a Caucasoid female of 18 years. Living stature was 5′ 5½″ to 5′ 9½″, with a most likely height of 5′ 7½″. Weight was 120 to 130 lbs. Time of death was approximately two weeks ago. Cause of death is unknown.

A detailed analysis follows.

Preliminary Treatment

Preliminary examination in your presence revealed an unclothed partial human body with considerable decomposed soft tissue present. The bones were cleaned of soft tissue, and segments of skin and muscle from both buttocks and the right lateral and posterior thigh were preserved in a 10% Formalin solution.

Bones Present

The partial skeleton consists of the pelvic girdle, including both pelves, the sacrum, and the fifth lumbar vertebra. The coccyx is not present. In addition, the proximal three inches of the right femur, extending to the distal end of the lesser trochanter, are present.

Condition

Exposed edges of bone show heavy abrasion, probably from contacts with rocks in the creek. The right acetabulum is perforated, apparently post-mortem, probably as a result of buffeting by the head of the femur, caused by the fast-moving water of the depositional environment. The break in the femur is splintered and abraded.

Pathological Conditions, Antemortem Trauma, Anomalies

None noted.

Sex

The angles of the sciatic notches and the subpubic angle indicate that the skeleton is that of a female. The diameter of the head of the femur (41mm.) supports this view.

Age

The aging criteria for female skeletons of Gilbert and McKern were applied to the pubic symphysis and indicate an age of no less than 14 and no more than 18. The complete fusion of the proximal femoral epiphyses, and of the pubis and ischium, and the complete ossification of the acetabulum indicates an age of 17+. The most probable age is therefore 18.

Race

Whereas the pelvis provides accurate skeletal evidence of sex and age, its bones are among the least reliable in determining race. However, interspinous and interiliac diameters were measured (22.2mm. and 26.6mm., respectively) and make it possible to draw tentative conclusions in regard at least to the three

120

major racial groupings: The skeleton is most probably that of a Caucasoid, but possibly that of a Mongoloid. The wide diameters, and also the lower symphysis of this pelvis, make it unlikely that the skeleton is that of a Negroid.

Stature

Determination of height is problematical, inasmuch as the pelvis and vertebrae are of no help, the single lumbar vertebra is unreliable, and long bone representation is limited to the proximal end of the femur. Nevertheless, height was estimated by applying Steele's regression formulae. The resulting estimate of height is 169 cm. ± 5 cm. or 5 feet 7½ inches ± 1.97 inches.

Weight

The skeletal remains give no indication of obesity or thinness. They do, however, indicate a person of slender, gracile frame. Assuming no extreme of obesity or thinness, and taking into consideration the estimated age of 18, it is estimated that living weight was from 120 to 130 lbs.

Time of Death

Assuming the body to have been continuously in Pyrites Creek from the time of death to the time of discovery, and assuming the water to contain a reasonable complement of fish and other flesh-consuming organisms, the estimated time elapsed since death is two to four weeks, with two weeks the most likely estimate. Any variation in the above assumptions would greatly modify this estimate.

Cause of Death

No evidence of cause of death is provided by the skeletal material.

Not too bad, Gideon thought. Not as definite as he'd like it to be, but there wasn't much to go on. Minor would love it. It was nice and bureaucratic, with enough passives to make it sound official.

Minor came in. "I heard the typewriter stop. May I assume you're done?"

He sat down, placed the report on the table in front of him, aligned the two sheets with each other and the edge of the table, straightened his immaculate cuffs, and began to read.

121

Gideon could see his eyes moving back and forth with rigid precision. When Minor finished, he put the first sheet back on top and straightened the papers again.

"Height, weight, sex, age, race, time of death," he said. "That's a great deal to tell from so few bones."

Gideon said nothing. If Minor wanted to argue about it, he'd have to argue with himself. Gideon had done the best he could with the material, had indicated his reservations, and wasn't going to quibble over his findings. Minor could take them or leave them. Gideon frowned, surprised at himself. His defenses were certainly up. The Hornick analysis must have bothered him more than he'd realized.

"If I understand correctly," Minor continued with polite dubiety, "your estimation of height is based on a single three-inch fragment of femur?"

"That's right," Gideon said carefully.

"The femur is the leg bone?"

"Yes, the thigh bone."

"Dr. Arthur Fenster maintains one should never try to estimate stature with fewer than two complete long bones."

"Dr. Arthur Fenster is correct. I support Dr. Arthur Fenster and applaud him. But we don't have two complete long bones. We don't have one complete long bone. We don't have *half* of one long bone. We have seven lousy centimeters, from the *caput femoris* to the . . . the . . ." He'd forgotten the Latin term for the lesser trochanter. Why was he speaking Latin, anyway?

Minor smiled for the first time, a pleasant, self-effacing smile. "I surely do take your point," he said. He glanced back at the summary. "It certainly looks as if it's the Hornick girl, doesn't it?"

"I don't know. Could be."

"You don't know? Didn't you look at the stats?" He indicated a file folder that he'd earlier left on the table for Gideon.

"No. If you have a missing person's stats, you tend to find what you're looking for."

"Well, then," Minor said, "I really *am* impressed." He opened the folder. "Eighteen on the nose, five-seven on the nose—no, I guess you missed by half an inch there." He smiled again. "What can you expect from seven lousy centimeters? And she weighed one-thirty. And of course she disappeared September 28. Two weeks ago. It must be she."

"It sounds like it."

"Yes." Minor's mild, slightly whimsical air vanished as he studied something in the folder. "Have you ever seen her picture?"

"Not that I can remember."

Minor handed a photograph to Gideon. It was a small black-and-white high school graduation portrait. The girl wore a black gown and a mortarboard set unfashionably straight on her head. She looked directly into the camera with a soft smile that showed a chipped incisor. Her hair, long and straight and carefully fanned over her shoulders, appeared to be light brown. She looked like a million other kids. Gideon had the feeling that under the gown she was wearing grubby jeans with torn knees, and dirty tennis shoes.

A convulsive shudder ran slowly up his spine and jerked his shoulders. Twelve-thousand-year-old skeletons, dry and brittle and brown, were more his line. No meat on the bones. No smiling photographs. He handed the picture back to Minor. "It's a shame. She looks like a nice kid."

"You bet it's a shame!" Minor said with sudden vehemence. "A goddamn shame!" As if embarrassed by this display of emotion, he visibly collected himself, ran a finger around the inside of his collar, and said, "I'd like to thank you for your excellent report, Doctor. You've been most helpful."

Julie had left a note for him on her office door. "I've gone home," it said. "Could you drop by when you have a chance?"

When she let him in, he was at once concerned. Her face was pale, almost gray, with the area around her mouth a dead white. She had changed from her uniform to a nondescript blouse and pants.

"What is it?" he asked. "The body?"

She nodded. "Come inside. Let's sit down."

Worried, he followed her in. The sight of her bare feet padding along as strong, brown, and healthy as ever reassured him slightly.

"Was it Claire Hornick?" she said when they were seated on the sofa. Her clenched hands rested on her thighs.

"It was the Hornick girl, yes."

Her eyes flashed. "Not the Hornick girl . . . Claire! She had a name; she wasn't a laboratory specimen!" She unclenched her fists and placed a hand on his knee. "Ah, Gideon, I'm sorry. I just . . . it didn't really come home to me before, but this one . . . There really are murderers out there. I don't care if they're Indians or what. . . . It scares me to think of you trying to find them."

"I know, Julie." With his own hand, he covered the hand on his knee.

"Gideon," she said, not looking at him, "don't go looking for them. I don't want to go, and I don't want you to go." She was very near to crying.

"I don't think there's too much to worry about," he said gently. "Remember, I don't even know where to look."

She squeezed his hand impatiently. "I want you to promise me you'll leave all this to the FBI. You can study them *after* they're caught. Promise me you won't go." Before he could answer she said, "No, I'm sorry. I *am* possessive, aren't I?" She tried a tentative, weepy smile, and his heart melted.

"You sure are." He tipped her head back to kiss her forehead. "Now stop being all female and trembly. I have to go back to Dungeness and get on with my dig, and I want a proper kiss good-bye."

She put her hands on the back of his neck, and he wrapped her in his arms. They kissed a long time, leaning back against the soft, old cushions, breathing in and out without moving. When he finally lifted his face from hers, she was Julie again, soft and smiling; no white skin around her lovely mouth, no tremulous muscles near her eyes. "Gideon, Gideon," she said, slumping lushly against the cushions, "you're very good medicine for me." She smiled tiredly at him.

124

"That's better," he said. "Now, are you or aren't you going to invite me back down for next weekend?"

"Why don't I come up there instead and spend a few days? Wouldn't you like a hand on your project?"

"Was that a bawdy pun? I must say, I'm very surprised."

She laughed. "You're terrible. Gideon, may I come? Or do you already have a mistress tucked away in your little cottage?"

"Two, but I'll get rid of them. Come, please, Julie. Sure you can help me on the dig. And it will be fun for you to meet Abe. Fun for him, too." He paused and felt himself tense. "Julie . . . I want you to know I . . . like you a hell of a lot." Disconcerted to find himself stammering, his cheeks growing hot, he stopped. For three simple, monosyllabic words, "I love you" was giving him a great deal of trouble.

Julie was smiling gently at him with a quizzical expression. "I like you too," she said. "I'll see you next Friday, then."

On the way back to Dungeness he stopped at Port Angeles to buy a large tin of Earl Grey tea and a five-pound box of Scottish shortbread and preserves, and mailed them to Mr. Pringle. Then he had a razor clam dinner at a seafood restaurant on Fountain Street. By the time he got to Bayview Cottages it was almost dark. He poured himself some Scotch, grumbled at himself for forgetting to make ice cubes, filled the tumbler with water, and took it out to the edge of the low cliffs, where a few folding chairs were set out overlooking the straits.

He had meant to think about Julie, not the Indians, but he couldn't get them out of his mind. The bloodthirsty little band that murdered any strangers who came within reach didn't square with Pringle's scrawny, frightened group sneaking back to his cabin with gifts of thanks for his great benevolence in not shooting them.

He was, although he tried to convince himself otherwise, not as keen as he'd been on finding them. The Hornick affair had left him still feeling sick, and he found little kindness in his heart for the people who had murdered that harmless, pretty girl. He wondered if they had stabbed her with one of their crude bone spears, or clubbed her.

He shook his head to clear away the images. Let John find them; it was his job. And probably a good thing, he thought moodily. The rainy season was about to arrive, and Gideon was, as Julie had pointed out, no woodsman. A jungly wilderness in the rain was no place for him.

He had finished his drink but was too gloomily comfortable to go inside and get another. A heron floated down to the shoreline below, sending the gulls squawking away, and wading a few elegant steps into the quiet, dark water, there to stand staring absently at the distant lights of Victoria on the Canadian shoreline.

He must have dozed, because when the telephone rang in his cottage, he jerked upright, startling the heron, which croaked roughly and rose on slow, lolloping wingbeats into a sky of burnt crimson.

"You're back?" Abe said. "And you didn't call to say even hello?"

"I got in late, Abe. I didn't want to bother you."

"Eight o'clock is too late to bother me? What am I, an invalid? You ate dinner?"

"Yes, I stopped in Port Angeles."

"So come on over for a glass tea and a Danish, maybe. Bertha went to a movie in Port Angeles. I'm all alone."

Gideon looked out the window at the darkening straits, now a misty mauve. He was in a somber, solitary mood. He wanted to fix another drink, take it back outside, and watch the evening turn to night. Maybe the heron would return. "Actually, it's been a long day, Abe," he said. "I'd like to get to bed early. How about tomorrow?"

"Tuesdays the warden doesn't let us have any visitors. Only Mondays. Come on, a glass tea, a piece cake, tell me how come it's been such a long day. And then . . ."

"The last time you gave me one of those 'and then's' I wound up on center stage at the great American Bigfoot debate."

"No, no, nothing like that. I just got something interesting to show you. You'll see."

126

13

"KBYO, SEATTLE. WHAT is it, a TV channel?" Gideon asked, looking at the return address on the thick envelope Abe had wordlessly handed to him after listening absorbedly to his account of the past three days in the Quinault Valley.

"Radio," Abe said. "You sure you don't want some honey cake? It goes good with the tea."

"No, thanks." He pulled the stapled sheaf from the envelope and looked at the title on the first page: *The Joe Ambeau Show, February 28, 1982.* "Is this a script?"

"A transcript. I just sent for it. I remembered a few months ago I was listening to this talk show—"

"You listen to talk shows?" Gideon was unable to keep the disapproval from his voice.

"Why not?" Abe looked honestly surprised. "I'm not interested in my own culture? I'm only supposed to listen to Ph.D.'s and professors? Truck drivers and old ladies ain't worth my time? Gideon, you got elitist leanings, you know that? For an anthropologist you got some funny ideas. Did I ever tell you?"

"Many times."

"It's not a joke," Abe muttered. "Go ahead and read. Start on page seven, where the check is."

Gideon found Abe's spidery red mark and settled back in his chair.

MR. AMBEAU:	Joe Ambeau. You're on the air.
CALLER:	Hello, Joe? Am I on?
MR. AMBEAU:	You're on the air, ma'am. Go ahead.
CALLER:	I just wanted to tell you that there are creatures that we don't know about that hide in the rain forest. But they're not like gorillas, they're just funny little brown men.

127

MR. AMBEAU:	Ma'am, we've been on this subject all morning, and I'm getting just a little tired of it. So here's a notice to you and any other kooks out there. Unless you can prove what you're talking about, don't bother me or our listeners with any more fairy tales about monsters in the woods.
CALLER:	But I do have proof, Joe.
MR. AMBEAU:	And what kind of proof would that be?
CALLER:	I wrote down what they said in my diary, which I just happened to have with me.
MR. AMBEAU:	Happened to have with me. Uh-huh. This wouldn't by any chance be my old friend who saw the giant flying saucer land at Copalis Beach last summer, would it?
CALLER:	Well, yes.
MR. AMBEAU:	I thought so. It's Looney Tunes time again, folks.
CALLER:	Now, Joe, don't be funny. I was near that old trail they closed up, near where Seldes Creek runs into Finley Creek, panning for gold a few summers ago—
MR. AMBEAU:	Panning for gold. Yes, uh-huh.
CALLER:	Yes, and I got a little lost, and I fell asleep, and I heard some voices—
MR. AMBEAU:	Glory, hallelujah.
CALLER:	And so I opened my eyes, you know, just a little? So they wouldn't know I was awake. And I saw them sort of sneaking among the trees, looking at me.
MR. AMBEAU:	That's really fascinating, ma'am. I could just sit and talk with you all day, but we only have another thirty seconds.
CALLER:	Well, I lay there very quiet, and I heard what they said. One of them, anyway, a little old man. He said, "kooknama reemee."
MR. AMBEAU:	I see. You sure these were little brown men? You sure they weren't little green men from that flying saucer of yours? Wearing space suits?
CALLER:	Oh, no, they were little brown men. And all they were wearing were little aprons, sort of.
MR. AMBEAU:	Gotta go, dearie. Time for a commercial. Give us a call next time the moon's full, hear, now?

When Gideon looked up, Abe said, "So what do you think?"

"I don't know. It might be true, but—forgive my elitist leanings—my credulity is not enhanced by the flying-saucer bit."

"Good," Abe said. "A nice, healthy skepticism. Now, the first question is: Is there such a place as—what was it?—where Seldes Creek runs into Finley Creek?"

"The answer is yes."

Abe's moist eyes widened. "You *know* this?"

"No, but I can see you have a topographic map unrolled on the dining-room table, and something tells me that you're about to lead me over there and show me that, verily, there is such a place." But it wasn't only that. Finley Creek had a familiar ring.

As soon as Abe jabbed his finger onto the map, Gideon remembered. And he knew they were onto something. "That's where Pringle found the spear head; right where you're pointing!"

Abe clucked softly. "So. What do you think of that? You wouldn't happen to remember where those two hikers got lost five or six years ago? The ones who got killed?"

"I don't think I ever knew. They were found in the cemetery. That's only a few miles from there."

"I did a little looking in the old newspapers. It looks like they were both on a new trail that just opened up, the Matheny trail, that runs from the Queets River—what a name—all the way up Matheny Creek"—his finger slowly traced the line from left to right—"and then to this North Fork Campground along Big Creek. In between, for a few miles, it runs—guess where?—down Finley Creek."

"Why doesn't it show on the map?"

"It's not there anymore, not officially. It opened up in 1976 and inside of a month those guys disappeared. They closed the trail—a good thing, it looks like—and they never bothered to reopen it. Now the Park Service says it ain't really necessary, and they ain't got funds to maintain it, and so on and so forth. So it's not on the map, and the signs are all down, and it's all overgrown, and nobody knows it's there. If you want my opinion, Mr. Skeleton Detective, that's where your Indians are."

129

"But what about the ledge we found? That was up on Pyrites Creek, over ten miles away. So was Claire Hornick's body. And that's where Pringle found two of his points. You're not going to say there are *two* groups in there, are you?"

Abe waved off Gideon's comments. "Use your noodle. Think about what you know about the Yahi—"

"What do the Yahi have to do with it?"

"I'm just giving you an example," Abe said. "Keep your shirt on. When the Yahi were hiding in California all those years, they had two villages. In the summer they lived up on Mount Lassen, where it was nice and breezy. In the wintertime, they came down and lived in the valleys. Much warmer. Why shouldn't *these* Indians do the same thing?"

"You think the ledge on Pyrites Creek is their summer home, and when it turns cold they move down to Finley Creek?"

"Why not? And if you do a little checking, which I did, you'll see that the two hikers on the Matheny trail, they got killed in the winter, when the Indians would have been there, near this Finley Creek. But the Hornick girl, according to you, she's dead two weeks, right? Late summer. The Indians would still be *there*." He pointed at Pyrites Creek. "But now that the weather's all cold and crummy, you can bet your life they went lower down, where it's not so cold. Here." The finger thumped Finley Creek.

That would explain why the ledge had been deserted. The Zanders must have happened on it just after the Indians had left. The same day, apparently, if they'd smelled smoke. The Zanders had been lucky.

"Why are you looking so glum?" Abe said. "Cheer up. Now I really got something to knock your block off. Come."

Gideon followed Abe back into the study. Abe whistled tunelessly under his breath, a sure sign he was enjoying himself. The old man seated himself stiffly in one of the wing-backed chairs in front of the wall with the photographs and reached for a book at his side. "Come look."

Gideon pulled up the other chair. The book was a bilingual dictionary: one column was English, the other an unfamiliar language, definitely not Indo-European.

"The lady of the talk show," Abe said. "You remember what she said the old man said?"

" 'Moona Kameemee?' "

" 'Kooknama reemee.' Now look here."

Gideon followed the knobbly forefinger down the page to the last line, where it hovered. " 'Ku'naamari'mi,' " Gideon read with interest. "Close enough."

"And what does it say it means?" The forefinger shifted slightly.

Gideon read it aloud. " 'Old woman.' Son-of-a-gun. What kind of dictionary *is* this? What's the language?"

Abe closed the book so Gideon could see the plain gray paper cover: *A Yahi Dictionary.* Compiled by Edward R. Chapman. University of California Publications in American Indian Linguistics, Volume 13, 1914. "Fascinating, huh?"

"Yahi!" Gideon said, his blood stirred. "But that's . . . There aren't any more Yahi. . . ." His hand went to his shirt pocket and found the small notebook there. He flipped rapidly through it, searching for the notes from his talk with Pringle. "Look at this, Abe: *cara* and *sin-yah*. See if we can find them."

In ten minutes they had them both. In Yahi, *kara* was "please," and *ciniyaa* was "no."

"Well, well, well," Abe said quietly.

"Abe . . . they speak Yahi. *Yahi!*" His mouth had gone dry. "How . . . who are they?"

"Don't get so excited," Abe said, flushed and excited himself. "Don't jump so fast to conclusions. Listen, a minute ago in that notebook, when you were flipping, I saw a picture. Show me again."

Gideon turned back to the drawing he had made of Pringle's baskets. "This?"

"Let's go in the library," Abe said suddenly.

Abe had had the wall between the family room and the master bedroom knocked out—he and Bertha slept in the smaller bedrooms—and had created a huge room which he'd filled with secondhand metal library shelves, freestanding in rows as well as along the walls, and blocking the windows, so that the whole was satisfyingly like a fusty corner of the stacks in some graduate library of anthropology.

The books, some fifteen thousand of them, Gideon had once estimated, were shelved in amazing disorder of which only Abe could make sense: books behind books, books in piles on their sides, books overflowing onto the floor in three-foot stacks. Gideon strongly suspected the existence of a precise but arcane cataloging system specifically invented for the bafflement of visitors. If there were one, it had successfully baffled him.

He stood respectfully in the doorway while Abe scurried about the labyrinth. Every few moments there would be a "feh!" or a "phooey!" and Abe would scuttle sourly around a corner of the shelves to disappear down another cluttered lane. After a while, "bingo's" began to outnumber "phooey's" and Abe emerged regularly to put an old, dark, serious-looking volume in Gideon's hands. In ten minutes he had an armload.

Abe came out with a final thick book, frowningly plumped it on the top of the stack Gideon was holding, and looked at him as if he were startled to see him. "What for are you standing there like a *shmegegge*? Put them on the table so we can see."

With the books on the dining-room table, Abe propped Gideon's open notebook in front of them and thumped it with his forefinger. "This basket pattern I've seen before."

"But it won't tell us anything. Pringle said a student told him it's a California design. They must have traded for it."

"Of course it's a California design. Any dope could see it's a California design. That's why these are California monographs we got here. So start looking."

Right, Gideon thought. Any dope. He opened the volume nearest him, *Material Culture of Aboriginal California,* and turned to the index. "Basketry," he read, "36–41, 122–23, 174–83 . . ."

Abe wasn't bothering with indices. He was starting at the beginning of each book and turning the pages with amazing rapidity, using just a flick of the finger. After every fifteen or twenty flicks, barely pausing, he would moisten the finger with his tongue. He was in the middle of his third book as Gideon finished his first.

"Bingo," Abe said. He turned the open book so it faced Gideon. "Is this it, or isn't it?"

It was definitely it: the same double, stepped columns of dark rectangles on a light background.

Abe's face was glowing. He closed the book so Gideon could see the cover: *Basketry of the Indians of North Central California, Vol. VI. The Yahi.*

"The Yahi," Gideon murmured, conscious of the slow, powerful pounding of his heart. "But is it possible Abe? Ishi was the last. No one's ever mentioned a splinter group."

Abe's voice was dreamy. "Five hundred miles they must have walked, always hiding. Over the mountains. Across the Columbia Gorge. Out of the land of Canaan, the warm, plenteous valleys of California, five hundred miles to the wettest, darkest place in America."

"And one of the most isolated places in America. The settlers were hunting them down in the nineteenth century, remember, killing them off." And the twentieth, according to Pringle.

"Hah," Abe said softly, and Gideon could see how much he wanted to believe in the incredible possibility. So did Gideon. "Hah," Abe said again, then shook his head. "No. No, it's too bizarre, too romantic. No."

"I don't recall," Gideon said, "that such pedestrian considerations ever caused you any concern before."

Abe slapped the table with his hand. "Right you are. You're absolutely right. I think we got something here."

He pointed suddenly at another book. "Hand me that, will you?"

As Gideon did so, he saw that it was *Yahi Archery* by Saxton Pope.

Abe flicked rapidly away. Halfway through, he stopped and stared. "This settles it."

On page 119, in neat, economical lines, was a drawing of a Yahi point. It was an arrow, not a spear, and it looked like stone, not bone, but the shape and the technique of manufacture were unmistakably the same as the ones in Pringle's collection, the one the Zanders had found, and the one in Norris Eckert's seventh thoracic vertebra.

"That settles it," Gideon agreed. He drew a deep breath. "The Yahi." They were both quiet for a while, lost in their own thoughts. Then Gideon spoke. "Abe, something's wrong. The Yahi were never a vicious people, and everybody who wrote about Ishi was struck by what a gentle, kind person he was. And Pringle's story suggests the ones he saw weren't exactly ferocious. But the ones in there now—they've murdered at least three people, probably more—all harmless campers or hikers. One was a young girl—"

"Listen, Gideon, in the 1850s they weren't exactly angels. Believe me," he said, as if he'd been there, "all the atrocities weren't on one side. Besides, who knows what their minds are like? A hundred years of isolation, of fear, of hate. Who can tell what goes on in their heads?"

"Abe," Gideon said suddenly, "I'd like to borrow these books, at least the ones that deal with the Yahi, if that's all right with you."

"You mean tonight? What's the hurry? You got till next spring."

"No. The FBI will want to find them long before that. I think the best thing would be for me to tell John Lau what we know, and then go in with them, or maybe a little before, to sort of smooth the way, open communication, that kind of thing. . . ." He waved his hand uncertainly.

"Sure, that kind of thing," Abe said, imitating the vague gesture. "You sure you know what you want to do?"

"No."

Abe chewed the inside of his cheek. He pointed at his glass of tea. "I don't want any more of this stuff. I want some Wild Turkey. A double. You, too. You know where it is?"

When Gideon returned with the bourbons they clinked glasses in a silent toast.

"What a thing," Abe said.

"What a thing," said Gideon.

"All right," Abe said, businesslike. "Let's think about what's going to happen after you find them. You and the FBI."

"I've *been* thinking. I can't believe the government would want to put them in prison. And they can't just let them stay out in the rain forest, obviously. For one thing, they're dangerous, and for another, it would be inhumane to leave them in that climate. I think it would be good if you started talking to some of your contacts in the Bureau of Indian Affairs. Maybe it's possible to get them some small piece of land of their own, off in a wilderness area."

"A reservation? Gideon, you take primitive people from their own land, no matter how hot, or cold, or wet, or dry, and put them someplace else, even with all the modern conveniences, and they wither away. You know that."

"Yes, I know that, but they're already withering. And what's the alternative? Lock them up in some big concrete building? They'd die for sure. This way we might be able to save them. Not just the people, but what's left of the culture."

"Maybe," Abe said doubtfully. "All right, I'll talk to the BIA, but I don't know. Maybe it takes an Act of Congress to create a reservation. And this would be a pretty funny reservation. You couldn't let them leave it."

"It's a pretty funny situation." Gideon looked at his watch. "Eleven-thirty. It's been a full day, Abe. I'm going to be getting along."

"Finish your bourbon. You can't waste Wild Turkey."

They touched glasses one more time. "Here's to Ishi," Abe said.

"And the Yahi."

They drained their glasses.

It was midnight when Gideon got back to the cottage, but his mind was too active for sleep. He turned on the small electric wall heater against the damp chill that had been building up during the past few days, pulled on an old woolen sweater, and sat down at the little Formica table with Abe's books spread out in front of him. In a few seconds he was up again,

135

hunting for the tea kettle. He had been the kind of child who ate his vegetables and potatoes first, so the meat could be looked forward to all through the meal. He was the same kind of adult, and to hold off the pleasures of research a little longer he brewed a pot of Earl Grey tea—he'd gotten some for himself when he'd bought Pringle's—and rummaged in the refrigerator, finally bringing out an apple. Then, humming, enjoying the feel of the rough, warm sweater in the cool room, he sat down again and began.

He started with a dull article on Yahi technology, moved on to a scholarly and interesting paper on social norms, and then spent three painstaking hours with the incredibly complex Yahi language. By 4:00 A.M., although pleased with the linguistic progress he'd made, he was too tired for any more serious study. He threw down his pen, rubbed his eyes, and stretched. His bed was neatly made and beginning to look inviting, but he knew he still wasn't relaxed enough to sleep. What he needed, he decided, was a hot bath. A hot bath and some easy reading, something to browse in. He turned on the tap and, yawning, reached for one of the volumes he'd thus far ignored, *Indian Days in Old California,* a 1920 collection of popular observations and reminiscences, no doubt one of the many stimulated by Ishi's startling appearance a few years earlier.

Once settled in the deliciously hot water, he opened the book, drying his hands first so he didn't wet the old paper. The first section consisted of pieces written in the 1860s. One was a newspaper account of the bloody killing and scalping of a Yahi family who had stolen a sheep. The next two were more of the same, and the fourth was a learned endorsement of an 1861 court case in which it had been decided that the legal principle of "justifiable conquest" applied to the appropriation of Indian land by white settlers. It was no wonder that the Yahi had chosen to disappear at about that time. Other old articles confirmed in macabre detail Abe's statement that by no means all the murders and mutilations in Old California were perpetuated by whites.

Gideon had just about decided he'd chosen the wrong book

136

for relaxing with when he came upon a 1919 article called "My Indian Friend Denga," in which a St. Louis woman recalled her childhood in Red Bluff more than fifty years before. Her father and mother had run the general store in the little northern California town, and she had gotten to know some "city" Yahi who sometimes did odd jobs for the store, taking their pay in flour and tea. She had made friends, after a fashion, with one of the Indian children, and had even learned some Yahi, a feat that impressed Gideon considerably.

The affectionate, rambling story was a pleasant counter to the newspaper stories but provided little pertinent information until the last two pages:

> I remember the last time I saw Denga. He came to the yard in back of the store with his uncle, old One-ear. I thought it was strange that One-ear didn't leave him there to play with me, and go inside to help my father, but the two of them just stood there. Denga's eyes were full of tears, and One-ear was very serious.
>
> "Denga cannot play anymore," One-ear said. I was surprised, because that was the first time he ever really said anything to me. Usually he just grinned and shuffled his feet. I guess he finally figured out I could understand Yahi.
>
> "Is he sick?" I asked.
>
> One-ear looked confused, and I thought maybe I hadn't used the right words. "Not sick," he finally said. "We have to go away."
>
> At that Denga started to cry. "I have to go to the Dark Place," he said.
>
> One-ear kind of shook the boy's shoulder to make him stop blubbering, and just then Father came to the back door and called One-ear to help him with something. The old Indian went to the door, dragging Denga by the arm, but Father separated them and took One-ear inside. Denga just stood by the door, trembling and miserable. I ran right up to him and asked him what in the world it was all about.
>
> That started him crying again. "We're never coming back here. We have to go away forever."
>
> "But where is the Dark Place?" I asked him, thinking

maybe he meant they were going to die. "Is it Heaven?"

He looked sideways at the ground. That's the way they said no. Then he said, "It's far away, on the other side of Mount Lassen. There are no people, and the ferns are as big as trees, and the trees are as tall as mountains, so tall that you can never see the sun, and day is the same as night. And the air is made of water, and it rains all day long."

It sounded awful. "But why do you have to go there?" I asked him.

"So the *saltu* can't find us."

Saltu was their word for white people, and it was the first time I'd heard that the Yahi had any reason to be afraid of us. Of course, later on I found out that they had plenty of reason.

One-ear came out then and glared at Denga; he knew he'd been telling tales. He stared hard at me, with a strange look on his face, as if he wanted to ask something, but then he just took hold of Denga's arm and dragged him away.

Naturally, at the time I didn't believe the story of the Dark Place, but then Denga didn't ever come back, and neither did the others. Father must have thought I knew something about it, because he kept asking me where they'd gone, but I remembered that last begging look of One-ear's and held my tongue. Until now, fifty-two years later, I have kept that story locked in my heart.

The Dark Place no longer sounds awful to me. It sounds like a good place to be, cool and dim and calm. I like to think of my little friend Denga there, and ugly old One-ear, beyond whatever earthly or heavenly mountain range it lies, enjoying the tranquil, halcyon days denied them in their ancestral homeland.

With an odd tightening in his throat, Gideon closed the book and laid it on the rim of the tub. He stepped out of the cooling water, put on a warm velour robe, and went into the kitchen to prepare another pot of tea, but changed his mind. Turning up the robe's collar, he opened the cottage door and stepped into the night. There was no wind, but a cold, velvety mist, smelling of the ocean, drifted in the air. The night was at its blackest and most silent, so that the gentle hissing of the tide on the pebbles of the beach forty feet below seemed much closer, like old leaves rustling a few inches from his ear. Far away a night bird, an owl, hooted twice, mournful and hollow. Much nearer, in the water, there was a sudden small splash, and then a scrabbling sound. Then the slow flapping of big wings. Another night hunter, this one finding its prey.

His hair was wet with mist, and droplets had collected on his eyelids. He stood looking down at the black water hé could not see. The Dark Place. The name echoed in his mind, doomful and sinister, melancholy and strangely beautiful. He shivered again, not from the cold this time.

Tranquil, halcyon days. He smiled grimly to himself. Over a hundred years of self-imposed isolation, over a century of fear and loneliness and privation. He tried to imagine the appalling significance of the new trail to them. To what horrendous proportions must the stories of the *saltu* have grown in four generations of retelling? What must have gone through their minds when the snorting, snuffling bulldozers and shrieking saws came and cut a swath along Finley Creek, perhaps within sight of the village that had been their home beyond the memory of many of them, or of their fathers' memory?

The machines would have gone away after a while, but then the walkers would have begun to come, not with frightening monsters that ripped the trees groaning from the earth, but alone and vulnerable. And the Yahi had killed in desperation and killed again. The walkers had stopped coming. Then the girl had somehow stumbled onto their little territory, and once again they had killed. And now, after over a hundred years, the *saltu* stalked them again.

This time, however, there would be no bloodshed and mutilation. Not if he and John got there before the reward-seekers and the Bigfoot hunters. And they would, because Gideon knew where they were.

He went back into the cottage but stood at the open door to inhale the misty, salt-laden air one more time before he finally lay wearily down. He fell asleep quickly and slept through the gray dawn and long into the drizzly morning.

14

WHEN HE AWOKE at ten he called John's number in Seattle, but the FBI agent wasn't in, so Gideon left a message asking him to return the call. It was raining—not heavily, but steadily, as if it were going to go on for a long time. He stood at the window awhile, sipping hot coffee from a mug and wondering what it would be like to huddle over a primitive drill trying to light a fire in weather like this.

He scrambled three eggs, fried some bacon, and toasted a few slices of bread in the oven. Then he sat down at the table, trying not to feel guilty, and propped the Yahi dictionary in front of him.

"*Ya'a hushol*," he said between mouthfuls of eggs and bacon. "Hello." He shook his head and tried it again. How were you supposed to pronounce apostrophes? The dictionary had been prepared before the invention of the international phonetic alphabet, and the explanation—"apostrophes may represent any number of concurrent glottalizations"—wasn't much help. "*Ai'niza ma'a wagai*," he said, trying to glottalize concurrently. "Me friend." Verbs, cases, and other nonessentials he could do without.

The telephone rang, and John was already speaking as Gideon got it to his ear. "What's up, Doc?"

Gideon washed down a piece of toast with a gulp of coffee. "*Ya'a hushol*," he said.

"*Yakahooshle* to you too. That was a good report on Hornick. Thanks. What did you want me to call you about?"

"When you come down to Quinault, you're planning to go in after those Indians, aren't you?"

"Sure. First thing I'm going to do is check out that ledge."

"I want to go with you." But they're not at that ledge, he al-

140

most added, then thought better of it. It would be best to see where John stood first.

"Doc, I can't do that. You know that."

"I can speak their language," Gideon said, feeling that a certain amount of overstatement was excusable under the circumstances. "And I know something about their customs."

"No, Doc, no way. These guys are killers. I'm not taking you along. What would be the point, anyway?"

"I could talk to them, kind of ease the way, make sure there isn't any shooting—"

"Who's talking about shooting? This isn't cowboys and Indians. We're just going to bring them in. If we find them."

"And if they don't want to come? If they start throwing spears? These are people from the Stone Age. They're not going to understand who you are, or what you are, or what you want to do to them, or why you want to do it. You're going to need someone—"

"For Christ's sake, Doc!" John was annoyed. "Do I tell you how to do your job?"

"Every goddamn chance you get."

"Goddamnit . . . !" Then, as Gideon knew he would, John burst into his easy, childlike laughter, melodious and infectious. And as always, Gideon couldn't help smiling himself.

"Okay," John said, "maybe I do a little. But this is different. Me and Minor and the others, we're a team. We can all predict what the other ones are going to do, you know what I mean? If we brought in someone who's not trained, who doesn't know the way we work, it'd be dangerous for everybody. Including the Indians."

When Gideon didn't respond, John said, "Okay, what are you thinking?"

"Nothing. I'm just pouting."

"No, you're not. You're hatching something. What do you want to do, find them yourself?"

"I was thinking about it, yes."

"Well, what the hell for?"

141

"What do you mean, what the hell for? I want to talk to them, convince them we mean them no harm."

It sounded lame to Gideon as he said it, and lame-brained too. It did to John as well; a disgusted snort and a muffled "Jesus Christ" were audible over the telephone. Gideon could imagine his eyes raised to the fluorescent ceiling of the office in Seattle.

"Look, Doc, they already killed three people. You think you're going to walk up to them and say, 'How. Me friend,' and they're going to fall all over you with joy? They'll spit you on one of those spears like a big barbecued chicken."

"Now, look, John—" Gideon said crossly, stung by the brief but uncomfortably cogent dismissal of what was, after all, his only-begotten plan so far.

"Doc, you're not going with me. That's all there is to it."

Gideon's mouth tightened. If that's the way he wanted it, that's the way it would be. "Okay," he said, "you win."

It was too easy, and John was immediately suspicious. "What's that supposed to mean? They're not there, are they? At Pyrites Creek? Doc, if you know where they are, tell me. How are you going to feel if they kill someone else? You know something, and you're not telling me."

"Now, John, you engage me from time to time to do skeletal analyses, and not, as you point out freely and often, to do your detection for you. Of course, if you agreed to take me along. . . ."

"Not a chance, but if you know—"

"I don't know nuttin' and I ain't sayin' nuttin'."

John sighed. "You're a damn difficult man to deal with. Look, let's leave it at this: I can't get down there till Friday anyway, so you go do whatever dumb thing you're going to do. But on Friday I'm going to expect you to tell me everything you know about this. I mean it, Doc."

Gideon hesitated a moment, and John said irritably, "Come on, man, I'm giving you three days. Against my better judgment. Don't make me go all legal on you. Let's stay friends."

"All right, John, fair enough."

"Okay. And do me a favor, huh? If you find these guys, be careful, will you? They're not exactly noble savages."

"Don't worry. Believe me, I know exactly what I'm doing." The hell he did, thought Gideon.

"The hell you do," said John.

The coffee was still warm, and the bacon and eggs weren't quite cold, so Gideon propped the map on the table and munched while studying it. Finley Creek was not much more than a mile from the road along Lake Quinault's north shore but it was a mile of unbroken, trailless rain forest. Impossible to get in that way. He'd be lost in five minutes, even with a compass. Instead, he'd have to drive to the North Fork Ranger Station seven or eight miles farther on and walk back along the abandoned Matheny trail. Surely it would still be passable; it couldn't have grown over in six years. All told, including a three-hour drive and allowing for a rough trail, it would take him eight or nine hours to get to Finley Creek from where he was sitting. If he left now he'd arrive in Yahi territory at about dark. Not the most enchanting idea in the world. It'd be better to take the rest of the day to learn some more Yahi, and leave early Wednesday. He thought briefly of calling Julie and spending the night at Lake Quinault, but she'd worm out of him what he was doing down there and then either try to dissuade him or insist on coming along. No, it would be best to work right where he was all day, go to bed early, and get on his way the next day at 4:00 A.M. or so. That would put him on Finley Creek with plenty of daylight to spare. Much better. He folded up the map, took one more bite of cold toast, and got out the Yahi dictionary.

By late afternoon, his head was so full of the strange morphemes he was afraid that if he tried to cram in one more syllable there would be an explosion, and *hoori'ma'a'nigi*'s and *zicin'mauyaa*'s would go ricocheting off the walls. He closed the book wearily, stretched, and made himself a ham and cheese sandwich, which he ate standing at the sink, washing it down with a glassful of milk, blessedly vacant of mind.

Then he slipped his poncho over his head, dashed through

the rain to his Rabbit, and drove down the wet and blackly shining road toward Sequim, ten miles away. He needed to do some shopping for his expedition.

The rain shadow gods were at work. Directly over Sequim there was a big, bright blue, raggedly circular hole in the thick clouds, through which sunlight streamed in visible rays, suffusing the streets with tawny light. The effect was that of a Tiepolo fresco. All it needed was a rosy-nippled shepherdess peeking through the hole, and a couple of buttery cherubs on top of the lamppost at East Washington and Sequim Avenue.

He stopped first at Southwood's Department Store to buy a five-dollar lightweight plastic tube tent, which someone had told him was a useful thing to have in the rain, a bottle of liquid purporting to waterproof shoes, and a day pack. Package in hand, he was making for the exit when a discounted box of necklaces made, apparently, from ball bearings caught his eye. Trinkets. How could you go looking for a lost tribe without trinkets? He bought four of them for a dollar apiece, then went back to the cosmetics section. Mirrors also were *de rigueur*, and he bought two purse-sized ones.

A few yards of cloth would round out the obligatory items, but Southwood's didn't stock it, so he got a packaged set of kitchen curtains, yellow with red fleur-de-lis, instead. On the spur of the moment he went to the toy section and bought a $1.09 rubber turtle named Squeekie who, predictably enough, squeaked cheerfully when squeezed. A fair sampling of the wonders of civilization for $10.88.

"This it?" the grandmotherly clerk said, punching at the cash register. "A few goodies for Daddy's little darlings?"

"Yes," Gideon said, smiling. "And I'll have one of these, too." He picked up a throwaway plastic cigarette lighter for sixty-nine cents. If that didn't convince them that civilization had something going for it, he didn't know what would.

He put his purchases in the car and walked a block to the Mark & Pak supermarket. The blue hole still was directly overhead, and he enjoyed the sunshine. He bought a small loaf of wheat bread, a pound or so of grapes, and ten cans of sardines (in tomato sauce, mustard sauce, and olive oil for variety). Not the most appealing menu imaginable, but nutritious and protein-rich. He didn't have a camp stove, didn't want to buy one, and didn't want to carry one on his back for ten miles each way. Or carry pots and utensils. It wouldn't kill him to eat cold food for a couple of days.

In the evening he was in a lighthearted mood. He had just finished a note to John describing what he was planning to do. He'd drop it off at John's Quinault office tomorrow morning, and if all went well, he'd be back before John saw it. And if not, the prospect of John thundering after him was reassuring. He put the note in a manila envelope, enclosed a Forest Service map with his route marked in fluorescent ink, and sealed it. Then he loaded his pack, applied the liquid to his shoes (it seemed to work), puttered happily until 9:00 P.M., and went to bed.

When the alarm rang it was a different story. No one is a hero at 4:00 A.M., a wise man has said, and Gideon found it true. He had lain under the covers for fifteen minutes, reluctant to leave his warm bed, and then, more reluctant still to face the black, slanting rain, he had managed to use nearly an hour making and consuming a pot of coffee with toast.

Now, three hours later, having swung by Quinault to tack the note to John's door, he slowed to a stop in the deserted North Fork campground. If he was not precisely reluctant, then he was not exactly anxious, either, to walk off into the dark and dripping forest.

The campground was closed for the winter, and the camp sites were all empty. Small wonder. Who'd be out in weather like this? It was barely light. The only sounds were the pattering of the rain on the hood of his poncho, and the dripping of rain from the limbs of the trees, and the trickling of rain down the runnels at the edges of the gravel paths. For a man who had always liked rain, Gideon found the scene dispiritingly gloomy and forlorn. Already he regretted his decision not to bring a stove. A hot cup of coffee would have gone a long way to brighten things.

Finding the trailhead took more time than he expected. Only

145

after an hour's prowling of the barren campground, when he was beginning to fear he wouldn't find it—or to hope he wouldn't; he wasn't so sure which—he came upon it, not in the campground itself, but a hundred feet back down the road. It was an unmarked, decayed trail, corroded and rutted by six seasons of hundred-forty-five-inch rains, obliterated in places by robust intrusions of ferns, bead-ruby, and cloverlike oxalis. Still, it looked passable and easy enough to follow. The towering green walls of moss-draped cedar and spruce that hemmed it in would make it difficult to lose, even where it was overrun with smaller plants.

He struck out determined to walk off the slightly down-at-the-mouth feelings he'd awakened with, and, with his usual resilience, soon did so. Potholes and obstructive vegetation notwithstanding, he quickly settled into an easy stride and found himself humming and thinking with pleasure about meeting the Indians, talking with them, befriending them. The walking warmed him, and the cool rain sliding down his face was fresh, and sweet-tasting when it ran into his mouth. Except for his face and hands, he was as dry as toast.

After a couple of miles the trail began to climb gently. Must be skirting the southern flank of Finley Peak, Gideon thought sagely, trailwise and proficient in the ways of contour maps and rain forests. Eyes to the uneven path, he noticed that the air had lost its green, underwater cast, and he looked up to see that the trees had thinned. He was indeed on the flank of a mountain, with a clear, stupendous view to his left.

He found a relatively dry spot under a mossy rock overhang and sat down to look at the scene before him. It was like a photograph taken from a small airplane, the opening picture of a jungly *National Geographic* article perhaps titled, "Four Months on the Matto Grosso."

Below him lay the Quinault Valley, an endless, wet, billowing blue-green carpet, humped and bulging in places, like a stupendous, lumpy mattress tossed carelessly down between the mountain ranges. Here and there the Quinault River glinted dully through the green. Off to the west a flat, crescent-shaped seg-

146

ment of Lake Quinault could be seen, mirroring the sky's gray but pinkly tinged and luminous, like a disc of abalone shell.

Gideon suddenly realized he was hungry; all he'd eaten was the slice of toast before dawn. He opened a can of sardines in olive oil, found them delicious, and had another with a few slices of bread and some water from a stream that gushed down the rock a few feet away.

When he was done he got out the map and compared it to the terrain, nodding complacently to himself. The trail wasn't on the map, of course, but he knew approximately where it should be, and he thought he knew just where he was. The mountains directly across the valley had to be Colonel Bob and Mount O'Neil. Off ahead five or six miles the southeast shoulder of Finley Peak edged gracefully into the rain forest, just as the contour lines said it did. On the other side of that, according to the map, in the little canyon between it and Matheny Ridge, ran Finley Creek, and there the Yahi would be. It didn't look difficult to get to. With mountains as reference points on either side, he'd be able to find it easily, even if the trail petered out, which it gave no sign of doing.

Revivified, content, and feeling very much the outdoorsman— city person, indeed!—he started confidently out once more.

Twenty minutes later he was as lost as he'd ever been in his life. The trouble was that the trail descended at once, back into the rain forest, and there it *did* peter out, or at least become so overrun with huckleberry, horsetail, ferns, and even some fledgling trees that it required more concentrated attention than he gave it, engaged as he was in reciting Yahi vocabulary.

When he finally realized that he was no longer on the trail, he looked up to find his mountain reference points. All he could see were trees: massive trunks of Sitka spruce, like monstrous elephant legs; slim, soaring hemlock; rough-barked fir. No mountains, no reference points, not even any sky.

Gideon's first reaction was mild amusement, removed and tolerant, a sort of "Oho, it looks as if the Great White Hunter isn't the woodsman he thought he was." Then he turned very slowly in a complete circle, searching for anything that might

147

help him find the trail. There was nothing. More unsettling, he wasn't certain exactly when he'd turned all the way around; he was no longer sure which way he'd been heading, and he didn't know which way he'd come.

That shook him a little, and he felt a prickle of uneasiness. The rain was falling more heavily now, and the enormous folds of club moss hanging from the branches were not translucent archways but thick, sodden draperies, slimy and spinachlike. A green, swampy mist, thickening perceptibly, swirled over the ground, theatrical and sinister. That was a good description of the whole damn rain forest, he thought: ominous and unreal. No, he said to himself, that was no frame of mind to get into. Positive thinking was in order.

All right. Think positively. He couldn't have been off the trail more than a few minutes, so it was nearby. He would walk in an expanding spiral, keeping the big cedar with the droopy branch as the central point.

To his astonishment, as soon as he took his eyes off the cedar he lost it. It vanished, became exactly like a hundred others. And when he instinctively spun around to look for it, he once more lost his sense of direction; he couldn't tell which way it lay.

The uneasy prickle became a stabbing worry. This was not his element; he was an intruder, a foreigner who didn't know the rules. He wiped the rain from his streaming face. "The air is made of water," the little boy Denga had said. It seemed like it, all right. Hard to see through, difficult to breathe, confining, constraining, restricting . . .

Positive thinking. If the spirals wouldn't work, he would try another tack. He would once again take a big tree as a point of reference—and learn what it looked like this time. He chose a spruce, fixing in his mind's eye the configuration of a convoluted set of limbs high up on the trunk and the big, ragged tear in the club moss that hung from them. Good. Now he would choose as a landmark another large tree a hundred and fifty feet away, the absolute limit of his vision about seventy-five feet above the ground. (At ground level, the undergrowth made it much less.) He would walk toward the tree in as straight a line as he could, con-

148

tinually checking back over his shoulder for his home spruce. If he did not find the trail by the time he reached the tree, he would go back to the spruce, choose another landmark tree down a line at right angles to the first one, and so on. With four such explorations he would be bound to cross the trail if it was within a ninety-thousand-square-foot area . . . unless, of course, the trail curved, which he wouldn't think about just yet. If all of this didn't work, he could expand the area, using the landmark trees as new focal points.

What he didn't anticipate was the number of trails—elk trails perhaps, or deer, or maybe Yahi, for all he knew. Some seemed to be natural, meandering channels through the undergrowth. He followed five false leads, one of them for a quarter of a mile, before he stumbled onto the one he was looking for, only fifteen feet from where he'd begun. It had taken him an hour and a half.

Humbled and much more observant now, he began walking again, carefully following the trail. After an hour it began to climb again. He was beginning to recover some of his confidence when he was stopped short by the opening up of a long view over the valley toward Mount O'Neil and Colonel Bob—the same view he'd seen before. Exactly. At first nothing registered but puzzlement. Could it be possible that he was on a loop trail? That he had been walking in a circle? It must be; there was the rocky overhang under which he'd had the sardines.

When the truth hit him he came near to sitting down in the rain and crying. He had, of course, been simply and stupidly walking in the wrong direction since he'd rediscovered the trail. He'd gone back the way he'd come and never even suspected it! On second thought he did sit down, his back against the rock wall. He sat there awhile, slumped over, wet, and miserable. The wind had sharpened so that the overhang was little protection. The temperature was dropping, too. His hands were red and raw, and from the feel of it, so was his face.

There was now no chance that he'd reach Finley Creek in time to find and talk with the Yahi today. He'd have to camp out in this cold and funereal jungle—and he wasn't going to get much coziness from his five-dollar plastic tent or much warmth

149

from his butane lighter. Certainly, he wasn't going to be able to ignite any of the ubiquitous but waterlogged deadwood of the forest floor. It might make more sense to walk back to his car right now—it was less than two hours away, notwithstanding the five hours he'd been bumbling through the rain forest—and drive off to have a decent dinner somewhere, then find a warm bed someplace, and return in the morning, fresh and—

He cut off the thought with a shake of his head and hauled himself to his feet. He knew very well where his mind was leading him: A good dinner somewhere meant the Lake Quinault Lodge, and a warm bed someplace was Julie's. No, he was more resolute than that, or more stubborn. He wasn't going to melt in the rain, goddamnit, and there was plenty of daylight left in which to make more progress. He adjusted the uncomfortable pack and strode firmly back down the hill. He wasn't ready to admit he was done in yet, not by a long shot.

Three hours later, dispirited and weary, he was ready to admit it. A choppy, erratic wind drove the rain needlelike into his face, stinging his cheeks and eyes, and sometimes even streaming upward into his nostrils to make him cough and sputter. His trousers, poorly protected by the flapping poncho, were soaked, and the waterproofing seemed to be wearing off his shoes. The rough up-and-down trail had long ago slowed his stride to a foot-dragging, mindless trudge.

When he found himself under a little open sky, he stopped and looked gratefully at it. It was malevolent and yellowish-gray, but anything was better than that tossing, dipping roof of solid green. Even the rain didn't seem so bad here, falling more gently, in fat, soft blobs. He was somewhere along Big Creek, still probably a good four miles from Finley Creek, and, he thought dully, it seemed a good place to stop for the day. He found a flat, open space ten or fifteen feet off the path, still with a view of the sky, but surrounded by thick brush and trees that blocked the wind and offered a little protection, more psychological than real, against the rain.

For a few minutes he simply stood there with his eyes closed, catching his breath, thoroughly sick of the rain forest and the endless rain; sick even of the Yahi, though he had yet to meet them. He had, for that matter, yet to confirm their existence. How, he wondered muzzily, had he come to be here? What impossible chain of events had brought a quiet, comfort-loving professor to stand alone in gray-green mist, drenched and shivering, deep in the only damn jungle in the Northern Hemisphere?

Swaying slightly, with the rain pelting his eyelids and thrumming on his poncho, Gideon waited for sensible answers which didn't come. The hell with it, he thought stolidly, I'm here and I'll see it through. Not that he had a choice; he didn't have the energy to make the long walk back to the car.

By shrugging and twisting, he moved the pack around to his chest, keeping the pack under the poncho to protect it from the rain, and managed to dig out the ridiculously unsubstantial-looking tube tent, packed flat in a square not much bigger than a handkerchief. The principle was simple, the salesman had told him: Lay the blue plastic cylinder on the ground, tie ropes to the grommets at each end, tie the other ends of the ropes to supports, and presto, instant tent.

He had neglected to bring a ground cloth, but the spongy forest duff drained well and kept the ground from being muddy. Thank God for small favors. He laid out the tent, ran ropes through the grommets, and found a low, stubby tree limb to serve as one of the anchors. It was massive and sturdy-looking, but when he pulled tentatively on it, it squashed like papier-mâché, oozing water between his fingers and dropping in pulpy fragments to the dark forest floor.

This bothered Gideon more than it should have. The entire rain forest seemed suddenly more deceitful, more untrustworthy. He looked around him, noticing for the first time that he had chosen to spend the night in an area in which most of the trees had long ago sprung from what Julie had called nurse logs. These were great, fallen trunks on which seedlings had taken purchase, gradually straddling them with roots that ran down to the ground. Eventually the original trunks had rotted away, leaving the roots straddling nothing but air. The effect was grotesque. Gideon felt as if he were surrounded by the mighty hands of giants, their splayed, gnarled fingers gripping the ground, their powerful forearm-trunks rising to the forest roof.

Now he was getting silly, and he certainly wasn't going to allow himself to be spooked by trees. He tied the two rope ends around a couple of young maple trunks, testing them first to see if they were solid. The tent now looked something like a tent, even if it smelled like a brand-new beach ball. The plastic stench would be overpowering once he tied the ends against the rain.

Which he couldn't do, he realized with a heart that sank a little more with each passing, rain-soaked minute. He hadn't brought any extra rope. Uncharitably, he cursed the salesman for not reminding him. He laid his sleeping bag, which even under the poncho had somehow gotten damp, inside the tent and used twigs to hold together the three grommets at each end, but he could see it wasn't going to work. The sleeping bag would be drenched. Already little puddles were forming on the plastic floor of the tent.

What a night this was going to be, but he was too tired and hungry to think much about it; he would eat something and then try to sleep, even if he had to do it sitting up in his poncho against a tree.

When he got out his plastic bag of food, he found that the bread was thoroughly soaked, more like a wet mush than bread at all, and that the grapes weren't there; he had apparently left them when he'd stopped to eat that morning.

That did not leave much of a dinner menu: *M'sieu* would like the *sardines à la sauce moutarde? Non?* Perhaps then the *sardines à la sauce de tomates?* He opened a can with the mustard and glowered unenthusiastically at the contents. They were very large sardines, only three to a tin, and they looked more like cold, dead fish than sardines had a right to do.

Huddled over the can in the rainy, deepening darkness, Gideon couldn't remember a time when he'd felt so extravagantly glum. He smiled unconvincingly; this would no doubt be most amusing told over a steak dinner in a warm, dry restaurant. But it didn't seem funny now, he thought, looking at the spreading water in his sleeping bag and at his raw, wet hands. And those oily fish.

He couldn't locate the plastic fork he'd brought, but he managed to find a pointed, fairly solid sliver of wood to serve as a knife. He steeled himself to impale one of the soft, grublike bodies in the can. Ah, well . . .

He stiffened, suddenly alert, the back of his neck tingling. There had been a sound, audible over the unvarying, sharp rattling of the rain. A rotten branch breaking under the weight of accumulated water? A large bird startled into flight . . . but by what?

It came again, a scuffling sound, and then again; someone or something moving, brushing against the foliage. He jumped to his feet and jerked down the hood of his poncho to listen. The sound had come from the direction of the path; he was fairly certain of that. He stood staring, blinded by thick, gray cords of rain. He could hear his heart pounding crazily. *"Ya'a hushol!"* he shouted. *"Ai'niza ma'a wagai!"*

The sounds stopped abruptly, then continued more firmly, someone moving toward him. He could hear the squelch of footsteps now. His breath came fast and hard.

Between the huge fronds of a head-high brake fern he caught a brief, startling glimpse of a dark, bundled figure moving purposefully through the underbrush—toward him, he was sure. The figure vanished behind foliage, and Gideon stood staring at the spot where it had been, trying to see through the sheet of water that ran down his face. He stopped his breath, got his feet more firmly under him, tensed the powerful muscles of his arms and shoulders.

A moment later the fronds of a lady fern were abruptly thrust aside. With a violent jerk, Gideon spun toward the motion, crouched and straining, the pointed wood sliver clenched in his hand.

Enveloped in a bulky parka and loaded with a huge pack, Julie walked into the clearing.

"Dr. Oliver, I presume," she said, smiling.

153

15

IT TOOK HER five minutes to set up the amazingly roomy A-frame tent she'd had in her pack, and another five to rig a rain fly over it. Fifteen minutes after that, a pot of beef stew was bubbling on the tiny Optimus stove. Gideon sat in a warm corner of the tent near the stove, grinning foolishly, content to be out of the rain, and out of his musty poncho, and to watch Julie bustle competently about.

"What was that you were squeaking when I came up?" she said over her shoulder, stirring the stew.

"I wasn't squeaking. I was speaking Yahi."

"Yahi? Why Yahi? How do you know Yahi?"

He explained while she stirred thoughtfully. "Well, you scared me," she said. "I thought maybe it wasn't you. I didn't know you squeaked."

Gideon laughed. "I guess I might have been a little jumpy."

"Yes, maybe just a little. I didn't know whether you were going to stab me with that twig or hit me with that horrible fish."

Gideon laughed again, beginning to thaw out. "I thought you weren't supposed to light a stove in a tent."

"You're not, but you can get away with it if you're careful."

"And if you're the chief ranger."

"That too." Julie spooned the steaming stew into a couple of plastic bowls and handed one to Gideon. She was as hungry as he, and for a few minutes they sat cross-legged on the floor of the tent without speaking, energetically cramming the hot vegetables and beef into their mouths.

When the heat began to flow through him, Gideon sighed luxuriously and slowed down, looking up from his bowl to watch Julie eat. She was wonderfully healthy and happy, her skin golden and rosy, her eyes sparkling. She caught him looking at her with her mouth full, and she waved the big spoon

154

happily at him. She laughed while she chewed, without opening her lips. In a baggy, shapeless sweater, with her cheeks stuffed like a chipmunk's and her damp hair pasted flat to her forehead, she looked so heartbreakingly beautiful he could hardly swallow.

"I love you, Julie," he said.

Finally.

Her mouth was too filled for her to speak. She frowned, chewing harder, and swallowed prodigiously, then washed the food all the way down with some hot tea.

"I heard you the first time," she said, smiling.

"The first time?"

"In the sleeping bag. You were speaking to the back of my neck at the time, but I assume you meant the rest of me too."

"You *heard* me? I thought you were asleep."

"I was, but there are certain things you don't miss even in your sleep."

"But why didn't you say anything?"

"Well, it wasn't exactly the sort of thing to sweep me off my feet. 'I love you, I think.' " She laughed and shook her head.

Gideon laughed too and spooned a chunk of potato into his mouth. "It does lack somewhat for lyrical expression, doesn't it? But," he said more soberly, "there aren't any qualifications this time."

"Are you sure? It's not just my beef stew and my tent? You're not just glad to have a warm female to take care of you on a cold, wet night?"

He shook his head. "No qualifications. I love you, Julie Tendler. And that's something I don't say very often, believe me." Not once out loud in three years.

" 'I love you, Julie Tendler'?" she said. "Why would you say that very—?"

"Shush, you." He leaned over to kiss her softly. They moved apart and looked at each other, then kissed again, longer this time but no less gently. Her fingers rested on his cheek, radiating shivery tendrils; his hand cupped the warm, downy nape of her neck. When they paused at last to breathe, he brushed the tip of her nose with his lips. "Now," he said, "what was that about taking care of me on a cold night?"

"Men," she said. "It's one thing after another. Get them dry and they want food. Get them fed and they want . . . well, something else."

"Precisely," said Gideon. "Maslow's concept of human needs as a hierarchy of prepotencies. Very succinctly expressed."

"Is that what I said?"

"Yup."

"What does it mean?"

"It means let's go to bed."

She laughed. "Don't overwhelm me. I can stand only so much lyrical expression in one night. Let's clean up the dinner things first."

They did it quickly, scraping the pots and dishes and putting them outside to rinse in the rain.

"I think," she said, looking out into the pouring near-darkness, "that we'd better bring your sleeping bag inside."

"It's already wet. Doesn't matter. It was a $12.95 special ten years ago. Made of genuine, reconstituted Kleenex."

She closed the tent flap and crawled back on her knees. "Some anthropologist. *El cheapo* sleeping bag, five-and-dime tent, sardines for breakfast, lunch, and dinner. Are you ever lucky I came along and found you!"

He smiled. Then his brow furrowed. "Julie, what the heck are you doing here?"

She began to undo the ties on the sleeping bag. "Coming after you. I had visions of you sitting wet and cold and hungry in the dark . . . absurd as it may seem. My nurturing instincts were aroused. I even thought you might get lost. It's a rough trail. *Did* you get lost? You haven't gotten very far."

"Of course not," he said disdainfully. "All you have to do is follow the path. Did *you* get lost?"

"Uh-uh," she said with transparent honesty, unrolling the bag.

"And so you lugged all this stuff on your back, hiked all this way . . ."

"For you," she said simply, with a soft, quiet smile. "I love you too, you know."

The muscles in Gideon's throat tightened. Once again she had made his tears come close to spilling over. "But how," he said gruffly, "did you know where I was?"

"I saw the envelope on John's door. I recognized your handwriting and I opened it up."

"You opened my letter to John?"

"Don't look so shocked. I knew you were going to do something like this, and I thought that's what the letter was about. So of course I opened it. Wouldn't you have done the same thing if you thought I was out here alone?"

"You better believe it," he said, "but I thought getting anywhere near the Yahi was the last thing you wanted to do."

"I changed my mind. Woman's privilege." She patted the bag into place and sat back. Her expression became serious. "Do you . . . do you think they're near here?"

Gideon smiled at her. He loved her when she was an efficient, capable park ranger, and he loved her—maybe even a little more—when she seemed a frightened little girl with big black eyes. "No, I think they're miles away, and I don't imagine they'd be out wandering around on a night like this."

"But what about tomorrow?"

"Tomorrow, Julie, you're going back to Quinault."

"The heck I am! If you think I came all the way out here for nothing—"

"Nothing? You've brought me sustenance, physical and spiritual, you've—"

"Damn you, Gideon, don't talk to me like a child!" Her cheeks flushed a dull red, and he could see she regretted saying it, but she remained silent.

"Julie, tomorrow—"

"Let's talk about tomorrow tomorrow," she said.

"Fine," Gideon said. They were both testy now. "I'm tired. Let's call it a day."

There wasn't room enough to stand in the tent, and with the sleeping bag and gear in a corner, there was hardly any floor space. They sat back to back on the sleeping bag and undressed themselves.

"You get in the bag first," Julie said, not turning around.

Gideon scrambled in and squeezed over, leaving her ample room. He lay on his side looking at her smooth, naked back, waiting for her to make a peace offering.

"Close your eyes while I get in," she said flatly.

"Why?"

"I don't know. Because I feel bashful."

"Why would you feel bashful?" An inane remark but a good question. Why did *he* feel bashful?

"Just close them, please."

He shrugged, although she couldn't see him. "Fine," he said, unhappy with the tiny, silly tension. He could see from the mopey way she moved that she was sorry too.

He watched her, of course, through his eyelashes, as she crouched on her knees to loosen the top flap of the sleeping bag. It was not quite dark, and her smooth thighs were dusky and gleaming. She bent forward to throw the cover back, and her small, perfect breasts swayed gently, pointed and exquisite, only a few inches from his face.

"You're peeking, aren't you?" she said, looking hard at him. He could tell she was searching for a way to make friends again, as was he.

"I can't help it," he said honestly. "You look . . . I can't tell you how beautiful you look, leaning over like that, your breasts pendant—"

"Pendant? *Pendant?* What do you mean, pendant?"

"Don't get angry. I'm trying to say something nice."

"I hope I never hear you say something rotten. Pendant!" She jabbed him in the ribs with a knuckle. The spat, if that's what it had been, was over, and he grabbed for her, getting his arms around her back and bringing her breasts down to his face. She pummeled him a little more and then stopped, stroking his hair and watching him with avid eyes while he slowly moved his head back and forth, brushing her breasts over his forehead and cheeks and against his eyelids. He kissed each

158

nipple gently, feeling her tremble, and looked up at her face with a smile and a sigh.

"When I said pendant," he said, "I didn't mean it in the sense of 'droop,' I meant it in the sense of 'depend from.' "

"That's better," she said. "I like it when you talk like a dictionary."

They both laughed, and she slid into the bag alongside him. Gideon moved his hands down her sides and cupped a round buttock in each palm, pressing her close to him. She kissed his throat and rubbed her cheek against the hair on his chest.

"Julie, Julie . . ." he murmured.

"Oh-oh, I think I hear a lyrical flight coming."

"You're right. Let me rephrase it." He pretended to think. "Okay. You have a big, beautiful ass that I love to squeeze. And I really like it when your breast droops over my arm like that. How's that?"

He had said it to make her laugh, but she lay on her side and looked at him with liquid, ink-black eyes. "I love you so very much," she said tightly, and pressed her head to his chest again. To his surprise, and to hers, too, he was sure, they fell asleep like that.

In the morning they made love the moment they awakened, or perhaps even before. When they were dozing afterward and Gideon lay sprawled on his back with Julie's head on his shoulder, he jerked suddenly.

"What's that?" he said.

Her lashes brushed his shoulder as she opened her eyes. "I don't hear anything."

"No . . . maybe I was dreaming. . . ." He realized abruptly what it was. "It's not raining anymore."

The only sound was the soughing of a gentle breeze in the high branches. They dressed in the chilly, gray light inside the tent, unzipped the flap, and stepped out. With his first breath Gideon's antipathy to the Olympic rain forest vanished. The air smelled of moist green leaves and pine bark, and the light breeze had a touch of faraway ocean in it. What they could see of the sky was a brilliant robin's-egg blue, but it was early, not yet seven, and a morning mist clung to the forest in vertical, pearly sheets, one behind another, with clear spaces between them.

It was so beautiful it seemed contrived, a sfumato masterpiece from the Renaissance, with everything diffuse and muted yet marvelously crisp. Every surface was fresh and clean and covered with droplets of dew like clear glass beads. Nothing seemed sodden. The draperies of club moss and vine maple were translucent and ferny again, and the leaves and pine needles glowed with a thousand different greens—emerald, turquoise, Irish, olive, aquamarine.

"Don't I hear water running?" Gideon asked.

She nodded. "Big Creek. I think it's just a few hundred feet away, beyond that rise."

Her hand reached out to his and he took it, and they both stood basking in the freshness. After a while some birds began to sing. The sound was so perfect they looked at each other and laughed. "Winter wren," Julie said.

Ten or twelve feet away a tiny squirrel with its cheeks packed appeared on a log and sat up on its haunches, looking surrpised to see them. At Gideon's burst of laughter it scampered off into the brush toward the creek.

"I couldn't help it," he said to Julie, still laughing, "I feel like I'm in the middle of a Walt Disney cartoon, with the sun coming up and all the forest creatures beginning to stir. Honestly, I thought that squirrel was about to rub its eyes and yawn and maybe start singing."

He turned to her, smiling and serious both. "Julie, you're not going any farther. I'm going alone."

"No," she said firmly. "If it's not dangerous, then I want to go. If it's dangerous, then I don't want to go, and I don't want you to go either."

"It is *not* dangerous, and I am going by myself." He spoke at his deepest, most resonant pitch, and he backed it up with a no-nonsense scowl. "And it is not open for discussion."

"Baloney," she said brightly. "We'll talk about it over breakfast." She picked up a pot and thrust it at him. "Go and get some water for coffee. I'll scramble the eggs."

160

"Now, listen to me, Julie—"

She stood up tall and tucked in her chin. "It is not," she growled, "open for discussion. Now, git!"

The squirrel, cheek pouches bulging with tiny spruce cones, skittered over the rough ground, its gray tail floating behind it in a graceful, serpentine curve. Almost home, just a hundred feet from its nest in the old cedar, it halted abruptly, startled, and raised itself on its hindquarters. It stood trembling, nervously jerking its head from side to side. Then, reassured, it dropped to all fours and sprinted for the tree again, only to stop once more after a few feet. Again it stood erect and quivering, its forelegs hugged to its pale, furry chest, its nose twitching.

The shining, buttonlike eyes focused on the still, brown heap before it, nearly invisible among the huckleberry and ferns, and the squirrel's body froze, as if suddenly turned to stone. So it remained for a long time in the quiet, sunshot undergrowth, staring at the unfamiliar, motionless pile. Finally the nose twitched, the whiskers waggled once, twice, and the squirrel, choosing the better part of valor, gave the strange heap a wide berth and scampered for home on a roundabout route.

When it had gone, the heap gathered itself together, got to its knees, and became a man. The man crouched behind the thick brush, brown and rough-skinned, like a part of the ancient forest itself, with damp fragments of bark and dead leaves clinging to the grease that coated him.

Through a screen of matted hair, deep-set eyes watched the *saltu* clamber down the slope to the gravel bar, then walk to the water. The nearly naked brown man swayed slowly back and forth with a high-pitched, singsong muttering. His shoulder muscles jumped and twitched, and on the hand that held the stone ax the tendons stood out like ropes.

Big Creek was not very big, but it flowed fast and satisfyingly noisily. Schools of small, brown fish, invisible against the brown pebbles on the bottom, briefly twinkled silver when they veered sharply in unison, then vanished again. On the surface, brown leaves billowed and spun slowly on the tiny swells and were borne away toward Lake Quinault.

At the stream's edge, Gideon immersed the pot. He remained on one knee for a few moments, lulled by the splashing, purling water, and by the warm morning sunlight on the back of his neck. As he rose he was conscious of a small movement behind him. Julie, probably, come to—

A tremendous concussion jarred his skull, and his head was filled with a great white light that quickly broke into tiny, yellow pinpoints on an endless field of velvet black. He was floating, tumbling slowly in the dark, and there was an odd, faraway noise, an inexplicable scraping sound. He was losing touch with his mind and fought to hold on against the overpowering fascination of the pinpoints, which had become smoothly revolving spoked wheels. The noise, he realized cunningly, was the pot clattering on the gravel. How absurd, how tasteless, he thought, that it should make so mundane and ordinary a racket at a time like this, at so presageful a moment, so augural a juncture, so, so . . .

He began to spin faster, in the opposite direction from the wheels, too fast to continue his interesting reflections. The wheels gradually contracted again to pinpoints, and slowly, one at a time, blinked out.

16

HE WAS LYING on his side, his left shoulder under his head. There was a soft breeze, and the air was sweet and fresh. The sharp gravel pressed uncomfortably against his side. He had no idea how long he'd been unconscious. His head hurt.

He opened his eyes and looked up into the timid, brown face of an old man crouched on his haunches ten feet away, peering apprehensively at him, as if Gideon were a beached shark that might or might not be dead. When Gideon looked at him the old man shrank convulsively back. Up shot the gray eyebrows and down fell the toothless, sunken mouth in a near-caricature of terror.

Gideon searched through a dazed and cloudy mind for the Yahi words. "*Ya'a hushol*," he said, each syllable thumping in his head like a hammer. "*Ai'niza ma'a wagai*."

The old man uttered a shocked sound between a gasp and a whimper and began to back away rapidly, brandishing a not very large stone ax in a pathetic counterfeit of ferocity.

A *stone ax!* Despite his whirling, chaotic mind, something in Gideon exulted, some tiny homunculus-anthropologist tucked away in the corner of his brain: *They existed. He had found them.*

The man was crippled, Gideon saw, with a terribly atrophied left leg and a foot that was no more than a knobby lump, so that he moved sideways, jerking the foot after him at each step. He was almost naked, clothed only in a breechclout with a small deerskin apron in front, and some tattered rabbit skins tied over his shoulders. Authentic winter dress, noted the inner anthropologist with satisfaction.

Gideon sat up, wincing at the pain in his head. At the movement, the old man stopped, petrified, chewing his gums frantically, his eyes rolling, and then scrambled for dear life toward the trees.

"Wait!" Gideon called stupidly in English, but the old man hopped up, surprisingly nimbly, onto the thick forest floor and disappeared instantly into the bushlike willows at its edge.

Gideon rose painfully to his feet and put his hand to his head. The fingers came away sticky with blood, but the skull was whole. "*Ya'a hushol!*" he shouted at the forest, trying to make his voice friendly, but how the hell did you sound friendly in Yahi?

"There," Julie said, pressing the adhesive strip into place with cool fingers. "It's not going to hold very well on account of your hair, but it'll do. You'll live."

Gideon nodded vacantly. He was sitting on a tree trunk in

163

front of the tent. During the cleaning and dressing of the wound he had been docile and dreamy.

"Gideon, you *are* all right, aren't you?"

"All right? Julie, I'm wonderful! Paleolithic people! That could have been a Cro-Magnon looking at me, or even a Mousterian Man . . . except for the race, of course," he emended properly, "which wouldn't have been Mongoloid. But, my God, a stone ax, a deerskin breechclout, a body greased against the cold . . ."

She laughed. "Somebody sneaks up behind you and whomps you on the head, and you couldn't be more pleased." She snapped the first-aid kit shut, straddled the log, and sat down at his side. "Gideon," she said seriously, "what would be the point of hitting you on the head?"

"I must have gotten too close to their village. Maybe they thought I saw them."

"But then why not kill you? What good would it do just to hit you and then leave you to tell the tale? All they had to do was bop you again while you were unconscious." She illustrated with a dip of her wrist. "Bop."

"It seems to me," he said, gingerly fingering the bandage, "you're taking a rather cavalier attitude about my head. Bop, indeed. Anyway, they probably thought I was already dead."

"I doubt it. With all due respect to your head, it isn't that bad a wound, and you didn't bleed a lot. I don't think you could have looked very dead. Do you think it was the old man who bopped you—"

"Julie," he grumbled, "I wish you wouldn't keep saying 'bop.' It trivializes a very painful—"

She leaned forward and kissed him on the mouth. "You're funny. How about 'clobber'?"

He kissed her back and nodded judiciously. " 'Clobber' is acceptable."

"All right, do you think it was the old man who clobbered you? Do you think he was creeping up on you to finish the job when you woke up?"

"No, I don't think so. He was scared to death. I think somebody else must have hit me earlier. Then the old man came

164

along and saw me lying there and was just having a very tentative, careful look when I terrified him by waking up. How long was I gone altogether?"

"Not even ten minutes, before I heard you yelling those funny Yahi words. So you couldn't have been unconscious very long."

"Hmm," Gideon said. "It seemed longer."

"Well," Julie said after a pause, "what do we do now?"

"I go find them—"

"Find them? After they've clobbered you—"

"A mere bop. If I could talk to them—"

"You talked to the old man, and that didn't get you anywhere."

"He was too frightened. But he understood me; I could see that in his eyes."

"All right," she said, "so we go and find them—"

"I go and find them. You walk back to North Fork and get in your car and go to Lake Quinault."

"You'd send me off, walking all alone, defenseless and vulnerable, in a forest full of naked men with axes and spears?"

"Hmm. That's a point."

There were other points: She knew the rain forest infinitely better than he did, knew how to read it and use it; two heads were better than one; and she was a reasonably expert tracker. Of the last point he was courteously skeptical, but the others made sense.

In the end, they agreed to look for the Yahi together. They would leave the tent and cooking equipment where they were and carry their personal gear with them. If they didn't encounter the Indians in a few hours, they would turn back so they could reach North Fork before dark. John could take over the quest the next day. They took Julie's sleeping bag with them in case they lost their way and had to spend the night.

They began by searching for signs of the old man where Gideon had last seen him. Julie quickly found some vague depressions in the ground cover and announced that they were human tracks made within the past two hours, possibly by a person with one crippled foot.

165

"And," she said, pointing downstream through the dense trees, "they lead that way. Let's go."

Gideon followed, impressed by her confidence but still not convinced of her expertise. His doubts were removed half an hour later, however. They had laboriously followed the faint indentations for about a hundred feet when they came to a large expanse of granite covered only by a skin of moss on which an accumulation of damp leaves had collected. Without soil, nothing remotely resembling a footprint was visible.

"Okay, expert," he said, "what now?"

Julie got to one knee, then lay full length on the ground and pushed herself about on her elbows to study the area from different angles. After a few minutes she emitted a self-satisfied "aha," stood up, and brushed the leaves from her. "He went thataway," she said.

Gideon studied the ground. He could see nothing. "Now, how can you tell that?"

"The leaves. The undersides of fallen leaves turn yellow first, and a stepped-on leaf tends to curl. If you get down next to the ground and look at them at an angle, sometimes the yellow edges of the curled leaves stand out. The amount of curl gives you some idea of how old the track is."

"I'm impressed," Gideon said truthfully. "You *do* know what you're talking about."

"Well, of course I do. Didn't I say so?" He could see that she was delighted.

In the next few hours, transformed into an attentive and respectful student, he learned that twigs stepped on by human beings are usually splintered, while those broken by the sharp hooves of elk or deer generally fracture cleanly; that the broken end of a twig is light-colored when first snapped but darkens with time; that trodden grass takes one to six hours to straighten again; that a spider web takes from six to eight hours to spin, depending on the type of spider.

The trail twisted many times, sometimes back on itself. Twice they had to crawl on their abdomens under masses of sword ferns only two feet high. The old man moved like a Yahi, all right. And a pretty limber one, considering his age and condition.

At a little before one o'clock, they found what they were looking for. They had been following the tracks along the foot of a cliff, and when they threaded their way between two big boulders, there it was. A huge mass of rock had fallen away from the cliff wall near its base, leaving a concavity about eighty feet long and thirty feet high—a shallow, roofed, flat-bottomed cave. In the limestone country of the Dordogne it would have been called an *abri*, and the hands of any anthropologist who saw it would have itched to get hold of a shovel and search for Cro-Magnon remains.

No anthropologist would have seen it, however, except through the most fortunate accident. The sloughed-off rock, a colossal, semicircular monolith, lay in front of the cave that it had created, completely blocking it from view and allowing ingress only at one point—where the giant boulder had split and separated enough to allow a person to get in.

It was a perfect place for the Yahi village, and there the tiny village lay. At the far end of the opening, surrounded on three sides by walls of rock, there were two dome-shaped huts like the ones on Pyrites Creek, but these were winter quarters, covered with skins instead of brush. In front of them was a fire pit shielded by cedar bark, and around the fire sat four Indians quietly absorbed in homely and simple tasks. One of them was the man Gideon had startled—and vice versa—at the gravel bar.

The scene was astonishingly domestic. It was like looking at a museum diorama: Everyday life in the Old Stone Age. Gideon recognized at once what each person was doing, although he had previously seen the tasks performed only in old ethnographic movies. The old man he had seen before was binding the two prongs of a fishing harpoon to its shaft with a length of sinew. Another man, even older, was heating wooden shafts against a hot rock from the fire and pressing out irregularities with his thumbs. A third was stirring something in a large pot or basket, and with the flat of his other hand was braiding grasses into rope by rubbing them against his thigh; that had been women's work among

167

the Yahi of old. The fourth man was bent over a rock in his hand, pressure-chipping it with a piece of antler.

"Gideon," Julie whispered, "they're so old."

They were; the youngest of them appeared to be in his mid-sixties.

"They don't look like killers," Julie said. "They look so . . . pacific. There must be others, mustn't there? Younger ones?"

"Maybe, but not many. There are only two huts."

The question was answered more definitively by a movement off to the left and above them. A fifth Indian was slowly rising from a sitting position in a cleft in the big rock that fronted the cave and was looking down at them with an expression that was far from pacific. Gideon could feel the hostility radiate from him.

Like the old people, he wore a breechclout, but his shoulders were naked, not covered by a ragged cape. Like them, he gleamed with grease, and his short hair was clotted with it. There the resemblance ended. This was a lithe, slender man of thirty or less, who might have been carved from dark marble. He stood, in fact, remarkably like a barbaric David, confident and arrogantly relaxed, his narrow hips canted, one sinewy hand hanging loosely curled at his side. The other hand was at his shoulder, but where Michelangelo had chosen to put a sling, there was a long, bone-pointed spear cradled almost casually.

17

THE INDIAN SAID something in a sharp, nasal voice, and the old people stood up quickly, if shakily, saw the two strangers, and stared, open-mouthed.

Julie's fingers, ice-cold, crept into Gideon's hand. "Be of stout heart," he said, clamly enough to surprise himself. "This is what we came for. He doesn't seem to be pointing that thing at us."

Julie surprised him too. "At least he doesn't have an atlatl," she said lightly, but her voice was barely audible.

"You stay here." He squeezed her fingers, dropped her hand, and stepped forward.

"Ya'a hushol," he said loudly, feeling stagey and embarrassed.

"Ya'a hushol," answered the Indian on the rock—the first real proof that Gideon could communicate with them. But the voice seemed to be heavy with mockery.

Gideon walked cautiously toward him. "Ai'niza ma'a wagai," he said. "I am a friend." He noticed for the first time that a stone ax was thrust through the Indian's waistband. The one that had nearly brained him? Instinctively, his fingers crept to the bandage on his head.

Without expression the Indian watched him approach. If anything, there was a faint look of disdain in the intelligent, black eyes. When Gideon was ten feet away, the naked shoulders tensed slightly, and the feet shifted to a squarer stance. The spear was more firmly grasped.

Gideon stopped and stretched his lips in a smile. "I come in peace," he said in Yahi.

In response he got a slight curling of the Indian's upper lip. The man was taller than Gideon had thought, massively muscled, slender only in the hips and legs. His face would have done better on a lordly Mayan than a lowly Yahi. Gideon had seen similar ones carved on the ruined walls of Tikal and Palenque: a high-bridged, lavishly curved nose, delicately angled, almond-shaped eyes, sensual, exquisitely formed lips. All were set in an oval, flat face of blank planes and angles, so that the total effect was oddly disturbing, as if a seductive and willowy youth peeked through the eye slits of a stony, brutally masculine mask.

"I come in peace," Gideon said again.

The sybaritic eyes behind the slits continued their leisurely inspection. The shapely upper lip curled once more. In Gideon's world it would have been a sneer.

Gideon felt an active dislike begin to simmer. That, he knew, would not do. He was not thinking like an anthropologist. What, after all, did he know of the nuances of Yahi posture and tone?

Nothing. The sneer, the arrogant pose were artifacts of Gideon's own ethnocentric perspective. How could he tell what they connoted in Yahi culture?

"Bullshit," he muttered to himself—the man, the fallible human being, addressing the schoolish scientist. "I know when I don't trust somebody."

The Indian on the rock suddenly turned loquacious. Gideon could not follow everything he said, but it seemed to be a sort of welcoming speech. He heard "friends" and "peace" more than once. When he had done, the Indian jumped lightly down from the considerable height of the rock and joined the old ones. He moved, as Gideon knew he would, with a casual, surefooted grace. Like a movie Indian, Gideon couldn't help thinking. The others were not like movie Indians. They huddled together in a woebegone clump, shoulder to hunched shoulder and elbow to elbow, quaking and terrified.

The young one shouted something and gestured with his spear, apparently urging Gideon and Julie to come forward.

When they hesitated, his full lips twisted—it was unquestionably a sneer; Gideon would bet on it. Ostentatiously the spear was flung to the ground and the Indian's open, empty hands were displayed to them. The ax in his belt remained where it was.

Gideon was far from easy, but he had come to meet with them, and meet with them he would.

He turned to Julie. "You stay here," he said. "See how it goes with me."

"No way," she said, and came from between the rocks to stand at his side.

"Now, you listen—"

"Gideon, we don't want to have a scene in front of them, do we?" She reached for his hand again. Her fingers were not as cold as they'd been.

"All right," he said, smiling. "I think it's going to be okay."

"Of course it will. But keep your eye on the big cheese."

"Don't worry, I will. Let's go." One more squeeze of her hand and they walked cautiously forward. Gideon took the opportunity to study the four elderly Yahi. The one who had been straightening the shafts was the oldest of them, with a fierce-eyed, hawklike patriarch's face but a spine so contorted by disease or injury that his torso was like a gnarled old tree trunk, lumpy and asymmetric, and twisted nearly into a knot.

The man who had been stone-chipping had a big, kindly face badly pitted by what appeared to be smallpox scars, and a squashed, meandering nose that sat on his face like a baked potato. His eyes were very large and very gentle. At about sixty-five he was the youngest of them and the largest, with a broad, fleshy chest that once must have been powerfully muscled.

The third person, Gideon realized belatedly, was an aged woman, with scanty hair cut as short as the men's, and flat breasts like wrinkled, empty paper bags. Her clothing was almost the same as the others': She wore a skirt a little longer than the small aprons that fronted the men's breechclouts, and her cape was of feathers rather than skins. In her hand she held the twine she had been working on, and Gideon's inner anthropologist recorded with approval that, among the Yahi, women's work was still done by women. Her head was tipped alertly, as if listening for something, and she stared fixedly off to the side. She was, Gideon understood, blind.

The other old man appeared to be no less frightened than he'd been at the gravel bar. As he had then made pitifully threatening motions with an ax, now he gestured feebly and intermittently with the wooden-pronged harpoon he'd been binding.

With every step of the two intruders, the four old people drew closer together still, drawing strength from each other's nearness. When Julie and Gideon, moving very slowly, were ten feet away, the oldest man could bear it no longer and spoke nervously to the young Indian. The others quickly joined in, so that all four of them were chattering at once in whispery agitation. The young one barked a few curt words and they stopped immediately, looking, Gideon thought, a little sheepish.

He had grasped enough of the words and body language to understand the exchange. The old ones were frightened and wanted to run off right then; the young man, surprisingly, had told them that would be unthinkably rude, *kuu Yahi*—not the

Yahi way. Guests were to be treated with respect. Gideon found himself wondering if Eckert and the others had been treated with respect but pushed the thought from his mind. It was, he decided, time for his *pièce de résistance*, the only complete and formally correct speech he had managed to memorize in Yahi.

"I bring gifts in your honor," he said. "I apologize for their being poor and worthless and not to be compared with your own belongings, but I beg you to accept them."

He delivered his little address with what he hoped were properly expansive gestures, but nonetheless he experienced a slight sinking sensation as he spoke. A rubber turtle in their honor?

The four older Indians, who were still huddled together, showed for the first time that they could understand him. Quick glances moved among them, and the man with the big, gentle, pockmarked face looked him shyly in the eye for an instant before shifting his gaze downward.

Even the young Indian seemed a little taken aback. The curl left his lip, and he too stared Gideon in the eye, for once without insolence. "No," he said. "First we eat. Then gifts." He was being very proper—the Yahi way again—and he was speaking very slowly and simply, apparently so that Gideon could understand.

"What's going on?" Julie said. "Are we in trouble?"

"Only if the food's bad. We've just been invited to dinner."

The food, at least to begin with, was far from bad. The woman, with some help from the old men, uncovered a pit-oven—a hole in the ground lined with rocks and covered with damp branches—releasing a cloud of fragrant steam. From the hole she scooped out four small fish with a green stick that had been looped and tied at one end. The fish were placed at Gideon's and Julie's feet in a much-used platter-shaped basket. There was no ceremony and no speech. The food was simply plumped down in front of them as it might have been by a tired counterman in an all-night diner.

The young Indian suddenly threw himself to the ground and sprawled on one elbow, watching them. He was, Gideon noted, in easy reach of his spear. The others followed his lead and squatted on their heels, clasping bony knees in skinny arms. Their faces were impassive.

Gideon and Julie sat down on the ground Gideon reached for a fish.

"Gideon!" Julie said. "You're not going to eat this, are you? They've given us their own dinner."

"Of course I am," he said, picking up a fish, pushing back the skin with his fingers, and biting into the tender white flesh of the back. "Eat up, Julie. If you don't, it would be implying that it isn't good enough for you, or that they don't have enough for them and us both."

"Well, they don't."

"But it would be rude to suggest it. They're being very mannerly, and we should be too. For all we know, three people have already been killed because they weren't sufficiently decorous. Now shut up and eat."

The Indians had been watching them silently. When Julie and Gideon spoke to each other, it aroused not a flicker of interest. The Yahi appeared not to notice. It was as if they were a couple of dogs muttering to each other.

Gideon held up his fish and smiled at the Indians. "Good!" he said in Yahi, smiling and chewing. There was no response.

"Gideon," Julie said, reaching irresolutely for a fish, "do you really think these people are killers? They're more frightened of us than we are of them. Except him." She tipped her head toward the reclining Big Cheese, who seemed bored and impatient with watching the *saltu* eat. "You can practically see the hatred oozing out of him."

Gideon nodded. "Yes, the others don't look exactly bloodthirsty. I think that as long as we're not alone with Big Cheese we're safe."

Julie clawed a tiny piece of meat loose, popped it in her mouth, and licked her fingers. "Even if we were alone with him, I wouldn't be too worried. I don't think you'd have much trouble with him. Just don't you leave *me* alone with him."

Sitting there, living through one of the century's anthropological summits, the distinguished professor glowed just as much,

173

and for precisely the same reason, as he had when he was thirteen years old and Ruthie Nettle said she bet he could beat up Meat Baumhoff. He picked up another trout, bit it, and waved it directly at Big Cheese. "Good fish!"

"Can't you talk to them?" Julie asked uneasily. "It's awfully uncomfortable sitting here with them just staring at us."

"I don't think you understand how little Yahi I know. It's strictly Me-Lone Ranger-You-Tonto."

"Well, what about that? Wouldn't it be polite to ask their names? Tell them ours?"

"No, it'd be rude. And they'd never tell. No white person ever found out a Yahi's name."

"What about Ishi?"

"That wasn't his name," Gideon said. " 'Ishi' is a nickname. It's just what Kroeber dubbed him. It means 'man' in Yahi." He sucked the last shreds of meat from the ribs of the fish, taking pains to show noisy appreciation, and picked up another. The Indians watched stolidly. "To them the purpose of a name isn't to label someone, it's a placation of a dead ancestor, a magical source of power—"

Surprisingly, Julie burst out laughing. "Here we are in the middle of this scene right out of *King Solomon's Mines*, and you're delivering a lovely, stuffy lecture from *Introduction to Primitive Kinship Systems*."

To show her he wasn't at all stuffy, he suggested they assign the Yahi nicknames and suggested Shy Buffalo for the soft man with the big body and the gentle eyes, and Startled Mouse for the small, tremulous man he'd seen at the gravel bar. The young one, of course was Big Cheese. Julie chipped in with Gray Sparrow for the old woman, and Keen Eagle for the patriarchal old man.

When they finished the fish, Gray Sparrow groped for the basket she'd been working over earlier, a well-woven, watertight cooking basket with the Yahi stepped design on it, and began stirring again.

"The next course, I think," Gideon said. "Have you ever had acorn mush?"

"No. Am I about to?"

174

"Yes," he said, making a face. "A rare treat."

Every few moments Gray Sparrow would use two sticks to deftly lift a heated, round stone from the fire, dip it quickly into a small pot of water to wash off the ashes, and drop it into the basket. One of the sticks was used to keep the stones rolling about so that the basket wasn't burned, and in a very few minutes the pale mush was boiling. The stones were removed, and the large basket was set down in front of Gideon and Julie.

This course was to be communal. First Big Cheese slouched over offhandedly and sat down near the basket. Without waiting for the others, he dipped two fingers into it and slurped up the yellowish-white porridge. Then, by means of a brusque gesture with the same hand, he told Gideon and Julie to do likewise, which they did, Julie with only a momentary hesitation. A turn of his head over his shoulder and a few abrupt words brought the older Indians up to the basket like a family of shy deer ready to bolt at the first move of the *saltu*.

The bland, oily acorn mush was consumed in near-silence, with Gideon and Julie eating little. Gideon made friendly overtures several times, but the Yahi wouldn't even meet his eyes, let alone respond.

When it was done, another platter, of fish and root vegetables, came from the oven. This was politely if indifferently offered to Julie and Gideon, who declined.

"Too much," Gideon said in Yahi, patting his stomach and smiling. "Good."

The Indians ate, stuffing the food into their mouths but never taking their eyes off the strangers.

"Feel better?" Gideon asked. "It looks like they have plenty."

"Much better," Julie said.

Afterward, the old Indians crept away again and looked at them from a distance, but now there was a touch of expectancy, naïve and even charming, in their faces. They hadn't forgotten the gifts. Gideon opened his pack and looked through what he'd brought. If they'd never seen a mirror before, it would be a first-rate way to begin.

"Here goes," he said to Julie. "Unless I miss my guess, Big

175

Cheese is the kind of guy who'll find his own face the most fascinating thing in the world."

With a smile, he held one of the pocket mirrors out to him, tilting it so that the Indian would see his own reflection when he looked at it. But he wouldn't look at it. He turned his head away with his eyes closed, as a privileged infant might show his contempt for a proffered spoonful of mashed peas. When Gideon persisted, the naked arm flicked out in an impatient, back-handed swipe, sending the little mirror to the ground, where it struck a stone and cracked in two. The old Indians watched, blank-faced and reserved.

Gideon took a deep breath. "Not exactly a howling success," he said to Julie. "Let's hope some of the other things appeal to them more."

He took the four ball-bearing necklaces from his backpack and let them dangle from his hand. Big Cheese watched disdainfully, but the others craned their necks to see, nonetheless maintaining their prudent distance. Giving Big Cheese a wide berth, Gideon began to walk slowly toward them, holding the necklaces out and murmuring what he hoped were soothing sounds.

The Indians were obviously torn between their curiosity and the desire to run, but they held their ground and at last Shy Buffalo stretched out a tentative hand. Gideon, however, quickly slipped the necklace over his head so that it lay like a collar, burnished and sleek, on the dark, rough skin of his mantle. There was a shocked silence, and Gideon wondered momentarily if he'd violated some sacrosanct Yahi norm. But then Shy Buffalo's big face split in a slow grin, and his fingers moved over the smooth, heavy beads of steel.

Gideon held out the necklaces to the others, as if he were coaxing pigeons with bread crumbs, and they came. He gave one to each of the other three, and they placed them around their own necks, murmuring to each other in gentle surprise at the weight of the ball bearings. They were definitely beginning to thaw—except for Big Cheese, who remained off on one side, grim and uncommunicative.

"How did you know to bring four?" Julie asked.

"Dumb luck. Let's hope it keeps up."

It was the curtains that scored the major success, but not in the way expected. When Gideon tore open the package, there were murmurs of astonishment, and four pairs of hands reached not for the bright cloth but for the clear plastic wrapping. They held it up to their eyes, pressed it onto their faces, and crinkled and uncrinkled it. The curtains themselves were fingered politely and ignored.

In almost two hours, none of the old Yahi had spoken directly to the *saltu*, but Gideon's hangdog expression as he stood holding the unwanted curtains finally broke through the communication barrier. With no preliminaries, Keen Eagle suddenly addressed Gideon at length. Excited at finally making verbal contact, Gideon wanted desperately to understand, but not a single word was intelligible.

"I don't understand," he said miserably. "*Ulisi.*"

Keen Eagle gestured at the towel and repeated what he had said, this time shouting directly into Gideon's ear.

"I don't understand," Gideon repeated with a helpless gesture.

The Indians stared at each other and whispered incredulously. Their meaning was clear: Is it truly possible that a human being might not understand our language? Astounding!

Gray Sparrow also had a try at shouting into Gideon's ear, but Shy Buffalo solved the problem by spitting on the curtain, taking Gideon's hand, rubbing it over the wet spot, and gesturing expressively: What good is material that gets wet?

In the rain forest, it was a persuasive point. "Ah, I understand," Gideon said in Yahi.

"Ah, I understand," they repeated to each other, delighted, mimicking Gideon's outlandish accent but without malice. There was considerable good-natured laughter in which Gideon joined, with the feeling that the ice was broken at last.

When he dipped into the knapsack and fished out Squeekie the Turtle there was more laughter, which increased when he squeezed it to produce its soft bleat.

There was a rough, abrupt movement at his side, and a muscular arm swept down to knock the toy to the ground. Gideon

177

was considerably startled and sprang back; he had almost forgotten about Big Cheese. The young Indian stared at him, fierce and combative, his hand gripping the head of the ax at his belt. In the sudden silence the older Yahi melted back.

Gideon reached behind him and gently pushed Julie away. He didn't know what had angered Big Cheese, but if his hand so much as began to pull the ax from his waistband, he would spring. He'd go for the ax with his left hand and chop at the Yahi's throat with his right forearm. His eyes focused on the prominent Adam's apple in the muscled throat, and his body coiled. It was hardly orthodox behavior for an anthropologist, but that ax had nearly killed him once, and he wasn't going to give it another chance.

Big Cheese seemed to read his intentions. He dropped his hand casually away from the ax, an Old West gunman whose bluff had been called. His veiled eyes, always hostile, changed their expression perceptibly from bellicosity to mere contempt. The full lips, which had been rigid and pale, reformed into a derisive curl.

The harsh tension in the air eased. Gideon began to breathe again and heard Julie inhale deeply behind him. The four elderly Yahi, once again shrunken into their tight little knot, eased slightly apart. Gideon knew that he had won something, although he wasn't sure what, and it seemed like a good time to consolidate his gains. With a firm glance at Big Cheese, who watched him without moving, he bent to pick up the rubber toy and walked swiftly to the huddle of Indians. He'd seen Gray Sparrow's face light up when he'd squeezed the turtle, and he squeezed it again, then placed it in her hand, closing her fingers over it so that it made its little noise.

"Squeekie," Gideon said, and closed her hand over it once more. She tried it herself, and the worn, blind old face shone with pleasure. "Kweekee!" she crowed. "Kweekee!" She squeezed it some more, holding it up to her ear and emitting great peals of laughter, which exhibited a set of gray gums barren but for one nub of a brown molar on each side. Gideon laughed with her, and soon the others were laughing too. Asoundingly, even Big Cheese smiled slightly, and for a moment is feline eyes seemed to glow with something like warmth.

Pleased with their progress, Gideon presented the cigarette ighter. As expected, it brought gasps when he used it to ignite a ew twigs at the edge of the fire. Only two of the Yahi could be oaxed to try it, however, and neither Keen Eagle nor Shy Buffalo could get it to work. Their fingers were clumsy on the unfamiliar object, and they held it upside down, or in both hands, or dropped it altogether, in spite of Gideon's patient guidance. Both grew frustrated and sulky within minutes, and Gideon thought it best to put the lighter in the pocket of his jacket.

This caused a sensation. Pockets, it appeared, were as intriguing as clear plastic wrapping. Gideon was made to take the lighter out of his pocket and put it back in a dozen times, and oon Keen Eagle, Shy Buffalo, and Gray Sparrow were trying it. Startled Mouse hung skittishly back, as usual, and Big Cheese, who had threatened neither action nor speech since the affair of the turtle, was disdainful, miles above this *saltu* claptrap.

All in all, the presents had been a success. Most of the Yahi now milled about Gideon and even touched him with no apparent fear. Gideon thought it might be time to try to do what he had come to do.

"Chief," he said, using the Yahi honorific to address Big Cheese, "we talk now."

Big Cheese pointed at Shy Buffalo with his chin. "He is the chief," he said surprisingly.

Shy Buffalo smiled diffidently. "Yes, I am the chief." His manner of speaking was halting and slow, and Gideon could follow the intent of it, which was more than he could say for the throaty, rapid speech of the other older Yahi. Before they could talk, Shy Buffalo said, the *saltu* must also have gifts. He gestured for them to follow, turned, and walked slowly toward the larger of the two huts.

Inside, the hut was about twelve feet in diameter, larger than the ones on Pyrites Creek and tall enough to stand in, but otherwise like them. The curving walls, made of rushes tied over a framework of scouler willow poles, were smoke-blackened and

179

greasy with the fires of many winters. The sweet and pungent smells of smoke, human beings, and not too finically preserved meat were strong, but on the whole it was not unpleasant. Near the low entrance was a pile of baskets, some finished, some incomplete, some with the stepped Yahi design, some plain. There were cooking baskets, sifting baskets, and open-weave carrying baskets; all Gray Sparrow's handiwork, no doubt.

Along the wall was more basketry: lidded storage hampers. Some were open, showing plentiful supplies of dried, nearly black meat cut in strips, dried whole fish, and seeds and roots Gideon didn't recognize.

"I can stop worrying about them going hungry," Julie said. "There's enough right here for them to live on for three months."

Around the ashy fire pit in the center there were three rumpled, comfortable-looking blankets of sewn-together, brown rabbit skins. Other objects were scattered over the floor: a fire drill hearth with the drill upright in its hole, a scruffy deer's head filled with grass—hunting decoy, probably—two stone hammers, a few spears and harpoons leaning against the wall, stone knives, hand adzes, some unfinished notched wooden hafts. And an atlatl.

"Not exactly shipshape," Julie said. "I'll bet Gray Sparrow doesn't live here. It looks like bachelors' quarters."

"You're probably right," Gideon said, "but it really isn't too bad; kind of lived-in. It'd be cozy on a rainy day with the fire going. I could think of worse ways to spend a cold, dreary day than lying on one of those rabbit-skin rugs and munching dried fish around the fire."

Through gestures and words, Shy Buffalo told them that they were welcome to anything the Yahi possessed.

"I suppose we ought to take something to be polite?" Julie asked hopefully.

"Absolutely," Gideon said, smiling. "We wouldn't want to offend them."

She chose a beautifully woven, richly decorated little basket of the kind referred to by anthropologists as trinket baskets. Gid eon asked for one of the stone axes, which greatly pleased Shy Buffalo, who said with hesitant pride that he had made it.

Julie was not so pleased. "You're thinking," she said, frowning, "that might come in handy before we get out of all this?"

"Am I?" he said absentmindedly. Was he?

Outside, Gray Sparrow, still clutching Squeekie, smiled when Shy Buffalo told her what Julie had chosen, but went into the hut and came out a moment later with a large, pitch-smeared basket, undecorated and ugly. She thrust this on Julie and snatched back the smaller one, chattering all the time. Julie, the big basket in her arms, looked confusedly at Gideon.

"I think," he said, "that she's telling you the one you picked wasn't good for anything. Too small, impossible to cook in, useless for holding water. The other one is much more sensible."

Gideon interceded with his elementary Yahi, and Julie got to keep her trinket basket. Gray Sparrow grumbled good-naturedly at the foolishness of it.

Now, at last, with dinner done and gifts exchanged, it was finally time to talk. Evening was coming on and it was growing cool; they would talk in the big hut. Among the Yahi of a century before, serious talk would have meant man-talk, and, from the uncomfortable expressions on the faces of the men when Julie entered with Gideon, it still did.

Shy Buffalo began to explain in his hesitant, deferential way that she could not stay, but Big Cheese cut him off brusquely, speaking directly to Gideon. "Men talk with men," he said, again using a kind of simpleton's speech. "Women go in the woman's house."

Julie looked at Gideon for a translation.

"No dames," he said.

"What am I supposed to do?"

"I think you and Gray Sparrow are supposed to have a nice gossip in her house while we boys work things out. Julie," he said, suddenly serious, "be careful."

"Of Gray Sparrow?"

"Of everything. People have been killed, don't forget. For all we know, they're all involved."

His words seemed to startle her. "Do you know, I think I actually *did* forget? You be careful, too. Don't let Big Cheese get in back of you. He's always hanging around off to the side, as if he's waiting for his chance."

"Believe me, I won't. Besides, I have my trusty war club now." Actually, Gideon too had to keep reminding himself there was danger. The Yahi were not convincing murderers. Even Big Cheese, with all his surliness, hardly seemed about to assault him with his ax. Could the previous attack have been a misunderstanding? An error? Gideon touched his still-sore head. Some misunderstanding.

Inside the hut, with grunts and wheezing sighs, the three old Yahi sat down facing him across the fire: Keen Eagle supporting his turnip sack of a body against a bundle of spears, Startled Mouse with his ruined foot twisted under him, and Shy Buffalo, dignified and courteous. Big Cheese, as usual, lounged about to the side. Gideon shifted to keep him in view.

The jollity of the gift exchange had worn off, and the old men waited with nervous but circumspect expressions for him to speak. Gideon was suddenly and strongly put in mind of three aged and infirm rhesus monkeys, grave, scarred, and ill used by time, patiently awaiting whatever new indignities and abuses were to come.

"Noble Yahi," he said, politely, using the old, dignified form of address. "Noble people." So much for correct Yahi. "I have come to help you," he went on in his own fractured version. "The *saltu* are your friends, not your enemies."

18

"NO, I'M NOT kidding," Gideon said. "They thought it sounded like the greatest thing since canned peaches."

"Prison?" Julie said. "How could that be?"

How, indeed. He turned onto his back with his hands under

his head, looking at the slice of cloudy, moonlit sky beyond the curving edge of the rocky overhang, and thought about the remarkable conversation in the hut. They were lying fully clothed in the sleeping bag, at the base of the giant boulder that shielded the village—to the consternation of the Yahi, who had been flabbergasted when they refused the hospitality of their fire-warmed huts, preferring to sleep outside.

"It is the way of the *saltu*," Gideon had explained mysteriously, and they had gravely said, "Aah."

"Actually," Gideon said, "I hadn't wanted to talk to them about jail at all. The more I thought about it, the more insane the idea seemed. What possible purpose could it serve?"

She lay on her side, her cheek resting on her clasped hands. "I couldn't agree with you more."

"So I started telling them we might find them a reservation: land of their own, streams to fish, animals to hunt, a place where they could have their village, live their lives in peace, and so forth."

"You were able to say all that in Yahi?"

"Pretty much. At a kindergarten level."

"And?"

"And they didn't know what I was talking about. They said they already *had* all that right now. So somehow I got to talking to them about prison. I think I was trying to explain how much better life would be on a reservation than in a prison. And—" he burst out laughing—"well, I told them that prison was a big hut made of stone. . . . Clever, what? And they asked if it kept the rain out, and I said yes, it did. They asked if it was warm, and I said yes. They asked if it was light at night—I guess they've seen the buildings around Lake Quinault from a distance—and naturally I said it had lights. I could see the way they were looking at each other, especially Shy Buffalo and Keen Eagle, so I told them it was bad; they'd have to stay inside all the time and never go out."

"And that didn't give them second thoughts?"

"Yes, it did. Keen Eagle asked how they could get food if they didn't go out, and I told them—"

"—someone would bring their food to them."

"That's about the size of it. They can't wait to go."

"That's fascinating," Julie said. "All I did was learn how to make Yahi baskets. And I told Gray Sparrow my name, even if it's gauche. She liked it; it made her laugh. She calls me 'Dooley.'"

"Dooley," Gideon said. "I like it, too. She didn't tell you hers, did she?"

"No, she fell asleep after an hour, holding that silly turtle. She's really sweet, Gideon: shy, and happy, and ready to be friends. I'm glad I got a chance to meet her. I wish I could have talked to her."

She turned over on her back. The night was mild, and the sides of the bag were unzipped, giving them plenty of room. "What about Big Cheese?" she said after a while. "Was he so anxious to go to jail?"

"I don't know. He didn't say a word the entire time. Just watched, with that superior look on his face. Keen Eagle and Shy Buffalo did all the talking. Not that there was much talking, except for me."

Gideon sat up and clasped his arms around his knees. "You know, when I was telling them how we'd found Claire Hornick in Pyrites Creek, and Eckert and Hartman in the graveyard, I had the distinct impression that Keen Eagle and Shy Buffalo thought it was all a story made up for their amusement. They chuckled every time I mentioned something that was familiar—the villages, the graveyard, the creek—the way a child does when you tell him an exciting story and put him and his house and his street into it. But Big Cheese wasn't laughing; I wouldn't say he looked exactly worried, but pretty close; he certainly wasn't enjoying it."

Julie sat up and leaned her back against Gideon's shoulder, looking off into the night. "Were we right, then, do you think? Big Cheese has been doing the killing on his own, and the others don't even know about it?"

"Except for Startled Mouse. I think he knows. He spent most of the time looking at Big Cheese with a funny look on his face. You know, I'm pretty sure I owe him my life. Big Cheese must have hit me down on the gravel bar, and Startled Mouse must have come along and frightened him off before he—"

"*Frightened* Big Cheese? Startled Mouse?"

"Not physically frightened, of course. But he may be his grandfather, for all we know, or a great-uncle, and that'd give him a lot of authority in Yahi culture. Just being an elder would, for that matter."

Gideon swung his legs out of the bag and began to pull on his boots. "Let's move the sleeping bag," he said.

"Move it? Why?"

"Big Cheese knows exactly where we are. If he's planning anything for us tonight, I'd like to make it hard for him to find us."

"But the others wouldn't let him do anything, would they?"

"Who knows? Remember, we might be reading this wrong. Maybe they're all involved in it. Maybe this is their standard *modus operandi*: Feed the *saltu*, lull them into a peaceful night's sleep, and then, in the dark of the night, stalk out of their huts with those grisly spears—"

"All right. I'm convinced. Brr."

They found what seemed to be a good place atop the huge boulder itself: a fracture in the rock that provided a rough but nearly horizontal shelf about ten feet above the ground. The moon gave enough light through the thickening cover of ragged clouds to let them find their way quietly up the rock face, and they settled in quickly. They had a wide field of vision, so that anyone creeping toward them would be easy to see. Gideon had left Julie's jacket and his poncho below, laid out to resemble a sleeping bag.

"That's better," he said, placing the stone ax a foot from where his head would lie. "Let's hope it doesn't rain. We're out from under the overhang."

"Gideon," Julie said, "what do we do now? I mean tomorrow."

"Nothing, really. I think we've accomplished all we can. John will get my note in the morning and head right out. I think we just have to keep talking to them until he gets here. Then, at least, they'll be in custody—peacefully—and the killings will be over."

"And then what will happen to them?"

"Assuming that it's Big Cheese who's been doing the killing —I don't know what will happen to him. You couldn't just let him run loose. As for the others, Abe is working on getting some land; someplace remote. It's too bad they can't stay here. Or could they?"

"I don't think so. The Matheny trail is still in our development plan. They'll be starting to work on it again next year. Besides, how could you have a reservation in the middle of a national park?"

"You know," Gideon said, pulling a hazy item from his memory, "there was a case in Florida in which an Indian—a Seminole, I think—had killed a white man. The defense was based on the fact that the United States had never signed a peace treaty with the Seminoles, and therefore the killing was an act of war not murder. I wonder if something like that might apply here."

"How did the case turn out?"

"I don't remember."

"Very instructive, Professor." Julie finished unlacing her boots and got under the top flap of the sleeping bag. "Maybe we'd better get ourselves some sleep and worry about it tomorrow. I guess we ought to take turns staying awake, shouldn't we?"

"Right," Gideon said, sliding in beside her. He was on the outside of the ledge, toward the huts. "I'll take the first watch." He reached for the ax to make sure he knew where it was. "Not that I really expect anything to happen."

"All right," Julie said, already yawning, and snuggling up to his back. "Promise to wake me in two hours?"

"Promise. I'll wake you at eleven. Get some sleep, now. I love you."

"Love you, too. 'Night."

Her hand double-patted his hip and then remained there as she fell quickly asleep, with her breath warm on his neck. Gideon smiled to himself. How quickly they had gotten to this lovely old-shoe familiarity. Going to sleep with her at his side was already the most natural thing in the world. How had he done without her all these years? Gently he caressed the back of the hand that lay so easily and possessively on his thigh, and he

186

arranged himself to see better over the scene below. The clouds had thickened and the air smelled of rain, but the night was still clear and mild. Wide awake, he lay with his hand on the ax, waiting. Not that he really expected anything to happen.

Nothing happened. In two hours Julie woke herself and insisted on taking over the watch. Gideon dozed a little, and he had a hard time keeping awake on his second turn on watch, more from boredom than fatigue. The two huts were utterly still, as was the forest. There were no bird cries, no insect sounds, no murmur of wind. When 3:00 A.M. came around, he was happy to give over the watch to Julie. He curled up on his side, facing her, his right hand resting on her waist, his left under the soft line of her jaw. He could feel her pulse throb against his pinkie. With a long sigh, he let himself drift off to sleep. Dawn was only a few hours away. If Big Cheese had had anything in mind, he'd already have tried it.

He felt urgency in the grip on his shoulder and was instantly awake. "What?"

"The big hut," she whispered. "Somebody's moving."

He turned carefully onto his other side to face the huts. It was more difficult to see now. The misty rain had begun to float down again, and the air was soupy with it. There was a vague, diffuse moonlight filtering through the clouds, but it was no help, obscuring vision like headlights in the fog. His hair was wet with rain, the sleeping bag heavy with moisture.

He stared at the hut, blinking away the mist that had collected on his eyelashes, and listened hard. There was no sound. Nothing moved.

"Are you sure? Could someone have just turned over in his sleep?"

"I don't think so." Her whisper was sibilant, breathless. Again he could feel her breath on his neck, but now it was a shallow panting. "There!"

There had been a faint rustle. The poles at the hut entrance moved slightly, and someone crawled through. Gideon's hand found the handle of the ax. The figure rose and then stood, mo-

187

tionless and crouching. No, not crouching but crippled. It was Startled Mouse.

"Whew," Gideon said, realizing that he had hardly been breathing himself.

"But why is he out there?" Julie said into his neck.

"Shh."

The old man was not wearing his mantle, and the rain glistened on his skinny shoulders. He appeared to be staring directly at them, but Gideon doubted that he could see them in the rain. After a few moments, he turned to his left and limped quickly toward the other end of the cavelike shelf.

Gideon smiled. "Call of nature," he said. There was a toilet pit about seventy-five feet away, just out of sight.

"Boy," Julie said, hugging him from behind. "That really gave me a scare. Was he looking at us?"

Before he could reply, a second figure, its movements agitated and ferocious, came from the hut. It was Big Cheese, awesome and gigantic against the fragile huts, a slab-muscled, fairy tale giant, weirdly out of focus in the clinging mist. He ran quickly to where Gideon and Julie had lain earlier, immediately below the shelf. He was obviously startled when he saw the poncho and parka in place of the sleeping bag, and he kicked fiercely at the garments. Clearly, he was furious, trembling with rage, and he was a fearsome sight. The great muscles of the naked back twitched and coiled visibly, as clear as illustrations in an anatomy text, and shining with grease and rain. The savage head twisted violently from side to side as he searched for them.

Gideon looked directly down on him from a frighteningly small distance, no more than four feet, close enough to hear the heavy frenzied breathing. The Yahi lifted his face suddenly into the rain, and with his eyes closed and his voluptuary's lips stretched over his teeth, actually howled: a low, wolflike moan that raised the hairs on the back of Gideon's neck. With the sound, Julie buried her face between Gideon's shoulders and gripped his sides. He could feel her shiver convulsively. His heart pounded crazily. His tongue, rough and dry, seemed to fill his throat. He realized with a remote, annoyed disapproval that he was very

188

much frightened. Bracing himself against the rocky ledge as well as he could, he gripped the ax and got ready for whatever was going to happen.

The Yahi's moan died away, and the streaming face was lowered with its slitlike eyes closed. And then he was gone, bounding noiselessly through the mist and disappearing behind an outcropping of the boulder.

Julie's forehead was still pressed tightly to his back, her hands clenched on the cloth of his shirt. Over the hammering of his own heart, he could feel hers thumping against him.

"Shh," he whispered, stroking her arm. "It's all right. He's gone."

What had happened seemed clear. Big Cheese had seen the old man get up to go to the toilet pit—perhaps it happened every night, and the young Indian had been waiting for his chance. As soon as Startled Mouse was out of sight, Big Cheese had run to where he thought the *saltu* were sleeping. If they'd been there, Gideon thought, their heads would be smashed now, and Big Cheese would be back in the hut, rolled up in his skin and snoring, when the old man returned. In the morning, Big Cheese would be as surprised as the rest at the deaths of the strangers. Startled Mouse might be suspicious, but he couldn't know for sure what had happened.

"Wh . . . where did he go?" Julie asked without moving.

"I don't know. Hunting for us, I guess. He won't look up here."

Without confidence, Julie asked: "Why not?"

"Because," whispered Gideon, straining for lightness, "I chose this spot with the acumen for which I am so well known. Ishi told Kroeber no one slept under an open night sky. All sorts of spirits and disease lurk out there. It won't occur to a Yahi that we were batty enough to move out from under the overhang."

Julie rallied. "They're right," she said. "We're soaked." He could feel her relax a little, and it steadied him.

Quietly, he folded back the top flap of the bag and began to rise.

"Where are you going?" she asked sharply. "Don't—"

"Shh, I'm not going anywhere. I just want to stand up and

look. I can't see where he ran." He peered cautiously over the top of the boulder and was able to see all the way to the end of the rockbound enclosure, to the narrow cleft through which he and Julie had entered it.

"Do you see him?" .

"There's nothing. The sky's getting smudgy out that way, though. It'll be light soon."

"Thank goodness."

The entire little compound lay before him, permeated with a gray, predawn stillness. He wiped the moisture from his eyes. Already the strangely saturating mist had penetrated his shirt and trickled icily down the small of his back. Unless it was cold sweat, which was entirely possible. Where was Big Cheese? What had become of Startled Mouse? Gideon dropped his eyes to the ground at his feet. Where was the ax?

The two cries, urgent and horror-stricken, exploded in his ears one after the other.

"*Ciniyaa!*" someone shouted from behind him. "*No!*"

Behind him . . . on the *other* side of the big boulder, away from the cave! Big Cheese must have run out through the narrow entrance, doubled back, and come up behind him. . . .

Gideon spun violently just as Julie screamed, "*Gideon!* Oh, God . . . !"

The shining, naked figure crouching atop the rock swelled and reared up over him, gray and luminous in the murky light, the terrible stone ax raised to the zenith of its arc and already sweeping down.

Without thinking, Gideon leaped forward to meet it. His outthrust hand caught the plummeting wrist, caught it and brought it up short. Wild black eyes glared crazily at him, inches from his own, while the ax teetered and then toppled over, heavily thumping Gideon's shoulder and sliding down his back. Long before it hit the ground he had balled his right fist to ram it into the gleaming, dark abdomen. His shoulder muscles had already bunched to drive the blow home when the red, mindless haze of sudden violence abruptly cleared. He saw who stood before him.

Startled Mouse.

With a shudder of pity and revulsion he dropped the writhing, slippery wrist—as frail and scrawny as Abe's. The old man, too, shook himself, as if with disgust at the *saltu's* touch, and screamed what might have been a Yahi curse or only a wordless shriek of loathing. He ran a few feet along the top of the boulder, spiderlike and dragging his mutilated foot after him, to where a jumble of loose stone fragments lay in a rough depression, and tried to pick one up. It was too heavy, and the old man moaned his frustration. He grasped a smaller one in both hands and jerkily raised it over his head, grimacing with the effort.

Again there was a shout in Yahi from the other side of the boulder. "*Ciniyaa!*" Big Cheese stood below, his smooth face raised in the gray rain to the old man. Startled Mouse looked over his shoulder at the cry, and Gideon saw his sound foot slip a few inches on the wet rock. Off-balance from the weight of the stone, he began to tip backward over the edge of the boulder.

"The rock!" Gideon shouted. "Throw it down!"

Gideon sprang toward him, and Julie started from the sleeping bag, hands outstretched. Below, Big Cheese moved a step, his arms raised to catch the old Yahi. Gideon knew none of them would reach him in time, and knew that they knew it too.

Startled Mouse knew it as well. The rock was held aloft on rigidly extended arms. The collapsed old face was defiant, the flaccid, nervous mouth for once clamped shut. Like a bizarre statue toppling from its base—a tilting, pathetic Moses hurling down the tablets—the old man inclined slowly backward and hung impossibly over empty air. Gideon had very nearly reached him after all when the rock finally fell away, and Startled Mouse dropped headfirst after it.

Mercifully, the clatter of the stone drowned out the sound of fragile, thinly cushioned bone striking the rocky ground ten feet below. Gideon clambered quickly down the side of the boulder, but Big Cheese was there before him, on his knees.

The old man was dead. He had landed on the back of his head, and the brittle skull had ruptured, so that brains and blood were already mixing with the rain. His face was undamaged, but the mouth hung loose again, and the eyes were eerily askew, one nearly shut, the other open and unfocused.

Gideon heard Julie come up behind him. "Oh!" she said softly. Instinctively, Gideon knelt and gently closed the old eyes with two fingers. He looked up to see Big Cheese, his face streaming with rain, staring strangely at him. There was a long, long moment of silence. The Indian sat back on his heels. The sensual nostrils flared as he drew in a lengthy breath.

"You know," he said in flawless English, "he had a legitimate grievance."

19

"YEAH," BIG CHEESE said, "I'm Dennis Blackpath." The onetime graduate student leaned forward to blow on the dry shreds of moss and bark that had come from the deerskin pouch around his neck, and the crawling spark flickered, gasped, and puffed into flame. In the young Indian's hands the fire drill had been ridiculously easy to use. Now he added bits of wood, gradually increasing their size. When the fire was going well, the three of them, sitting on the ground, leaned close to it. Julie and Gideon shivered in their wet clothes. Blackpath, with the moisture beaded on his greased skin, didn't seem cold.

"You've been living with them all this time?" Julie asked, not bothering to conceal her astonishment. "Since 1975?"

"That's right," Blackpath said, adding more wood. "Nobody believed there were Indians, but I found them. And once I found them, I stayed. I'd had enough of the white man's rotten world. I went to live as my forefathers had lived, in harmony with nature. In tranquillity."

It was the sort of cant Gideon ordinarily found banal and tedious. But Blackpath was another matter. He had committed seven years of his life to it; he'd actually managed to bring it off. Except for the tranquillity.

"I suppose," Blackpath said moodily, flexing a long, thin stick like a fencer testing an *épée*, "you want some explanations."

"That would be nice," Gideon agreed.

"About the killings." His head down, Blackpath spoke to the stick, as surly in English as in Yahi.

"That seems like a good place to begin," Gideon said mildly, but his hackles were rising. If anyone had reason to be aggrieved, it was certainly *he*, with two attempts on his life and a painful dent in his head, and not this pampered student-*cum*-wild Indian. Something in his tone must have given away his feelings, because Blackpath suddenly looked up at him and snapped the stick in two.

Julie cut in. "You said that Startled . . . What was his name? I don't want to keep calling him that."

"Their names are private," Blackpath said curtly. "Startled Mouse is good enough." *For the likes of you.*

Julie did not respond in kind. "You said he had a legitimate grievance," she said quietly.

Blackpath tossed the pieces of the stick into the fire. "You saw his foot?"

"Yes," Julie said.

"It was shot away, a long time ago—"

"In 1913, when he was a little boy," Gideon said slowly, remembering. "And his mother was killed when they rifled a cabin on Canoe Creek. They stole two hard-boiled eggs."

"You talked to Pringle," Blackpath said.

"That's an awful thing," Julie said, "but—"

"But what?" He was answering Julie, but his stare challenged Gideon. "It's no excuse for killing people seventy years later?"

Gideon looked at him without speaking. Something sagged inside Blackpath. His gaze dropped to the fire. "Ah, hell," he said, "it's funny speaking English after all this time." He paused. "You're right, you're right. It's not an excuse." He seemed to be searching for the precise words he wanted, then gave up with a small shrug. The dawn had come; Gideon could see him more clearly and was struck anew by the strange beauty of the mask-like face.

"I really loved the old man. Really loved him." The words could hardly be heard. "He was the first one of them to accept me. He called me Grandson. I called him Grandfather." He cleared his throat. "But, God, how he hated the *saltu.* I think he's always been a little crazy." He was, Gideon thought, genuinely close to tears.

"I think he killed some people when he was young," Blackpath went on, "but when I found them he wasn't any kind of menace. Then they built that damn road right through here—"

"The Matheny trail," Julie said.

"Is that what it's called?" he asked without interest. "Well, he went wild. Killed the first hiker he saw."

"But he's so frail," Julie said, "so small—"

"This was six years ago, remember. He was stronger. Besides, he used an atlatl. A spear thrower." Blackpath was picking up moist earth, crumbling it in his palm, and letting it run from his cupped hand. "I talked with him again and again, tried to explain the killing couldn't do any good. I thought I had him convinced. And then he clubbed someone else."

"Hartman," Gideon said.

"Whoever. I found the poor guy on the trail with his head bashed in. A mess . . ." He stopped. Gideon knew he was thinking of Startled Mouse, who lay where he had fallen, covered with Gideon's poncho, on the far side of the boulder. Blackpath closed his eyes. "I took him back to the village. Back to here. Keen Eagle—that's a good name for him—remembered how to trephine, and I thought for a while the guy might live. But he died."

Blackpath stared into the fire. "I thought that was the end of it. But then a few weeks ago, after all those years, he must have stumbled on this girl near the summer village. You know about that?"

Gideon nodded.

"That was a bad thing. And now he tried to kill you. Twice." He sighed. "I guess it's best this way."

"What about the others?" Gideon asked. "They weren't involved? They didn't know?"

Blackpath shrugged again. "They knew and they didn't know

Like you didn't know about the Japanese internment camps. Like he Germans didn't know about Dachau. Look, they buried the two guys, didn't they? But no, they weren't involved in the killings, if that's what you mean. They're good people; harmless."

"What about you?" Julie asked suddenly. "You've been here seven years. Did you find what you came to find?"

"Sure," Blackpath said hotly. "Does it seem so impossible? What did I give up that was so wonderful? That world out there garbage! It's bad enough for a white man, let alone an Indian." His voice softened. "They helped me to become Indian, honest-to-God Indian. And I helped them."

"You helped them?" Gideon said.

Blackpath stared at the fire, seeming to muse aloud. "When I came, they lived like dogs, on filth, scrounging around camp dumps for food and old clothes. They'd forgotten how to fish, how to make fishhooks, how to cover their huts. They hadn't made a tool in decades. The old woman hadn't woven a basket since she was a little girl. They were fighting the eagles for rotten salmon. They'd forgotten how to preserve meat, how to make their clothes."

"And you," said Gideon, looking at him with increasing respect, "taught them the old ways."

Blackpath bristled. "Yeah, I taught them the old ways. What's wrong with that?"

"Look," Gideon said, "will you get it straight that I'm on your side? We came here to help."

"All right," Blackpath said. "I'm sorry. I know you did. Okay, I taught them the old ways. As much as I knew. Do you know, when I found them they all slept in one big hut? The woman in with all the men?" He seemed honestly scandalized. "Now look at the way they live. Their own tools, their own food, their own homes. I made them Indian again."

Not only Indian, Gideon thought, but indisputably Yahi. Dennis Blackpath had accomplished a phenomenal feat.

"But you're not Yahi," Gideon said. "How did you know the old ways?"

He shrugged. "Books."

"You've done a remarkable thing here," Gideon said.

Blackpath was uncomfortable with praise. "And what happens now?" he asked angrily. "Don't think we're going to live in some museum like Ishi all over again."

"There's a good possibility," Gideon said, "of a reservation—"

"Jesus Christ, can you see that? These people dealing with the BIA? Anthropologists all over the place with questionnaires 'And what is the nature of the informal relationship between the mother's brother and the paternal parallel cousins?' If—"

Gideon held up his hand, smiling. "I agree with you. All right what would you like to happen?"

"As far as you're concerned, nothing. Just leave us alone. Forget us. We don't want any help. We don't need any more squeaky turtles."

Gideon flushed, then smiled again. "But the old woman really got a bang out of it, didn't she?"

Blackpath smiled too. "Yeah, she did, didn't she? Look, you two are the only ones who know about us. Can't we keep it that way? Can't we just stay here?"

Julie shook her head. "The trail's going to be reopened There's no way of stopping it."

"God," Blackpath said, "do you really need another trail through here? More beer cans . . . I mean, how much longer can these people live? Can't you wait a few years—?"

She was shaking her head again. "No, it wouldn't work."

"Jesus Christ," Blackpath said, "I don't know what to do. We can't go back to our summer village. A couple of goddamn kids stumbled on it last week and almost found us. They must have told people, because the next day there were two more poking around—" He looked up suddenly. "That was you, wasn't it?"

"That was us," Gideon agreed, "and that funny feeling at the back of our necks was you."

"Wait a minute," Julie said slowly, "there is a place, about twenty-five miles northeast of here, near Hayes Pass." She spoke dreamily, her memory working. "Only about half the rainfall we get here. It was proposed for a trail two years ago and got turned down. Too expensive, too difficult to get to. Hardly anyone knows it's there. I only saw it once myself. A sloping, grassy valley, five miles long, with a lovely river running down it. There's a big, blue hanging glacier at the upper end. It was loaded with elk when I was there, and deer. . . ."

"It sounds like paradise," Blackpath said.

"It is. It's lovely. And there isn't a trail within five miles. Oh, it'd be perfect!" she said excitedly. "Why didn't I think of it before? I can show you where it is on the map." She frowned. "Rats. The map's back at our camp. It's two hours from here, at least."

"It's twenty minutes. You were following the old man's tracks, and he was being careful. That's one thing they didn't forget. Let's go."

"What about the others?" Gideon asked. "They'll be waking up. It's light."

Blackpath looked at the dripping, gray sky. "Not for another hour."

"You mean they don't get up at dawn?" Julie asked ingenuously.

"If you lived in a hut," Blackpath said, "and two out of three mornings were like this, what would you do?"

It took them exactly twenty minutes to get back to their camp. Julie spread the map on the floor of the tent, out of the rain, and Blackpath bent over it while Julie traced with a pen the best way to get to Hayes Pass. He nodded at last and looked up, staring into her eyes for so long that she finally dropped her own. Then he looked hard at Gideon.

The question was unasked, but Gideon answered it. "You can trust us," he said.

"I guess I have to." The veiled eyes studied Gideon longer still. "I do trust you," he said more firmly. "We'll go there. Now. As soon as we bury Clear Water. That was his name. Clear Water. Not Startled Mouse." It was an offering, a gift to them.

They were startled by a thumping drone and looked through the tent flap to see a helicopter skimming grasshopperlike toward them through the gray rain, coming from Lake Quinau.

197

"It's John," Julie said. She saw Gideon's surprise. "What did you think, they were going to hike in?"

That was just what he'd thought. He'd forgotten this was the twentieth century and had expected to have another five or six hours before John got there. "They won't be able to see the cave, but they'll spot this tent right away," he said. "They'll be down here in five minutes."

He grasped a suddenly distrustful Blackpath by the elbow and hustled him out of the tent, across the small clearing, and into the thick, green forest. Julie ran after them.

"We don't have much time," Gideon said to Blackpath. "Listen, it'd be better if you left Startled—Clear Water—where he is. We'd have a body to show the FBI, and they could close the case and forget about the rest of you."

"We can't!" It was the first time Gideon had seen him upset. "He's got to be buried. He ought to be cremated. His spirit can't rest until he's buried. I mean," he added quickly, "that's what they believe." Agitatedly, he looked up toward the rapidly increasing clatter, but the helicopter couldn't be seen through the forest canopy.

"I'll see to it that he's buried!" Gideon shouted over the noise. "And cremated! I promise!"

Blackpath was irresolute. Gideon had the feeling it was a rare condition for him. Again Blackpath looked up toward the sound. The helicopter was hovering. The tent had been seen. He nodded quickly and stuck the map in his waistband.

"Thank you!" he shouted. Obviously, it didn't come easily.

He began to turn away. The invisible helicopter was coming down, apparently on the nearby gravel bar. Julie touched the bare arm and leaned forward to speak in his ear. Gideon read her lips. "Tell Gray Sparrow good-bye."

He nodded. "Thank you!" he shouted again, but the words were lost. He turned and darted into the brush.

Gideon wondered how long it would be before he spoke English again, or if he ever would. He glided smoothly among the trees, the rain glistening on his naked back, and melted into the dripping, green forest. Already he seemed to have shed the per-

198

sona of Dennis Blackpath and left it at their feet, becoming part of the rain forest again; a Yahi, Ishi in reverse.

"What will he do when they all die?" Julie asked.

Gideon shook his head. "Beats the hell out of me. I hope he can find another lost tribe. Let's go greet John."

Julian Minor bustled prissily about the body along with another agent, a big-nosed, solemn young man named Simkins. A few yards away, John stood talking quietly with Julie and Gideon. Gideon's eyes strayed above John's shoulder to the cleft where the sleeping bag had been. It was no longer there, but lay wet and crumpled on the ground. Blackpath must have thrown it down, realizing that anyone who climbed up to where it had been would have seen the huts on the other side of the big boulder. The gifts—the ax and the basket—were not there either. He and Julie would have to come back someday to see if they were in the cave. Someday. Not for a long time.

"Doc," John was saying softly, his head tilted to one side, "your story doesn't make a whole hell of a lot of sense." He was referring to Gideon's considerably abridged description of the night's events, from which mention of anyone but Clear Water had been pruned. He was leaning with one hand against the huge monolith, on the other side of which—no more than twenty feet away, if one knew how to get to it—lay the deserted Yahi huts.

"I know, John. Look, would you believe me—and just let it go—if I tell you that little guy really is the murderer? And if I can guarantee there won't be any more killings?"

"I don't know. Is it true? No one else was involved?"

"It's true," Gideon said. Depending on what you meant by involved.

He said it a little too hesitantly. "But there *is* more to it," John said flatly.

"Yes, there's more, but it isn't relevant."

"It isn't, John," Julie said. "Really."

John shook his head. He was hatless, as they all were, and a few rivulets of rain ran down his wide forehead. "I don't know," he said. Gideon could see he was offended at being excluded. And rightfully so. He and Gideon had shared a lot of sensitive secrets.

"John, I'd be glad to tell you the rest as a friend. In fact, I'd *like* to tell you. But the problem is, you're also a special agent of the FBI."

John nodded. "And with my well-known, true-blue integrity, you know I'd report anything you told me, and then whatever you didn't want to get out would get out."

"That's it. But I'll tell you anyway, if you want."

John laughed and relaxed. "Nah," he said. "If you tell me the killings are over, and we've got the guy who did them, that's what counts, right? Don't tell me any more. I put enough strain on my integrity as it is. You can tell me the rest after I retire."

"I will," Gideon said.

"Fine. I'm going back to the chopper in a few minutes. Got to fly back and get a medical examiner. We'll give you guys a lift."

"Great," Julie said.

"No, thanks," said Gideon. "We'll walk back."

John's eyebrows went up. He waved a hand at the wet forest. "In *this?*"

"We have things we need to talk about," Gideon said. "A nice long walk will give us the chance."

John wiped the collected moisture from his face and flicked it to the ground. He addressed Julie. "You're really going to walk back?"

"I guess so. He's very masterful, you know."

"Suit yourself," John said. He shook his head, looking at Julie. "You're getting to be as crazy as he is." He clapped Gideon on the back and squeezed his shoulder. "Let's all get together for dinner at the lodge—if you're back by tonight." He shook his head again and went back to the others.

Hand in hand, they walked silently through the drizzle for a few hundred feet. "Gideon," Julie finally said, "what do we need to talk about that will take six hours?"

"For starters, how about the next forty years?"

"All right," she said again, her voice as misty as the rain. "That'll do. For starters."

27 million Americans can't read a bedtime story to a child.

It's because 27 million adults in this country simply can't read.

Functional illiteracy has reached one out of five Americans. It robs them of even the simplest of human pleasures, like reading a fairy tale to a child.

You can change all this by joining the fight against illiteracy.

Call the Coalition for Literacy at toll-free **1-800-228-8813** and volunteer.

Volunteer Against Illiteracy. The only degree you need is a degree of caring.

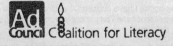

Ad Council Coalition for Literacy